BLOOD CRIES

BLOOD CRIES

a novel

by
Chris Hope

Blood Cries
© 2019 David Brasfield
All Rights Reserved
First Print Edition
This book is a work of fiction. Though certain aspects resemble actual people, places, things, events, and situations, none should be mistaken for their factual counterparts.
ISBN: 978-0-578-49312-1
Author Website: christamar.com

For Lois

Then the Lord said to Cain, "Where is your brother, Abel?"
"I do not know," Cain replied. "Am I my brother's keeper?"
Then the Lord said to him, "What have you done? Your brother's blood cries out to me from the ground."
Genesis 4:9-1

The Reverend
by Louella Harper
Copyright 1978

Prologue

Jackson City, Alabama stands on the front steps of the Piedmont plateau in a space between the pines formerly occupied by a Creek Indian village. Here, the Old South begins its slow collision with Appalachia. The hilly land is thick with timber, but the ground is fit for nothing, the locals say, but holding the world together, which it does by means of red clay packed between igneous rock and glittering with fragments of quartz.

At the start of the 20th century, a textile mill was established to satisfy the regional demand for undergarments. In 1920, the mill's founder, Langston Carmichael, along with his son Preston, invented the article of clothing now commonly referred to as the sweatshirt, which served as their entrance into the business of manufacturing sports apparel, a market Carmichael Mills would come to dominate. The Carmichael Corporation, as it is now known, boasts of factories across the South and as far away as Central America.

In 1922, the Alabama Power Company dammed the Muskogee river and formed Lake Robert along the southern border of McGillivray County. At the time, it was the largest manmade lake in the world. The presence of the lake immediately launched a real estate business to be dominated, naturally, by the Carmichaels. They took the best lakeside plots for themselves and their friends, erected fabulous houses upon them, and divvied out the rest while charging on a sliding scale.

A multitude of people have benefitted from their connections to the Carmichaels. They, in turn, have fortified the local economy, which remains as vibrant as any small-to-medium-sized town in the state. In addition to the textile mill and the cement plant, an array of small businesses and the timber industry provide dedicated individuals a means of acquiring capital.

None, however, have acquired more capital than the Carmichael family, and it is upon the steps of their domicile (figuratively speaking) that the social ladder rests. Their friends and family members inhabit the uppermost rungs. Passing them on the way down, one meets businessmen, judges, lawyers, doctors, preachers, teachers, firefighters, policeman, factory and mill workers, along with many others engaged in a hundred forms of meaningful employment or otherwise contributing to society as law-abiding citizens, including—and despite considerable obstacles—many black citizens, some of whom have climbed high enough to crack the professional ranks.

Despite some gains, blacks continue to lag behind whites economically, and most churches and some businesses remain segregated. The funeral business provides one of the most unpleasant examples of separate and unequal facilities persisting within the private sector.

If a white person dies, the friend or family member designated with making the necessary arrangements will pay a visit to the Robertson Family Funeral Home, directed by "Somber Tom" Robertson, who will ensure that their loved one will pass into the ethereal realm with the respect and dignity accorded to their race.

If a black person dies, the executor or next of kin will have to go see Ernie Smith.

Ernie is a squat, gruff, black man of indeterminate age and a reputation for unscrupulous business practices. He often stands on the ash-stained carpet of his funeral parlor, smoking his cigar, and peppering his conversations with bereaved family members with obscene language.

As a sideline, he runs The Colored People's Ambulance Service. The CPAS is a business developed to fill a gap in the market and to maximize profits generated by Ernie's back-up hearse. In the event of an emergency, a pink 1952 Cadillac Superior, affixed with rotating cherry beacons and a tornado siren, will arrive screaming onto the scene. Two hulking men dressed in the fashion of hospital orderlies will emerge from the vehicle ready to treat their patients with as much care or apathy as their temperament allows.

On the afternoon of April 7, 1957, Ernie and a young apprentice named Kevin Summers entered the home of 63-year-old Theodore Hall and emerged moments later carrying Hall on a pallet. After shoving him into the back of the hearse, Kevin climbed aboard and proceeded to connect him to the CPAS's first oxygen tank, which had been delivered to the funeral home earlier in the day.

"Don't worry," Kevin said, leaning over the man. "We'll have you at the hospital in no time."

Mr. Hall's eyes darted from side to side. The clear plastic mask he wore over his nose and mouth clouded with every tenuous breath.

The driver's side door slammed shut. Ernie adjusted the rearview mirror until his face loomed in the reflection. He chewed on the stub of a cigar. "What's the diagnosis, Dr. Kevin?"

"Shit."

"Come on, Summers. What do you think is wrong with the man?" Ernie yanked down the gear shift and steered onto 11th Street.

"I don't know. A heart attack?" Kevin looked down at Mr. Hall "My uncle had a heart attack three years ago. He came out of the hospital better than when he went in."

"You know good and well that man died on the operating table," Ernie said. His eyes pivoted from the mirror to the road. "Hey, Teddy, how old are you?"

Mr. Hall's face turned from side to side. His eyes blinked rapidly.

"What about it, Kevin?" Ernie asked.

"I don't know. Late sixties maybe."

"Might as well take the scenic route."

Kevin adjusted the oxygen mask. "He's only joking, sir."

"I ain't joking, motherfucker, and stop wasting all that oxygen. That man is breathing fine on his own."

Kevin shrugged and did as he was told. As he twisted his body to stow away the gear, Mr. Hall reached out with a trembling hand and raked the side of his shirt.

"He's breathing funny," Kevin observed.

"That's his problem," Ernie said. "Now stop thinking and start using your head. We have to decide what to do with him."

"I thought we were taking him to the hospital."

"I mean we have to weigh out the values. How much money do you think we'll make for transporting Teddy to the hospital?"

"I don't know. Twenty dollars?"

"That's about right. We've got a five-dollar transport fee, five dollars for labor, two-fifty for gas and maintenance on the ambulance, the pallet fee..."

"We charge him for the pallet?"

"For using it. I ain't running no charity. I've got to clean the sheets, don't I?"

"You make me do that. Every month."

"So, there's a fee for cleaning the sheets. Then, I've got to charge him for the oxygen."

"He's not on oxygen." Kevin looked down at the patient. "I think he's turning blue."

"Once he uses some, I've got to charge him for the full amount. That's just business. Now, it used to be in the old days we'd be lucky to get thirty-five dollars for the whole trip. We'd take a guy like Teddy here—spent his life cleaning toilets, ain't got a goddamn cent to his name—we'd fix him up, take him to the hospital, then after he'd get released, I'd have to spend all my spare time chasing him down for the money that was owed. I might even have to break his pinky finger or put a knife between his legs to show him the nature of my intent.

"But then, two years ago, the federal government stepped in, offering to pay for the deadbeats, but they limited the payout to twenty dollars, so I'll still have to go to this joker's house to collect the other thirty-five."

"If the government pays, how come you still collect from him?" Kevin asked.

"Just because the government pays don't mean he don't have to pay too. How else am I going to afford to pay you to clean those sheets?"

"I don't know."

"Then, there's the funeral side of things. On a funeral, I can clear over a hundred dollars profit just on the casket. Then, you've got a service fee, the fee for renting the funeral parlor, the fee for flowers, the fee for the bulletins, the fee for cleaning up the parlor afterwards. All totaled, we clear almost four hundred dollars, and I don't have to cut nobody. It's a winning situation for everybody."

"For everybody but Mr. Hall and anyone who loved him."

"Then there is the insurance consideration. As it happens, Teddy's wife, Betty, believes in life insurance. I know because she came down to the parlor not two years ago to order a casket for her mother, and she got upset she couldn't afford the one she wanted. I recommended a policy agent, and she gave him a call."

"How do you know that?"

"Because he told me."

"Oh."

"And he let me take out a policy on him as well."

"On Mr. Hall?" Kevin pointed to the man lying beside him.

"Yeah, Man. He worked for me for a while, you know, cleaning toilets. All I had to do was sign his name to a little form. When he dies, his family will get some money and so will I."

Kevin considered this information "How much will you get?"

"About seven thousand dollars."

Kevin looked at Mr. Hall in a new light. "You mean if Mr. Hall dies, you get seven thousand dollars?"

"No, I'll get five. You'll get the other two."

"Me?" He looked down at Mr. Hall. "But I'd be the one doing the dirty work. I should get half."

"Half of what?"

"Have of all of it: the ambulance, the funeral, and the insurance."

"You must be crazy. I got a business to run. I got expenses."

"Half the insurance then."

"I'll give you twenty-five hundred, and I'm over-paying."

Kevin considered the offer. "Okay," he said and then looked down at the patient. "You were a good man, Mr. Hall." He pulled the pillow out from under the man's head, letting it fall against the pallet. "I hope you go to a better place."

The old man tried to cry out, but only a feeble moan escaped his lips before the pillow came down over his face and smothered him.

Later the same year, Ernie found himself in court facing charges of first-degree murder after an elderly former employee burned up in a house fire and Ernie was found to have taken out three insurance policies on the man. The case turned against him when the accomplice he paid to get the old man drunk confessed under police interrogation.

When told of the confession, Ernie shouted, "That nigger is lying," but the jury believed him, and they believed the fire marshal who testified that a "fast hot fire" was a sure sign of arson. The judge handed down a life sentence.

Ernie went to prison not knowing the full force of his impact upon his community. His influence was felt beyond the suffering of his victims and their families. Greed, narcissism, and the willingness to do wrong by others persisted in Ernie's unwitting apprentices.

Together, these men form but a few links in a long line of weak and evil men that stretches back through the centuries, each generation another coil in the body of the Biblical serpent. With a tail rattling somewhere in the depths of human history, the head weaves forward through the present, testing the air with its flickering tongue. By the late 1960s, it was reared back over McGillivray County, poised to strike again.

Chrissy
2009

The first time I saw Melvin Little, he reminded me of a garden gnome. There was a split second when I thought he might actually be a gnome, or a small troll, instead of a little old man, sitting in his office, behind a cherry-top desk. He had a hump on his back that rose above his right shoulder and thick gray tufts of graying eyebrows with sprigs sticking out in all directions. There were sprigs sticking out of his nose and ears too. And he had these big jowls, one of which drooped down lower than the right. From a stroke maybe.

In the dim lamp light, his eyes appeared to be closed, and his little pot belly rose and fell in a slow rhythm that made me think he might be asleep. I wondered if I should just keep standing there in his doorway, staring at him, or if I should clear my throat or something to let him know I was there. That's what I did; I cleared my throat.

Nothing.

His little pot belly rose and fell.

It must be nice to have a belly like that, I thought, a built-in table to set cups on. And what was the deal with that hump? What causes a hump anyway? Is it contagious? What would happen if I touched it? Would it give me good luck? Or bad?

I never got the chance to test the idea because I took one step onto the Persian rug, and the floor creaked, and suddenly he was awake, and words went sputtering out of the side of his mouth in grunts and mumbles.

"Normally I stand when a lady enters the room," he said, and then muttered something about his arthritis.

I couldn't see his legs behind his desk, but in my imagination, they were thin and floppy and just sort of hung from his body, like Muppets. I pictured someone carting him around the office in a wheel barrow. I'd love it if someone would ride me around like that.

He pointed a crooked finger toward a leather padded chair in front of his desk and invited me to take a seat.

"How's your mama?" he asked in a voice that sounded like it had gone through a meat shredder.

"Good," I said. "She retired two years ago."

"She was a fine attorney."

I nodded, not knowing what else to say, and then looked around the office. Behind his desk, the wall was filled with degrees and accolades, newspaper clippings highlighting his brief stint in the state legislature, and a framed quote which read, "If you don't know the truth, then make something up."

This was my first trip back to my hometown in almost twenty years and it felt strange. Jackson City is one of those small southern towns that never seems to change, and yet, it felt different to me. I was eight when my father died, and my mother closed down her struggling law office and moved our dog Apples and me to Montgomery. She'd landed a job clerking for a judge on the Alabama Supreme Court. We moved from a big lake house in an all-white neighborhood to an apartment that rented mostly to families of foreign officers training at the Air War College. I'd always felt at home in Jackson City, but now I was in Montgomery and I felt like I was an alien. Twenty years later, I was back, and I still felt like an alien.

I'm weird, I know. People tell me that all the time, though I'm not sure what to do with that information.

"Well, you came here to find out about the Reverend, so I guess we should get on with it," Melvin said. He twisted a finger through the thicket of hair growing out of one of his ears. "I suppose you know who Louella Harper is."

"I sure do."

Every literate person in Alabama knew about Louella Harper. Her novel *Murder of Innocence* was required reading in schools throughout the state. A friendly librarian suggested the book to me when I was nine years old and still adjusting to my new life in Montgomery. I started reading it at school that day and within three pages I never wanted it to end.

I read between assignments, at the lunch table, while walking to and from classes, and on the bus-ride home. When I got to my house, I went straight to my room and read it underneath the covers until suppertime. I finished it that night and then started reading it again the next morning. I read it again and again and again, and at least once every year for the next twenty years. What can I say about *Murder of Innocence*? Within its pages I found the friends that eluded me in my real life and the moral clarity that doesn't seem to exist anywhere except within the boundaries of a fictional universe.

To Melvin Little all I said was, "That book changed my life."

"Uh huh," he said. "And you know about Louella's involvement in this story?"

"That's the reason I'm here."

A few weeks earlier while poking around on the internet, I came across a website that claimed Louella Harper had spent a year in Jackson City, writing a book about a voodoo-practicing serial killer who hunted members of his own family. As I stared at the computer screen, memories from my childhood flooded my head. I remembered sitting at the supper table, with my mouth hanging open as my mother told me about the killer who marked the doors of his victims with chicken blood and kept human heads in jars in his basement. His shelves were said to be lined with homemade dolls resembling family members, neighbors, and acquaintances. If ever he chose to stab one of the dolls with a pin, or light it on fire, or cut off its head, then the doll's real-life counterpart would suffer a similar fate.

One man experienced such serious leg pains he had to be confined to a wheelchair. Another man nearly had his arm burned off in a grease fire. Other people turned up dead, only no one could explain what killed them. They were the ones you could read about in the newspaper. "If you ever see the Reverend coming your way," my mother warned, "you better cross the street."

"Do you believe it?" I asked her. "Do you believe the Reverend has voodoo powers?"

"No," my mother said, smiling. "But it makes for a good story."

Fast forward twenty years to find me living in Atlanta, sitting in bed beside my sleeping boyfriend, with the only light supplied by the laptop computer balanced on a pillow on my lap, and I'm staring at that website, remembering my childhood. That's when I realized how great the story would have been had it been written by Louella Harper.

There was only one problem: after *Murder of Innocence*, Louella Harper never published another book.

I called my mother. "Did you know about this?"

"Know about what?"

"Louella Harper was going to write a book about Reverend Baxter."

"Who is Reverend Baxter?"

"You're no help," I said and hung up on her.

To find out what happened, I searched the internet. I read a million blog entries. I read Louella's unauthorized biography, even though everyone knows it's three hundred pages of lies. By all accounts, Louella went to Jackson City in 1978 and stayed for almost a year. She did her research and she wrote at least one draft of a book about the Reverend. No one knew why it was never published.

One thing you should know about me: I am not the type of person who will just let something like this go. Once I get an idea in my head, I have to follow it through to its logical conclusion, or, I don't know, I might explode!

I was going into Nancy Drew mode. I was going to solve the mystery of the lost true crime manuscript.

But how?

It's not like I could just call up Louella Harper and say, "Oh my God Oh my God Oh my God. I am such a huge fan of yours. I've read your book a million times. Would you mind signing it for me? Also, how come you never finished that book about the Reverend?"

I could not do that because I did not have her number.

So, I called my mom again.

"I remembered who Reverend Baxter was," she said. She was so proud of herself. "He was Melvin Little's client. I bet he could tell you all about him."

I found the website of Melvin's law office and then sent him an email asking if he'd be willing to talk to me. The next day, I received a reply.

"I'd be happy to talk to you about the Reverend. Give my secretary a call, and we'll set up a time."

The rest, as they say, is history. And now I was about to hear the whole story of the Reverend, the murders, and what happened to Louella Harper's lost manuscript.

"Before you start," I said, "Could you do me a favor?"

Melvin's eyes opened a millionth of a millimeter wider, which I took to be a sign I should continue. "Before all the other stuff, I was wondering if you could skip ahead and tell me what happened to Louella's book?"

I should probably mention, I am not a huge fan of mysteries, surprises, or suspense. I prefer knowing everything right up front.

"I know what you're thinking," Melvin said, "but I promise you that book will never see the light of day. She probably burned the damned manuscript. If you don't write this thing, then no one will."

"Um, I think there might have been a misunderstanding," I said. "I'm not planning to write a book. I just want to know what happened to hers."

"Un huh," Melvin said in a way that suggested he did not believe me. "Well, I'll tell you what I know, and you can do with that information what you will."

I found this acceptable, and I scrambled through my hand bag for the digital recorder I'd purchased on the way out of Atlanta. I placed it on the desk in front of him and pressed record.

Melvin cleared some of the phlegm out of his throat and began to tell his story. "Louella always said I was going to be the hero of her book. It would have been a good book too. One of the all-time greats..."

He talked for a long time, at least two hours, almost entirely about himself, while I did my best not to think about rubbing his hump. No matter how much I might have wanted it to, it wasn't going to grant me any free wishes.

From the Research Journal of Chrissy Hope

Oh my God! I can't believe I'm doing this! I am literally following in the footsteps of Louella Harper!!

Get it together, girl. Act like a professional.

Alright. Alright. I've got this.

Interview with Melvin Little Transcribed from a recording taken July 2, 2009

Interviewer
What else can you tell me about Louella Harper?

Melvin
In the public consciousness, Louella Harper has been elevated to sainthood. *Murder of Innocence* was so great, people decided the author must drop scented feces. The truth is the woman swears like a trucker, smokes two packs of unfiltered cigarettes a day, and drinks scotch on the rocks like a Southern Baptist drinks grape juice. I've known her for thirty years, so I can testify to these things just as I can testify the woman has a powerful mind and wit so sharp it can slice bacon.

One of her neighbors told me a story, must have been in the mid-1970s. One Sunday afternoon a woman led her two children onto the front porch of Louella's home and rang the bell. A minute later, the door opens up just about as far as a chain lock would allow.

"Louella Harper? Is it you? I just can't believe it."

(Transcriber's note: he's doing a funny voice.)

Louella eyed her through a sliver of doorway. "Yes, what do you want?"

"Oh, Ms. Harper, my children just love your book."

The children stared ahead with vacant expressions. Each held a copy of *Murder of Innocence*.

"I don't sign autographs," Louella said. All they could see of her was one eye, a patch of skin on the forehead, a patch on the cheekbone, and a sprinkle of hair spilling out from beneath a red bandana.

"I know it must be such an imposition having people come up to your door like this," said the woman, a former debutante who in Louella's opinion had been constructed from a tube of red lipstick, a can of hairspray, a pointy bra, and a gallon of sweet iced tea.

"You know, it really is."

"It's just that your book has meant so much to me and my family. It changed my life."

Louella's eyes fell to the paperback she held clutched to her chest, a pocket edition with an unbent spine and three hundred and seventy-five pages that had never been turned.

"Signing a book for you would be like putting up the Bat Signal. I'd never get any peace."

"Oh please. It would mean so much to us."

Louella closed the door long enough to remove the chain. The debutante beamed.

The door swung open, and Louella stepped as far as the doorway. For the first time, the debutante could see who she was dealing with: a forty-five-year-old woman with a face beginning to wrinkle and gray streaks replacing the black in her hair. She leaned against the frame, reached into the pocket of her apron, and fished out a cigarette.

"What is it going to take to make you understand?" She asked. She lit the cigarette with a disposable lighter.

"Excuse me?"

Louella blew a stream of smoke right into her face. "This is my house. I don't want you people coming to my house. You liked my book? I'm glad you liked my book. Someday I may even write another one, but in case you haven't noticed, I haven't published a word in fifteen years, and I honestly don't give a damn what you think of that book in your hand, or if you've even read it. Unless I'm mistaken—and I am not mistaken—nowhere in that book does it say it's okay to pester the author at her home."

The debutante burst into tears.

Her children had no idea know what to do.

"Oh, for heaven's sake," Louella snatched a book and a pen from the woman and scribbled down an autograph before sending them on their way.

       Interviewer

What did it say?

       Melvin

What?

       Interviewer

How did she sign the books? Did she give them a personalized message, or did she just sign her name?

       Melvin

She wrote the same thing in each of the three books: "Always try to learn from your mistakes, as I will try to learn from mine. With love, Louella Harper"

The Interviewer is literally crying right now.

Melvin

Louella grew fans like Alabama grows kudzu. All across America, teachers assigned *Murder of Innocence* to their classroom reading lists. Every year brought a new crop of fans and another printing of her book. There was the pocket edition, the classic edition, the pocket classic edition, all kinds of editions.

Louella made millions. There was no reason for her to ever do another day's work in her life. She just wanted to be left alone. That's all she cares about now—her privacy.

Louella Harper is a rock star!!!I can't wait to meet her!!

From the Diary of Louella Harper

06-13-77

Spent a lovely weekend at the lake with Maris and Brewer. Saturday night, we all went out on the deck and enjoyed the breeze coming off of the lake. Brewer grilled T-bone steaks while Maris and I enjoyed new cushioned reclining deck chairs until the food was ready. I don't know if Brewer is the world's top grill master or if the gin and tonics enhanced my taste buds, but I can say with certainty that it was the best steak and corn on the cob I have ever tasted. And, Maris served an eggplant casserole that was out of this world! The best part of course was the talking and just being together. We always laugh so much when we get together. It seems strange to say but spending time with my sister and her husband has brought more joy to my life than I probably deserve.

Sunday, my niece Madeline joined us for supper. She lives just down the road in Jackson City, where her husband has a job in the mayor's office. She came in with a newspaper and the story everyone in town is talking about: Voodoo in McGillivray County.

It's a tragic story. A sixteen-year-old was found dead beneath an automobile. It seems she was posed to appear as if she had been changing a tire when the jack slipped, and the car fell on her. No one could explain why the girl would change a tire while lying flat on her back staring up at the wheel well.

According to Madeline, the girl's stepfather is well-known practitioner of voodoo. He is suspected of murdering her as well as several other members of his immediate family. He'd been charged in at least one other case but has never been convicted of a crime.

"The blacks are all scared of him," Madeline said. "Whenever he drives through their neighborhoods, they all leave their porches and go inside. They think he's protected by voodoo magic."

Brewer found that anecdote hilarious and added his own racist tagline, which is best forgotten.

"You should write about this, Aunt Louella," Madeline suggested.

The poor girl was trying to be helpful.

"I'm sure the newspaper will cover the story well enough," I said, "but it's interesting that you should mention it. I've always believed I would make a wonderful true crime writer."

I was only trying to spare Madeline's feelings, but I realized immediately that I had put my foot in my mouth, as everyone seemed very excited at the prospect of me writing something again. Madeline insisted I bring the newspaper home with me.

After a two-hour drive and some time alone, I showed the article to Lydia, thinking we might share a laugh at the notion, but she was as bad as they were. "You *should* write another book."

"I think I'm experiencing déjà vu."

"Why not? The idea fell right into your lap? It's a gift from the Universe."

"That's not how it works."

"What are you talking about? That's literally how it's working."

"If you don't mind, I'd rather not talk about my creative process right now."

She dropped the subject, but several days later I sat down at the breakfast table to find my issue of the *New York Times* stacked beneath a copy of the *Jackson City Sentinel*. The banner headline trumpeted the latest shocking developments.

I sipped my coffee. "I see what you're up to." I was sitting at the table with my back to the kitchen, where Lydia was straightening up.

"What in the world are you talking about?" I could hear her stacking cups and saucers.

"The newspaper."

"What about it?"

"I see what you're up to."

Lydia dropped the silverware she was holding into a drawer and dragged a chair over, so she could sit close to me. "Come on, honey. It could be like Kansas again."

"You say that like it was a good thing. Besides, that was Cecil's book. I just went along for the ride."

"You know that's not true," Lydia said. "That book never would have been written if it wasn't for you."

The truth struck me silent, and Lydia recognized her advantage. She stroked my back. Her voice softened. "Isn't this the kind of project you used to talk about?"

"Sometimes I think it would be better if I never publish another book. Maybe I only had one in me."

"Lou, every morning after your drink your coffee and read your newspaper, you go into your office, and I have to listen to your blasted typewriter clacking away for the next four hours. It sounds a lot like writing to me."

"Yes, but once I get out and start asking questions, I'm going to have to start answering them too about why I'm doing this, and that's going to start creating expectations in people's minds."

"You have to stop worrying about other people's expectations."

"I do so have to worry." I was out of my chair now, pacing the kitchen.

Lydia remained anchored to her chair and the table. "This one is a crime story. It's completely different. Judging one against the other is like judging apples against artichokes."

"Oh, it will be judged," I said. "Believe me, it will be judged. I'm the artichoke in that scenario."

"Give people credit. Give your fans some credit. They'll love it because you wrote it. A lot of people love artichokes."

"You don't."

"You're not an artichoke," Lydia said. She was getting flustered. I could tell by her voice and the red splotches that appeared on her face and neck. "Now, you listen to me, Louella Harper. I know you. And I know you want to write another book. I believe fifteen years is long enough to wait."

"Exactly! It's been fifteen years. The expectations are going to be that much higher. There's only one direction I can go at this point—straight down."

"Why can't you just be open to the experience. See what happens."

"Let's say I do write another book. What do I have to gain other than money that I don't need and attention that I don't want? If the book fails, I get the same thing, plus it damages my legacy and lends credence to all the rumors that said Cecil wrote *Murder of Innocence* for me. It's a no-win situation."

"This isn't about winning, Lou. You're a writer. It's one of the reasons you were put on the Earth. You can't not write."

"I think you want to get rid of me."

"How can you say that?"

"Because it will be like Kansas again. You and I will never get to see each other."

"Didn't I come and visit you?" She leaned in again and stroked my arm. "Didn't we have a good time together?"

I clasped her hand against my shoulder. "I missed you."

"I missed you too. The being apart made the reunion that much sweeter."

"I don't know if I can do it."

"You have to try, Louella. I can't be the reason you don't publish. I can't be what stands between you and your destiny."

"Fine," I said. "I'll think about it."

From the Research Journal of Chrissy Hope

Interview of Melvin Little conducted by Chrissy Hope on July 2, 2009.

Melvin

Louella Harper's niece was working in the mayor's office at the time, and she mentioned to the mayor that her world-famous auntie was thinking about writing a book about the Reverend, and she would be coming down for that last big trial. Everyone got so excited after she accepted a dinner invitation from some of the town bigwigs.

Interviewer

Were you there?

Melvin

Of course, I was there. I was arguing the big case. We rented the Willow Creek Country Club's coziest banquet room, which extended out into the lake to provide views on three sides. The mayor and his wife were there, along with my wife Miriam and myself, Bill Thompson who was the chief of police, and some important business folks, including Russ Carmichael, who was president and CEO of Carmichael Mills at the time, and a grandson of the founder. He happened to be spending the summer at his lake house and heard about Louella's visit.

It was a big to-do. Everybody fawned over Louella and Madeline. We drank champagne and mixed drinks. Dinner consisted of filet mignon and stuffed lobster tails. The city paid for everything. Louella was the biggest thing to happen to Jackson City since they dammed the river.

From the Diary of Louella Harper

"What exactly is the point of this?" I asked Madeline when we sat down to dinner.

"They want to butter you up," she said, "so you'll make them look good when you write the book."

"They don't have to buy me an expensive meal," I said. "A kind word will do."

"I'm sure you'll receive a lot of kind words as well along with anything else you might ask for."

"I'm not asking for anything but a little honesty."

"Ladies, I couldn't help overhearing you," a voice said from across the table. I didn't know who he was then, but Melvin Little leaned toward us.

"I hope we didn't embarrass you, Ms. Harper. Around here, you're a star. We wanted to give you the star treatment. Of course, everybody was dying to meet you."

"I'm flattered you all find me so interesting, but I'm afraid I might let you down."

"That's not possible."

"I believe it is."

The mayor's wife broke the awkward silence that followed. "Ms. Harper, I just loved your book." She dabbed the meat juice running down her chin with a linen napkin.

"Thank you dear," I said.

"It must have been so exciting for you when you found out they were going to make the movie. What's Jimmy Stewart like?"

"Now, Nancy," Melvin said. "Ms. Harper isn't here to talk about her movie. She's here to work on her new book. She's here to learn about the Reverend."

"Oh, I don't know anything about that awful man other than what was printed in the newspapers."

"I bet the chief could tell you some stories," Melvin said, prodding Chief Thompson.

"Those cases were all outside my jurisdiction. You'll want to talk to Lonnie Maddox."

"Is he here?" I asked.

"Sherriff Maddox has had a rough go of it lately," Melvin said. "He lost his wife."

"And an election," Nancy added.

"Well, he's missing out on a wonderful evening," said Sheryl Carmichael, a woman who might've been a runway model if she'd been able to meet the height requirement. "I know there's no other place I'd rather be than right here." She smiled and somehow twinkled her nose at the same time.

"I'm sure he would be happy to talk to you, Miss Harper," Melvin said.

"How would you know, Melvin?" Mayor Randall asked. "He hates your guts!"

Melvin focused on Chief Thompson. "Now, Harry, I know you didn't let Glen Maddox have all the glory. I bet you're holding onto something you could share with Ms. Harper."

The police chief smiled graciously. "My department is at your disposal. You're more than welcome to stop by the station any time you like."

"I'll do that," I said, reaching for my glass of water with lemon.

"The doors to my office are always open too," Melvin said. "I probably have more files on the Reverend than anyone."

"Melvin was the Reverend's attorney for over ten years," Miriam said.

BLOOD CRIES

"We call his office building, 'The House that Baxter Built.'"

Nancy leaned in toward the center of the table, so we all did. "The people you really should be talking to," she said, "are the blacks. They were the ones most affected by the Reverend."

"Them and Melvin." The mayor said as he crammed a chunk of steak into his mouth. "Only they didn't make as much money."

Melvin shot him a look.

"Were any of them invited tonight?" I asked.

In the awkward silence that followed, I sipped my champagne.

The Reverend
by Louella Harper

Chapter One

Melvin Little awoke to the loathsome sound of a ringing telephone. He picked up the receiver, held it to his ear, and just slumped there, eyes closed, half asleep.

"Hello," said the voice on the other end of the line. "Is anyone there? Is this Mr. Little?"

"That depends," Melvin said. "Who's asking?"

"My name is Reverend Will Baxter. I need your help. The police are at my house. They say I murdered my wife, but I didn't do it."

Such is the life of a defense attorney. A man calls up needing help. He says he's innocent. A lawyer has no choice but to believe him. In America, a person is presumed innocent until proven guilty.

"I'm sorry to hear that Reverend. Have you been charged?"

"No, but I believe they are about to arrest me."

It wasn't easy being a black man in Alabama. Melvin was white, but he'd known for a long time how the system treated those it considered second-class citizens. He'd known it since he was twelve years old, back when his father rented land to a black man who subsequently lost his arm in an accident at the cement plant. Unable to work, he was fired from his job. Without income, Melvin's father ordered him off of the property.

Melvin was outraged, but argument proved fruitless. "Business is business," his father said. "You need to learn that, boy, if you ever hope to succeed in this world."

It was a lesson Melvin had no interest in learning. He swore when he got older he would help people. It didn't matter what color they were or how much money they had; he was going to help those who needed it. He proved as much during his term in the state legislature and he proved it in private practice while charging his clients what they could afford. And yet, somehow the lesson had been learned after all.

"Reverend, you are in a difficult spot just now, but I have a question I need to ask." His feet swung over the side of the bed and groped along the shag carpet for his slippers. "How do you intend to pay me?"

Helping people was nice, but so was buying a new car and taking the family on vacation.

"There's an insurance policy," the Reverend said. "I could pay you with that."

"How much is it worth?"

Melvin opened up the drawer of his bedside table and fumbled around for a pencil and paper to jot down notes.

"A hundred thousand dollars," the Reverend said.

Melvin celebrated silently. "You know you won't see a dime of that money if you get put away for murder? You understand that, right?" He said once he had recovered.

"Yes sir, I do."

"This could become very expensive."

"Yes sir. I expect it will."

"Okay then. I'll take you on."

Melvin worked hard for his clients no matter what they paid him—sometimes he worked for free—but it never hurt to have a little extra incentive.

He heard a voice in the background saying something that diverted the Reverend's attention. "Reverend? Do we have a deal?"

"Yes," he said. "That's fine."

"Don't you say anything. Do you hear me? I'll meet you at the jailhouse."

Less than an hour after hanging up the phone, Melvin stopped by the sheriff's office on a fact-finding mission. He found Sheriff Alonzo Glen Maddox sitting behind his desk, staring at some paperwork. He was a trim and proper man in his late fifties with fading red hair clipped close to his head and an abiding intolerance for defense attorneys.

"Morning, Sheriff," Melvin said amiably.

The Sheriff nodded without looking up. There were two empty chairs on the visitor's side of his desk, but he offered neither.

"I came by to find out why you arrested Reverend Baxter."

Maddox peered over the rim of his glasses at the thirty-five-year-old man standing in his doorway. He had slicked-back hair and wore an expensive suit with a silk handkerchief protruding from the breast pocket of his jacket. He had a face like a gibbous moon. "Here in the sheriff's department, we like to arrest people after they commit murder."

"I heard she died in a car wreck."

"She was beaten and strangled before she ever got behind the wheel of that car," Maddox said. "That's why she wrecked, you see. Dead people don't drive too good."

"My client had nothing to do with that."

"It's always the husband, Melvin. You know that."

"What's your evidence?"

"I'm not here to do your job. Go talk to your client. Maybe he can tell you who would testify against him."

Melvin turned over the new information in his mind as he made his way to the jail. If there was a witness, what exactly did they see?

Within a few minutes, he approached the iron cage containing his client. At one point, it had been someone's bright idea to paint the inside of the jailhouse yellow, but now most of the paint was faded, chipped, or rusted away. Melvin framed his face between the bars.

BLOOD CRIES

There were three men in the 8-by-15-foot cell: a vagrant, a petty thief, and his client. Melvin guessed the two men sitting on a short bench on the far end of the cell were the vagrant and the thief. One was dressed in ragged clothes and had his head buried in his hands. The other was muscular but had a fresh, dark bruises around his eyes that kept darting over to the third man before quickly looking away. Melvin noticed that the two men were about as far away from the third man as they could get.

The Reverend was sitting alone on the long wooden bench lining the wall. Despite the sweltering heat, he wore a black three-piece suit and a matching tiller hat tipped down over his face. His hands were folded across his lap. A soft snore emanated from beneath the hat.

Melvin cleared his throat.

The brim raised and there appeared beneath it a sliver of eyes shimmering white in the darkness.

"You must be Mr. Little," the man said in a drowsy voice. In the dimly lit cell, his voice seemed to emanate from the shadows

"I must be," Melvin said. "You must be ready to get out of here."

The man leaned forward into the light. His lips peeled back around glowing white teeth. "I'd like that very much."

"Okay," Melvin said, "but first come over here and tell me what happened.

The Reverend rose from his seat and smoothed out his suit jacket. He was six feet tall and thin as a piece of straw—all angles and elbows as Melvin's mother used to say. As he sauntered over to his attorney, his face took shape in the light. It was as long and thin as the rest of him and clean shaven except for a pencil mustache sharpened across his lip and oiled to a light sheen.

"I preached a revival in Auburn yesterday evening," He said. "I got home around eleven, but Mary Anne wasn't there. I assumed she was at her sister's house or visiting neighbors, but I was so tired, I went straight to sleep. I woke up around two in the morning and realized she still wasn't home. That's when I knew something was wrong. I started calling around asking about her, but no one had seen her."

"The Sheriff said he's got a witness against you," Melvin said.

"I don't know who that could be."

"I'll see what I can figure out. Right now, let's get you out of here."

Melvin would soon learn what the sheriff's investigation had uncovered. The Reverend had been fired from his job at Carmichael Mills on the same day of the murder. The night before the murder, he was seen riding around town in a brand-new Lincoln Continental with an 18-year-old girl in the passenger seat. It turned out the Lincoln was registered to him, though it was driven primarily by the girlfriend, Cassandra Woods. The only way he was going to keep up the payments, the sheriff surmised, was to kill his wife and collect the insurance.

This theory was seemingly confirmed by the statement of the Baxters' next-door neighbor, Calpurnia Murphy. She told police that Mary Anne had stopped by her house around eleven o'clock on the night in question. She seemed very worried. Her husband had just called saying he'd been in a car accident on the way home from the revival meeting. She was going to fetch him home and just wanted someone to know where she would be. The next morning, she was found dead in her car by the side of the road.

Melvin engineered several delays, but the day of the trial arrived eventually. His young son summed up his own prognostication when, after consulting with his magic 8 ball toy, he declared, "Outlook not so good." Calpurnia Murphy was set to take the stand.

Sitting in court, Melvin noted the look of serene indifference on the face of the district attorney, Henry Russell. With his white suit, white hair, and black-framed eyeglasses, the man looked about as intimidating as Colonel Sanders, but there was no denying he was a bulldog in the courtroom. He tended to stalk in front of the jury box and used his baritone voice and his six-foot-four, two-hundred-and-forty-five-pound frame to intimidate the hell out of witnesses.

"State calls Calpurnia Murphy to the stand."

The doors of the courtroom swung open, and Calpurnia Murphy strutted down the aisle like a peacock. Gone was the shy woman in drab clothing and tortoise shell glasses. Born was the woman in a turquoise dress and matching hat. She looked younger than thirty-five as she sashayed into the witness box, swinging her hips and smiling like she'd just won the church bake-off.

The sudden change in personality struck Melvin as odd, to say the least, especially considering the fact that, since losing her friend/next-door neighbor the previous year, she had also lost her husband. Six months after Mary Anne was found, Fred Murphy passed away following a protracted illness.

Rather than challenging the witness directly and risk alienating the jury, Melvin planned to tread lightly and focus on the dearth of physical evidence. No one could be sure what happened out on that road, since no one had been there to see what happened. He might yet summon the specter of reasonable doubt.

After the bailiff swore in the witness, Russell stood and began his examination.

"Are you Calpurnia Murphy, formerly Calpurnia Barrett of Hartselle, Alabama?" he asked.

Calpurnia leaned toward the jury and spoke like she was answering a question at a beauty contest. "I used to live in Hartselle. That's right. Now I live down Highway 22, about a half-mile past Corky's Bait and Tackle Shop."

"Do you know the defendant, William Baxter?" the prosecutor asked.

"Reverend Baxter's been my neighbor for nearly ten years," she answered, smiling. "His wife May Anne used to do my hair."

"And did you see Mary Anne Baxter on the evening of August 27, 1970?"

"I did."

"What time of day was it?"

"Around six o'clock in the afternoon."

"And did you speak with her?"

"I did."

"And what did she say?"

"She was mad because her husband was taking me to a revival in Auburn."

Russell, who had been doing his pacing routine in front of the jury box, stopped suddenly. "Could you repeat that?" he asked.

"She was very angry that Reverend Baxter was taking me to a revival meeting."

"And what were you doing going to a revival meeting with another woman's husband?" By now, Russell knew she was committing perjury. His only hope was to lay a trap and catch her in it.

"It was all perfectly innocent. I don't know why Mary Anne was so mad. The Reverend even said she was welcome to come with us, but Mary Anne wanted to stay home."

"You're saying you went with Will Baxter to a church revival that night?"

"That's correct," Calpurnia said.

"How did you get home?"

"Reverend Baxter drove me."

"And where was Mary Anne?"

"I don't know. She was already gone when we got there. I had just waved goodbye to him, and gone to check on Fred, when he knocked on my door and asked if Mary Anne was home. I said no, and then he said she must have gone over to her sisters, and then he went back home."

"And you hadn't seen Mary Anne since you left for the revival?"

"That's correct."

"Calpurnia," Henry Russell said in a scolding voice, "then, why did you tell the police she came over to your house talking about her husband having a car accident."

"I don't know anything about that," Cassandra said.

"You didn't make that statement to a sheriff's deputy?"

"I did not. They must have gotten confused. Or maybe it was a statement made by my late husband. Fred was often confused."

"You're saying your husband made a false report? Why is this the first I'm hearing of it?"

"Well, Fred and I have suffered a spell of bad luck lately, what with him dying and all."

"Why would he risk jail by making a false police report?"

"He was a very jealous man," Calpurnia said matter-of-factly. "He and Mary Anne had that in common."

"Were you two having an affair?" Russell asked,

"Objection, Your Honor," Melvin said.

"Calpurnia, why are you protecting Will Baxter?" Russell asked.

"Objection," Melvin said. "He's trying to impeach his own witness."

"Sustained," the judge said.

Henry Russell just stood there, looking stupefied.

"Your honor," Melvin said, "the prosecutor has no case. I move for a directed verdict in favor of the defendant."

"There is something amiss here, Your Honor," Henry Russell said.

"Well, you'll have to sort it out later," said the judge. "Do you have any other witnesses or evidence you can introduce now?"

"Not right now," he admitted.

"Then, I'm afraid he's got you, Henry. Motion is granted." He banged his gavel. "Case dismissed."

Russell stood frozen in the center of the courtroom like a deer caught in headlights. The only thing that snapped him out of a stupor was when Calpurnia stepped out of the witness box, and the light caused something to sparkle at the end of her ring finger.

"Now wait just a second," Russell said, seeing it for the first time. "Calpurnia, where did you get that diamond?"

"The case is over, Henry," Melvin said.

Calpurnia stretched out her hand to let the prosecutor admire her ring. "Will gave it to me."

"Will?" Russell asked.

Calpurnia could no longer contain her excitement. She let out a long squeal. "I'm going to be the next Mrs. William Baxter."

Henry Russell shook his head as the defendant strolled passed him to greet his fiancé, who jumped into his arms and gave him a big, fat kiss. "Did you know about this?"

"If I'd known, I would have insisted they get married right away," Melvin said. "You think I'd let a woman take the stand against her husband?"

Family members rushed forward to congratulate the happy couple. Henry snatched up his files and papers and stomped out of the courtroom.

The Reverend was off the hook for murder, but there was still the small matter of collecting the insurance payment. Baxter had taken out an accidental death insurance policy on his wife, but the insurance company had no interest in paying for what they considered to be a homicide. The Supreme Court of Alabama, however, had ruled that even a homicide was an accident to the person who was killed. Baxter received a verdict for the full amount of the policy.

The insurance company paid Melvin one hundred thousand dollars, half of which he turned over to the Reverend. That was a lot of money back in those days. Melvin figured it was the last he'd ever see of Reverend William Baxter.

Chrissy

After listening to Melvin tell his story, I had about a bazillion questions, but only one came out of my mouth. "Why didn't Louella Harper ever publish that book?"

Melvin looked at me through drooping eyelids but said nothing. It was two o'clock in the afternoon and quite possibly I was interrupting his regular naptime.

"I know," I said with the excitement that comes with a brilliant idea. "Let's call her right now and see what she says. Or, if you prefer, you could give me her number and I'll call her."

"She'll tell you to go to hell and hang up on you," he said.

"Well, then I'll have an interesting anecdote to tell my grandchildren," I said despite the fact that my boyfriend is afraid of commitment. There's a good chance I will never have grandchildren. I'm not feeling sorry for myself. I'm just saying.

Melvin shook his head.

Here's something you should know about me. When I get something stuck in my head, it stays stuck. Calling me obsessive is an understatement, but I like to think of my tendency—and it's really just a tendency—to obsess over things, and over people, is something that allows me to accomplish goals that other people might never bother to pursue because they require too much effort, or because they are deemed irrational.

CHRIS HOPE

My boyfriend says my actions sometimes fail to withstand logical scrutiny. He's also quick to point out that mental illness runs in my family. My great grandmother claimed the pilots of low flying airplanes were communicating with her through her braces. But I am not my Grandma Martha. I am a lovely young woman with nothing but good intentions and best wishes for everyone.

My big problem is I lack clearly defined career goals and I have no real prospects for the future. Before my trip to Melvin's office, my life was pretty monotonous. It involved going back and forth from my apartment to a job I hated, and then back to my apartment, where James and I would sit around and watch television, or poke around on the internet until it was time to go to bed, and then the process started all over again. Occasionally, James and I spent a night out with friends, but it wasn't enough, you know? I needed to do something more with my life.

So, I decided to find out what happened to Louella's manuscript.

Melvin put me in touch with an editor of one of the Montgomery papers, who, in the mid-to-late 1970s, was a cub reporter for the *Jackson City Sentinel*. When Louella came to Jackson City to research the story, he drove her around town, and they became friends. His name was Jim Easton.

Over the phone, Jim told me a little bit about the Reverend, but he got quiet when the subject turned to Louella. When I asked if he could get her a message for me he said, "I won't talk to her for you or anyone else. With Louella, privacy is a condition of friendship. People who talk about her publicly don't stay friends with her for long."

It was the same thing with everyone I talked to. Other than Melvin Little, no one would talk about Louella Harper publicly or privately.

I was ready to pull my hair out until I found the name of Louella's personal attorney in a newspaper article. I looked up her firm online, found a mailing address, and quickly typed out a long, rambling letter to Louella, telling her who I was and where I was from and that I was researching that whole Reverend story. I made it a big point to tell her that I go by Chrissy, but I once published a few short stories under the name Chris Hope. I guess I was hoping she would look them up online. I sent the letter to her in care of Melissa Taggert, attorney at law.

After a week, I received a letter in the mail with a PO Box number and Florentine, AL scribbled as the return address. Printed on an envelope-sized piece of cardstock underneath the monogram LH, the following message was written in an unsteady scrawl:

Dear Chris,
When I went down to Jackson City all those years ago, I found a mountain of rumors and tall tales and a molehill of facts. Perhaps the dust has settled by now. I wish you luck.
Louella Harper

As I read the note, I was doing cartwheels in my mind. Louella Harper wrote me a letter!

The note suggested that she had given up on the book, but the message was so short and vague, it left me with more questions than answers. How much did she write before she gave up on the book? What happened to her research materials? Would it be okay if I poked around in her garage and in her basement looking for remnants from her time in Jackson City?

Back in 1978, Louella lived in Jackson City for almost a year while she researched the Reverend's story. After a long day at the police station, the newspaper archives, the library, or interviewing witnesses, she must have stayed up late, typing up notes. She would not have been able to resist the temptation to explore characters and story lines. She was a writer—possibly the greatest writer who ever lived. She must have written something. Unless she threw it all away or burned it in her backyard like a deranged artist—instead of the super-down-to-earth-person I knew her to be—then that material must still exist somewhere, possibly in her house. If it existed anywhere, then I was going to find it.

I had to find it. Every cell in my body told me I was born to do this one thing. It was my purpose in life. I was Nancy Drew.

Again, I know how crazy this sounds, but allow me to explain.

Shortly after graduating from college, I informed my mother that I intended to become a professional writer. I wrote a few short stories and attempted a novel, but none of it was very good. I worked in restaurants to pay my bills, but I was usually too tired after a shift to do any actual writing.

I was still in my early twenties when I decided that nursing sounded like a pretty decent back-up profession. I liked the idea of helping people, and I had already earned all the science credits I needed during my undergraduate studies. In order to get into nursing school, though, I had to prove I was devoted to the cause, so I took a job working the midnight shift as an aide at a nursing home.

My job, basically, was to change adult diapers twice a night. It paid enough for me to live on and provided me with health insurance and 3-4 days off every week since I was working 12-hour shifts from 6 pm to 6 am.

As it happened, the company that owned the nursing home where I worked also owned an assisted living facility in Florentine, Alabama where Louella Harper had been living for the last year, ever since a minor heart attack brought her home from New York City.

"It's a sign from God!" I told my mother over the phone.

"It is not. It's a coincidence."

"Someone or something is communicating with me, Mother. It's telling me I have to do this."

This is the kind of thing that makes people think I'm crazy, isn't it?

Was it impulsive? Yes. I put in for a job transfer almost immediately. I never mentioned my reasoning or Louella Harper to my bosses. Now, that would have been crazy. I simply told them I wanted to be near some family I had down in South

Alabama, which is sort of true because after all the times I've read Murder of Innocence and all the books and articles I've consumed having to do with Louella, she kind of feels like family to me.

My employers were sorry to see me go because, you know, I'm awesome, but they also didn't try to talk me out of it or press me for any details.

James, of course, was against the idea.

"Let me get this straight," he said. "You're going to pack up all your things and move to Podunk, Alabama in the hopes that you might, *might*, meet an old lady who might tell you what happened to some book she may or may not have written forty years ago?"

"That sounds about right," I said. I was already packing my suitcase. In retrospect, part of the reason James was so angry was because I waited until after the transfer went through to tell him what I intended to do. James is very level-headed. I knew if I told him sooner, he would have talked me out of it.

"You're crazy," he said. "You're certifiably insane."

"What's so crazy about changing jobs?" I asked as I arranged a stack of neatly folded clothes on the bed.

"You are moving to another city to stalk an old lady. Do you know how creepy that sounds?"

"I'm not stalking. I'm investigating. I'm researching. I'm fact finding. I'm going to find out what happened to Louella Harper's book, and to do that, there's no better place to start than with Louella Harper herself. She spent a year researching the story. She didn't drive back and forth on the weekends. She moved there. Why? Because she was committed."

"If she was so committed, why didn't she finish the book?"

"I don't know," I said. "That's what I need to find out."

"You're never going to find out what happened to that book because you're never going to get anywhere near her. She probably has people around to protect her from people like you."

"I have to try," I said before doing a double-take. "Wait. What people like me? I'm nice. I'm not going to bother her. I'm going to do my job and bide my time. It might take a while, but eventually I'll meet her, strike up a conversation, which will lead to other conversations, which will lead to friendship, which will lead to the truth."

"That's not crazy at all."

"You're right. It's not crazy," I said, ignoring his sarcasm. "It's simple."

"And just how long do you intend to be gone?"

"I don't know." I looked down at the inside of my suitcase. "Six months maybe. A year at most."

The room was silent other than the alarm bells going off in my head.

"And what am I supposed to do during that time?" he asked. "Do you expect me to wait for you?"

"I assumed that you would come visit me," I said, "and that I would come visit you. Florentine is only four hours from Atlanta, but apparently pursuing my dream is so much of an inconvenience to you, you're ready to toss me out of your life completely."

"That's not fair."

"It is fair, James. You don't seem to understand that I have to do this. This is my chance to do… something."

"You're right," he said. "I don't understand."

It was brutal. That conversation was the reason I waited so long to tell him my plan. I knew not telling him was wrong, but I also knew there were no good options, and that he would try to talk me out of going, and that he would feel hurt and rejected, and that I would feel guilty about the whole thing, and that's exactly what happened.

When I loaded my car and drove out of the city, I had no idea if I would ever see him again. I was trading in a world of comfort and semi-security for an unknown destiny. Something was waiting for me at the end of this road, and it was going to change my life forever.

That was all I needed to keep going.

My first night in Florentine, I stayed at the only motel in town, the one across the street from the courthouse described

BLOOD CRIES

by Louella Harper in Murder of Innocence. I woke up early, crawled out of bed and into the dim light of my room, and peered through the blinds at that old cracked brick building.

This is so exciting!

After a quick shower and a granola bar, I rushed across the street to take a tour of the courthouse. For the low cost of six dollars, I was led through the building's original courtroom, no longer used for actual trials. I got to see the bench where Charles and Sydney Townsend—had they been real people and not fictional characters—would have sat while on trial for their lives. I saw the table where their lawyer, Terrence Digby, would have gathered his notes before delivering his impassioned closing argument. And I saw the judge's box where old Lowry Carter would have sat stone faced as he ignored Digby's pleas for leniency and issued a sentence so harsh and unfair that it would one day reduce a nine-year-old version of myself to a sobbing mess, causing her to throw her dog-eared paperback across the bedroom and bury herself beneath the covers for a good ten minutes before she could bring herself to scamper across the room to retrieve the book and finish the story.

After the tour, I was delivered to a gift shop filled with knick-knacks related to the masterwork. There were *Murder of Innocence* place mats, wall clocks, t-shirts, bed spreads, curtains, and pretty much everything else that could possibly be emblazoned with a hangman's noose: the same image used on the cover of the special edition paperback released to coincide with the fiftieth anniversary of the book's publication. Louella Harper-related tourism had become the number one source of commercial revenue in the city of Florentine.

Following an early lunch at the Innocence Diner, I spent another six dollars for the privilege of climbing aboard an old school bus that had been painted bright red, with a sign across the side advertising "The Louella Harper Mystery Tour." There were five of us including myself, an elderly couple, and an au pair killing time with the five-year-old girl under her charge. We drove down a picturesque street lined with magnolia and dogwood trees sprouting pink buds. The driver was a man with a large gut and a few strands of strawberry blonde hair atop his freckled head. His name was Gus.

Gus drove us to some amazing attractions, like the gas station that was built on the spot where the real-life counterpart of Terrence Digby supposedly faced down the angry mob ready to lynch the young men falsely accused of raping a white woman, and the billboard—recently decorated with the slogan "Rent this Sign"—that had been erected on the spot where Louella Harper's house once stood.

The woman who led the tour, Nancy, who was also Gus's wife, had short silver hair with black flecks hiding in the layers. Even though there were only five of us, she stood beside the first row of seats and spoke into a handheld microphone connected to a black box mounted above Gus's head. Each word she spoke stretched on for about five extra syllables as she told us where Louella Harper (it sounded like Hopper) went to high school.

The elderly man held up his hand. "When do we get to meet Louella?"

Nancy looked at him like he'd just asked her for a personal loan. Gus shook his head.

"You don't get to meet Louella Harper," Nancy said.

"She don't meet with anybody," Gus added.

"Do we at least get to see where she lives now?" asked the elderly man's wife. "We came all this way."

"We'll show you the landmarks and historical places, but that's where it ends," said Nancy.

As Nancy spoke, I sank down into my seat. It suddenly occurred to me that I had made a miscalculation by appearing in public. I was two days away from reporting for duty at the very same assisted living facility where Louella Harper resided. If this information came out, it would likely raise suspicions, and I might find myself out of a job before it began.

I wasn't the first person to come poking around Florentine looking for information about Louella Harper. Many others—usually journalists—had come before me, asking questions. The locals walked a fine line between guarding and celebrating their star citizen but were quite adept at misdirection and planting false information. I read one account of a journalist from a national publication who frequented the diner and asked each of the locals if they knew Louella Harper. One by one, they answered no, including Louella Harper herself, who had been having lunch there with a group of friends the whole time.

But it wasn't enough to stop the migration of newspaper folk and magazine writers, a few of whom took up long-term residence in Florentine while trying to get the scoop on the old woman who published one universally beloved title and then gave up literary celebrity for a life split between the anonymity of New York City and winters filled with grocery store trips and church socials back home. One of those writers even managed to do what I was now trying to do: she inserted herself into Louella's inner circle.

When the house next door to Louella's went on the market, she bought it sight unseen at asking price and moved in a week later. Louella did as many still do in this part of the country, she welcomed her new neighbor with a plate of homemade brownies, planting the seed of friendship that would grow for the next three years. By then, the woman decided she had what she needed. She moved home to New York and wrote a tell-all book about her time with Louella, who never forgave her.

In a strange way, the reporter's success gave me hope, while her underhandedness made me determined to do things differently. I had no idea what would happen, but I knew one thing: I would never betray Louella Harper.

After the tour, the time came for small talk and idle chit chat. I found myself telling fibs to cover up my true intentions.

"What brings you to town? Are you a fan of Louella Harper's book?" Nancy asked me.

"Well," I said, "I've been meaning to read it." This was true. I had been meaning to read it for the twenty-third time. "But mostly I was just looking for something to do."

Nancy's happy demeanor melted away. "Well, you have to read it right away," she said. "Gus will set you up with a copy for only $9.99."

A half-hour later, I waved goodbye with an extra copy of my favorite book, confident that my secret was safe.

I still had a lot to do that first day, starting with finding a place to live. Using the real-estate section of the *Florentine Gazette* as a guide, I made a list of seven potential homes and mapped out the shortest routes between addresses.

I eliminated one listing before leaving the tour group. Nancy assured me that Briarwood Estates—the only apartment complex on my list—was unsuitable to my needs. "It's no place for a single white woman," she said in a matter-of-fact tone before leaning close to my face and mouthing the word, "ghetto." As hateful as I found the underlying racism in her message, I reminded myself that I was not in Florentine to make a political statement, or to stand out in any way for that matter. I needed to maintain laser-like focus on my mission, so I took out my black sharpie and crossed Briarwood Estates off my list.

For the rest of the afternoon I crisscrossed the town looking for a suitable residence. I looked at several old houses available at astoundingly low prices compared to the Atlanta market. I scratched the first three places off my list because they lacked the southern charm I was looking for and several more were eliminated because they required me to share living space with families and/or lacked privacy.

I found what I needed at the end of a magnolia-lined street in an old, but well-kept neighborhood less than a mile from the courthouse. It was there that I pulled into the driveway of a stately brick home owned by Ms. Ruth Anne Stimpson, an elderly widow, who took me into her dining room and peppered me with questions to which I struggled to find answers.

"What brings you to Florentine?" She asked after sitting me down at the formal dinner table. "We get so few young people coming to town. Usually they're headed out." This had been the case with her three children, who fled Florentine at the first opportunity. When I explained that I had come to work in the assisted living facility, her expression grew even more perplexed. "Don't they have nursing homes in Atlanta?"

"They do," I admitted, "but they lack the charm and beauty of Florentine, Alabama."

Ms. Stimpson raised an eyebrow and continued the interrogation.

I told her the same thing I told the people at my old job—that I had family in the area—only now I was face to face with someone who knew everyone in the area.

"What are their names?"

"Who?"

"Your family."

"Um... Glover."

Ms. Stimpson named several Glovers she was well-acquainted with, along with the churches they attended.

I explained that my Glovers were neither Baptists nor Methodists, but free-thinking Universalists, most of whom had later migrated to Florida.

With a second eyebrow raised, she exclaimed, "I certainly don't know anyone like that."

I went on to explain that the only one of my relatives still remaining in Florentine, a second cousin, twice removed, was a shut-in with no other family besides myself, who had, for the last seventeen years, maintained residency at Lake View Estates Assisted Living Facility, where I was soon to take employment. I had taken the job, I said, as a way of fulfilling a promise I had made to my grandmother on her death bed.

I don't know what I was thinking, telling such a wild story. I guess I got carried away in the moment. Or maybe it was the fact that it was such a great house that had everything I needed: my own parking spot behind the house, a separate entrance by which to come and go, a full bathroom and kitchenette. If I played my cards right I might never have to even see or talk to Ms. Stimpson again.

My lies led to a new and painful thread of conversation in which she promised to make inquiries about my dear second cousin who would of course be added to her church prayer list. Second Cousin Sarah, as she was now called, could count on a stream of visitors in the near future. It took all of my powers to convince Ms. Stimpson that Second Cousin Sarah wanted nothing more than to be left alone, although a few prayers offered at a respectful distance might be appreciated.

I know. I know. So much lying. Just remember, I couldn't tell people I was on a quest for a lost manuscript because if I did that everyone would think I was crazy. If everyone thought I was crazy, I wouldn't get close enough to Louella to find out what happened to her manuscript. It was like a Catch-22 or something. I felt a little guilty, but I really had no choice but to lie. It was the only way to solve the mystery, and I had to solve the mystery because I was Nancy Fucking Drew.

From the Journal of Louella Harper

June 1977

I was in my motel room, sitting on the edge of the bed, talking to my agent, Amy, about the new project.

"How is that going to work?" she asked. "Are you going to include yourself as a character in the book?"

"Good Lord, no," I said. "I hate books like that. I am here strictly as an observer. I will collect facts and report them. As a character, I don't exist."

"Only you are a character. You're an important character. You're Louella Fricking Harper. The second you walked into town, you became the center of the story."

I thought about my country club welcome reception and frowned. "The last thing in the world I wanted to be."

"You could make this work for you, you know. Journalism is changing."

"It's in decline."

"No, there's plenty of good journalism out there. Nonfiction too. I know if you decide to throw your hat into the ring, I can go ahead and unscrew my navel because I'll know my ass is about to be blown off."

"Don't get too excited. I'm not even sure there's a story here."

"Oh, there's always a story if you look hard enough, but is it a Louella Harper kind of story? That's the only question I'm interested in hearing the answer to."

"I don't know that yet. I may need to travel a little further down the road."

"You take your time and let me know when you know. I have to run now, Darling. I'll speak with you in a few days."

I placed the telephone handset into its cradle, which sat in a circle of lamplight on the bedside table. Without thinking, I opened the drawer and found a fresh edition of Gideon's Bible. I kicked off my shoes and stretched out on the bed, and then opened the Good Book to a random page in Genesis. My eyes fell upon chapter 3, versus 6-7. "Then the Lord said to Cain, 'Why are you angry? Why is your face downcast? If you do what is right, will you not be accepted? But if you do not do what is right, sin is crouching at your door; it desires to have you, but you must rule over it.'"

Here was one of the oldest stories in the world, and it was still applicable. Cain only had one job—to go about his business and honor the Lord by not destroying his creation. Of course, we all know how that went. I made a mental note to reread the story of Cain and Abel to supplement my research. Besides, I might acquire a few guiding principles to navigate the ethically murky waters of this story.

On this night, however, I was absorbed in local history. I would soon fall asleep with Pickett's *The Story of Alabama* folded across my chest.

The Creek Indian War came to its bloody conclusion less than three miles away from my motel room. One hundred and sixty-five years ago, Major General Andrew Jackson and two thousand soldiers under his command trapped a thousand Creek Warriors on a small peninsula formed by the winding snake known as the Tallapoosa river.

After blasting their barricades with cannon fire, Jackson sent a small contingent of men to swim across the river and wreak havoc from the rear. When he saw plumes of smoke rising from behind the fortification and heard the sound of small arms fire, he ordered a bayonet charge, and within minutes, Jackson's men had breached the barricade of logs and mud and slaughtered all the "Red Sticks" on the other side.

The next day, the victorious soldiers counted the Creek dead by slicing off their noses. By nightfall, they had erected a small mountain of more than five hundred. Best estimates put an equal number at the bottom of the river.

Six months later, General Jackson defeated the British at the Battle of New Orleans. Five years after that, Alabama became a state. Ten years after that, Andrew Jackson became the seventh president of the United States. And one hundred and sixty-six years after that, I stayed at the Horseshoe Bend Motel on the outskirts of Jackson City, Alabama, a town named not for Andrew Jackson but for a former confederate officer who ran a railroad the townspeople wished to attract to the area, a ploy that proved successful.

As I huddled in my little motel room facing the woods, I compared my position to that of the men who fought at the battle of Horseshoe Bend. I'd ridden into town like a conquering hero, but I felt more like someone trapped behind a barricade, surrounded on all sides, and counting my final moments before the massacre.

Luckily, the next morning found my feelings of loneliness and self-pity replaced with a renewed sense of optimism. I was already dressed and ready to go out for the day, when someone knocked on the door. Outside, I found Melvin Little standing beside a young man who looked to be in his early twenties.

"Louella, I found this miscreant loitering outside of your motel room. I'm only kidding. This is Jimmy Easton. He covered the Baxter story for the *Jackson City Sentinel*."

"Call me Jim." The young man said. "I'm a big fan of yours, Ms. Harper." He was a big fellow, round in the belly, with curly red hair and a scruffy beard. He had a doughy face marked by pink splotches brought on by heat or embarrassment; I thought it impertinent to ask which. "And I wasn't loitering. We both just happened to drive up at the same time. I heard you were here, and I came to offer you my assistance."

"You might need someone to chauffeur you around while you're completing your research," Melvin suggested.

"Sure, I'd be happy to show you around," Jim said.

"You are very kind to offer. I accept" I said. "But before we go, I do have a few questions for you, Melvin"

"You know I am always at your service except for right now. I just stopped by on the way to meet a client. Why don't you stop by my office tomorrow and we'll do it proper?"

"That's fine," I said. "I take it you have some files to show me."

"Whatever you need," Melvin said. "I'll have Lorrie set you up."

With that settled, I looked at Jim. "Now, young man, are you ready to go?"

Jim offered me his arm. "I was born ready."

A few minutes later, I was riding in the passenger seat of his van, which he referred to as the Mystery Machine, a reference to the vehicle in the Scooby Dooby cartoons.

"Is this to be a novel then?" he asked.

"I've written a successful novel already, more successful than I ever could have imagined. This time I want to stick to the truth."

"Truth is an abstract concept to me. I don't know much about it."

"I thought you were a reporter."

"Truth depends on the observer," Jim said. "No two versions of it are ever exactly alike. I report things that can be verified."

"Just the facts then," I said.

We turned off of the highway and into the dirt driveway of a small, but well-kept, one-story house with a veranda. "A man named Evan Waverly lives here now," Jim said as he put the van in park, "But six years, the house belonged to Fred and Calpurnia Murphy."

"The Reverend's next-door neighbors." I pointed to the small brick bungalow next door. "Is that the Reverend's house?"

"That's it," Jim said. "From here, Calpurnia had a perfect view into his living room window. Evan bought this house from her not long after she moved next door."

"What does he know?"

"He's been telling everyone in town he has a story to tell, but after that he clams up. I'm hoping he'll open up to you."

As we climbed out of the vehicle, I realized we were being watched by a man sitting in a rocking chair.

"Mr. Waverly," Jim said. "This is Louella Harper, the writer I was telling you about."

With my purse hanging from my elbow, I stepped onto the porch and held out my hand just as my father taught me. "How do you do, Mr. Waverly?"

The man made no effort to take my hand. "Circumstances have changed since the last time we talked, Jim."

"What does that mean?"

"It means I can't part with this story for free."

I slowly withdrew my hand as it became clear that he had no intention of taking it.

"What are you talking about Evan? This is Louella Harper, probably the most famous writer in the country. If you've got something to say, this is the person to talk to."

"I'm holding out for the TV producer."

"What TV producer?"

"A man from Hollywood called me two nights ago. He said I could get seven thousand dollars for my story." He turned to me for the first time. "Can you beat that offer?"

I had already turned my back on him and was walking back toward the van. "Facts aren't things to be bought and sold," I said, looking at Jim. "To do so would call them into question."

It was only my first stop, but it had yielded zero information. I couldn't help feeling disappointed. I hoped the next stop would produce better results.

The Reverend
by Louella Harper

Chapter Two

In the dimly lit chapel of the Temple of the Smith, Carefree Kevin disco danced down the center aisle, slapping the tops of pews, and moving to music that could only be he heard in his head. On the tail end of a Bee Gees chorus, he spun around full circle, dropped to the rug with legs split front to back, and then bounced back up again. He let out a celebratory "Whoo!" on the up-step and shimmied on down the way toward his evening's employment.

When he reached the first pew, his right hand gripped the cap rail, and he socked his head to one side to listen to the staggered snores emanating from the pine seat beneath him. A festering lump of army jacket expanded and contracted at semi-regular intervals occasionally interrupted by fits of gasping.

He slipped his hand into the side pocket of his own fine, sporty model—the one his mother called his silver dinner jacket—and wrapped his fingers and thumb around the paper bag and bottle he had stored there.

He shifted into predator mode.

Silent as a stone, he ripped his weapon of choice—cheap Tennessee Mash—into *Psycho* knife-stabbing position.

"Hi-ja," he screamed in his high-pitched karate voice. Bottle met wood—thock—and that was the end of J. Christopher's rest.

"Good evening, sir. I bring you tidings of great joy."

J. blinked at the bottle and the man disrupting his slumber while his mind oriented to his surroundings. He wiped the sleepers from his eyes with the sleeve of his button-down shirt as he sat up in the pew. His feet met the floor inside a pair of unlaced hunting boots.

Seeing that he had the attention of his guest, Kevin led it to the deluxe model coffin at the top of the room, adorned on one side by an arrangement of carnations and lilies.

"When did that get here?" J. Christopher asked.

"We been in here sweating our asses off all afternoon. Your drunk ass slept through it all."

"It's beautiful."

"It's expensive," Kevin said. He stepped behind the podium and gestured to the coffin beside him. "This here is the deluxe model. It can meet all your heavenly needs for the retail price of three hundred and seventy-five dollars. Are you interested in making a purchase with us today? Seriously. What's it going to take to put you into one of these sweet babies?"

J. looked away. "You know I don't have no money."

"How come your brother won't share? Doesn't he know it isn't nice not to share?"

"I don't like talking about my brother."

"That's okay. I won't ask you to speak against your brother. Let's talk about that bottle sitting beside you. Did I buy the right brand?"

"Brand don't matter to me. It's quality that counts."

"Well, did I buy the right quality then?"

J. Christopher fingered the label of the cheapest pint of whisky you could buy at the liquor store. "It'll do."

"Don't cha wanna know who's in the coffin?" Kevin asked in his excited kid voice.

"I know who's in it. It's Etta Birch." With a twist of his wrist, J. cracked the paper seal of the whiskey bottle, and then set the cap down beside him on the pew. He took a long pull and sighed. "Why'd you bring me here, Kevin?"

"Can't I offer a helping hand to a brother in need without you doubting my intentions? I'm hurt, John Christopher. I'm really hurt."

"Is that what you think? That your helping me?"

Kevin pressed the backs of his hands to his hips. "This is just too much. I am shocked to hear you speak this way, J. Christopher. Here, I have given you a free place to stay. I brought you what I thought was your favorite liquid refreshment, and you have done nothing but complain." He reached out with open palms. "Did I not invite you to stay in this chapel? Would you prefer sleeping in the woods?"

"I am always thankful to receive shelter."

"Well it doesn't sound like it. Where would you be without me? Where would you be right now?"

"Probably sleeping in the church basement."

"They make you sleep in the basement?"

"There's a bed there for me. It's warm, and the sheets are clean. I can get my clothes washed and some food to eat."

"Poor John Christopher," Kevin said. "Are you sure I can't sell you this coffin?"

"I thought Etta Birch bought that coffin."

"She did. And tomorrow she'll be buried in it, and then later me or somebody else will dig it up again and dump Etta Birch back in the ground and cover her up. Then, we'll wash off the outside, wax it, freshen up the inside, and then I'll sell it all over again. I sold this same coffin six times already. Ernie gives me a fifty percent commission every time I dig it up."

J. flinched when he heard the name.

"What's the matter J. Christopher? Ernie's the reason you're here. Don't you know I only extended this hospitality on his behalf? I honestly don't give a damn where you stay."

J. fingered the label of the whisky bottle. "When did he get out of the penitentiary?"

"A few days ago."

J. tilted his head back and let the whiskey pour down his throat. When he put it down again, Ernie was standing beside him. He wore a black suit with a white shirt and no tie.

"I thought it was a sin to drink whisky in church," he said.

"This ain't a church," J. said.

Ernie laughed. "Kevin, do me a favor and bring this man another drink.

"I still have half a pint."

"That's okay. You weren't planning on going anywhere any time soon, were you?" Ernie stretched his arm across the smaller man's back and squeezed his shoulder.

"No," J. Christopher said. "I wasn't planning on that."

CHRIS HOPE

From the Journal of Louella Harper

On the 17th day of September 1972, Christopher Baxter was found sprawled in a patch of tall grass beside Highway 22. The authorities found no signs of accident or foul play. The official cause of death was listed as alcohol poisoning and exposure. When investigators later took a second look at the toxicology report, they discovered that the blood alcohol content in the blood stream of the deceased was more than five times the legal limit. Some have suggested that the only way a human being could have drunk that much liquor was if someone held them down and poured it down his throat.

Chrissy

Lake View Estates was very different from my previous workplace, which was set up like a traditional hospital with a nurse's station centered between a convergence of corridors stretching out like rays of sunshine on a child's drawing. Lake View was a hive of twenty luxury garden-style buildings separated from one another by hedgerows.

Most of the residents—we called them guests—led comfortable and fairly independent lives. As a new employee, I would not be working with them.

My guests were often suffering from chronic and sometimes terminal illnesses, broken legs and hips, arthritis and other debilitating conditions. Many were close but not quite ready to be transferred to a full-time care facility.

Following a mandatory three-week training period in which I received a refresher course in everything from taking blood pressure to changing sheets without removing the patient from the bed to administering CPR in emergency situations, I mostly assisted guests in the restroom.

I started out on the day shift. Each morning, I arrived at work by 6 a.m., stowed my things in a locker, and then made my way to the small office of the charge nurse to clock in. Next, I reported to a senior aide: an experienced nurse's assistant who would be supervising me until I learned the ropes.

My supervising aide's name was Dorothy.

At the beginning of our shift, Dorothy and I usually met in the breakroom for a cup of coffee and a discussion about the specific needs of the residents highlighted on our assignment sheet. We then made the rounds, going from building to building, helping guests with activities of daily living such as using the restroom, bathing, using the restroom, preparing lunch, using the restroom, a little light cleaning, preparing dinner, and using the restroom. It was a thankless, and somewhat disgusting job, but someone had to do it.

"I'm just glad they didn't stick me with a man," Dorothy said to me on our first day together. She was in her early forties, with two grown children. Having worked at Lake View for five years, she was something of an elder statesperson.

"Why don't you want to work with a man?" I asked. "Worried about sexual harassment?" The truth, I knew from training, was that in the state of Alabama, men were excused from assisting female guests in the restroom. Women were required to assist both males and females. Supervising a male nurse's aide would increase Dorothy's workload. It wasn't a fair system, and I wasn't exactly clear on the rationale, but I wasn't there to advocate for change.

"Don't you start," Dorothy said.

I was happy to have made a positive first impression, but I still had to prove to her that I could do the job. On that first day, I showed her how I handled unpleasant assignments like dodging Mrs. Winningham's punches during her sponge bath and smiling cheerfully as Mr. Melbourne called me the devil when I tried to take his temperature. By the afternoon, Dorothy and I were chatting like old friends.

"So, who do you think is the most interesting guest?" I asked, trying to sound nonchalant.

"'Let's see," Dorothy said. "Where do I begin?"

She proceeded to entertain me with stories from her time at Lake View, stories about Mr. Halpern—who thought he received visits from the ghost of his dead dog—and Mrs. MacDougal, who set her apartment on fire while burning trash on the porch of her upstairs apartment. (Thankfully, no one was injured.)

She had nothing whatsoever to say about Louella Harper.

In fact, through my first four weeks on the job I never heard anyone mention Louella Harper's name at all, and I began to worry that I'd gotten a job at the wrong assisted living facility. Had I come all this way—and thrown away a great relationship—for the opportunity to meet someone who wasn't even there?

I wanted to ask Dorothy about Louella, but I didn't want to draw attention to the fact that I was a humongous Louella Harper fangirl. Dorothy might mention it to the supervising nurse—referred to as Nurse K because of her unpronounceable name—who might not want a humongous fangirl anywhere near Lake View's most famous guest, assuming she was there. Basically, I had just moved two hundred and fifty miles to take a thankless, low-paying job I already had back home.

To raise my spirits, I gave myself a pep talk in the mirror every day before driving to work. "This is the day you're going to see Louella Harper. You can do this, girl!"

Then, at the end of another Louella-less day, I would look in the same mirror and say, "Okay, you didn't see Louella Harper today, but don't worry, you'll see her tomorrow. Also, you need to make an appointment to get your hair fixed so you'll look nice when you see her."

At least once a week I tried to give myself a treat, so I wouldn't get depressed, but it's kind of hard to give yourself the spa treatment when you live in a town that doesn't have a spa. There weren't a lot of places to go to get a manicure or a massage; and finding someone to cut your hair the way you like it in a small town in South Alabama is all but impossible.

My luck finally changed after more than a month on the job. As Dorothy and I made our morning rounds, a black Mercedes passed through the front gates and pulled to a stop in front of building eleven. Dorothy and I were making our way toward building thirteen, and I slowed my gait to watch the vehicle pull into its reserved parking place.

"Come on," Dorothy said. "I want to get through bathing Mrs. Winningham as fast as possible."

"I'm coming," I said, but I lingered on the sidewalk and watched as a middle-aged woman in an Armani suit and Chanel sunglasses stepped out of the driver's seat. She walked briskly to the passenger side door and opened it. With some difficulty, and assistance from her driver, an elderly woman emerged from the Mercedes.

She was stooped over and leaning heavily on the younger woman. Her hair was white and trimmed close to her head. She wore an old cloth dress and heavy black sunglasses of the type worn by someone who has had their eyes dilated. Even without seeing her eyes, I knew I was looking at the face of literary greatness.

"Let's go," Dorothy said. She stood in front of building twelve. "We haven't got all day." She came back down the sidewalk to see what was causing the delay.

"Sorry," I said. "I had to tie my shoe."

Dorothy looked past me at the reclusive author. "Just be glad we don't have her on our list," she said.

"What do you mean?" I looked at the sweet old woman hobbling toward her front door.

"Don't worry about it," Dorothy said. "You don't want to know."

But I did. I really, really did.

BLOOD CRIES

From the Journal of Louella Harper

I stopped by Melvin's office yesterday for our scheduled interview only to be told by his secretary that he was not on the premises and that she had not been authorized to share any files with me. A string of unvarnished thoughts and expletives directed at Melvin followed, and this may have been what compelled her to call her boss. She relayed a version of what I had said—a much sanitized recreation with less pacing around the reception area and no angry gestures—and then handed the telephone to me.

"I'm sorry, Ms. Harper," Melvin said in a groveling voice. "I was pulled away on unexpected business. I meant no disrespect. I hope you can forgive me."

"I am not the forgiving type."

"You have to let me make it up to you. Miriam will kill me if you don't join us for supper tonight. The saddest part is I won't be alive to defend her in court. It rises to the level of Shakespearean tragedy. Please, Ms. Harper. I'm begging you."

"Well," I said reluctantly. "We still need to do an interview."

"Okay. We can start tonight."

"Very well," I said, and he gave me the details.

We picked up our discussion at Melvin's two-story cabin in the prestigious Wind Lake subdivision. The deck featured a magnificent hilltop view of Lake Robert, and I was immediately ushered there for cocktails. It being June in Alabama, the heat was still oppressive at six o'clock and the humidity in the air brought out the mosquitos.

I declined Melvin's offer to douse myself in bug repellent, so Miriam suggested alternative accommodations. A moment later I was following her around the wrap-around porch to the shady side of the house, where a screened-in section overlooked the tree-lined valley separating the Littles' property from their neighbors. Inside the screen-room, I found a picnic table set with paper plates and metal utensils. Miriam commented that it just felt natural to serve dinner on paper plates when eating on the porch.

"All you need is a ceiling fan, and this room would be perfect," I said. I ripped a section of paper towel from the roll on the table and used it to mop the sweat from my brow.

Before the meal and throughout, Miriam fluttered in and out of the house, ferrying serving dishes, condiments, utensils, etc... along with some pleasant conversation. We dined on racks of BBQ ribs, white bread, baked beans, and coleslaw. The children were made to eat in the dining room, and then sent to the basement to watch television so that Melvin could relay, at length and in detail, his experiences representing Reverend Baxter.

Regarding the events stemming from the discovery of Calpurnia Murphy Baxter, who was found dead in her car alongside Highway 22 in the early morning hours of October 12, 1972, the interview yielded the following information:

Nine am found Melvin nestled in his bed, snoring like a gas-powered leaf blower—that part came from Miriam—when he was awakened by the bleating telephone.

Interview transcription to follow

Melvin

Miriam handed me the phone, and I held it up to my face though I was still sound asleep.

"Yeah... uh huh... uh huh... okay... I'll be there." I dropped the phone into the folds of my blanket and went back to sleep.

A second later, Miriam shoved me awake again and I sat up in bed. "I just had the craziest dream," I said. "I dreamed Reverend Baxter called and told me he had been arrested for murdering his wife. Again."

"That was no dream," Miriam said. "You have to go bail him out of jail. Again."

End of transcription

The second Mrs. Baxter was found dead about a half-mile from where they found the body of the first Mrs. Baxter. Neither woman was wearing a seatbelt, and both women left insurance policies naming the Reverend as the beneficiary. Calpurnia, or someone using her name, had taken out a series of policies totaling at least $120,000. Four of the policies included a double indemnity clause in the case of accidental death.

Melvin's story continued into the great room. A large oil painting of a beach landscape was mounted above the hearth, which was decorated with shells and other beach knickknacks. We settled into matching cream-colored sofas decorated with a large brown zigzag pattern. A 32-inch color television set sat the corner, trying to look unobtrusive. I settled onto my designated cushion and continued to take shorthand.

Transcription to follow

Melvin

No one believed the death was accidental, but this time there was even less evidence and this time no one would come forward to make a claim against the Reverend on or off the record.

Rumors spread. "Better not testify, or you might be next."

"He'll get away with it again, just like he did the last time."

"I heard they found a black cat on the passenger seat of Mary Anne's car. No one knows how it got there."

"I won't even say his name. That man is protected by evil spirits."

And so on.

Maybe they were scared. Maybe they were prudent. Maybe they just didn't know anything, but no one was coming forward with information. And this time, no one was even sure how the woman was killed. A grand jury was empaneled but refused to indict due to lack of evidence.

As far as I was concerned, there was only one problem: how to collect the insurance money. For some reason, the insurance companies thought they only had to pay out on accidental death policies if the person's death was caused by an accident. The judge that would've heard the case in McGillivray County was, in my estimation, inclined to rule in their favor, but, as luck would have it, one of the insurance policies had been issued free of charge along with a Shell gas card that had been applied for over in Butler County.

End Transcription

Butler County is notoriously unfriendly to individual plaintiffs and defendants who happen to be big corporations. Naturally, that's where Melvin chose to file suit.

Transcription to follow

Melvin

As I suspected, Reverend Baxter turned out to be one hell of a good witness. He started out very cordially. He was very charming. But when asked to describe the circumstances of his second wife's death, he got very quiet.

"I don't understand what happened," he said. His eyes welled up and his voice broke. "She wasn't sick. Maybe she had a cold or something a few days earlier, but she was fine when she left the house. She was just going to the store. I never expected..."

He stopped then and covered his face with his handkerchief. You could hear a pin drop in that courtroom.

"I never even kissed her goodbye."
(Melvin laughs)
Do you believe that? Even the judge was offering his sympathy.

End Transcription

When pressed for more details about the case, Melvin mentioned the testimony of Dr. Henry Poole, the pathologist who performed Calpurnia's autopsy.

Transcription to follow

Melvin

The insurance company lawyer (Mike Barrett) called on Poole to testify that the car accident had not caused Calpurnia's death. The condition of the lungs observed during the examination, he said, were similar to those of someone suffering from chronic bronchitis.

"Doesn't suffocation present the same way?"
"I object," I said.
"Sustained."
"Now, doctor," I said when it was my turn to cross examine, "let's assume that, prior to the accident, Mrs. Baxter appeared healthy, with no symptoms of respiratory problems. She wasn't even coughing…"

Mike objected to the hypothetical.

"This follows the evidence, Your Honor. The husband of the deceased testified that she was in good health. I'm just trying to establish the cause of death here."

"I'll allow it," the judge said.

"And Doctor," I continued, "let's further assume that Mrs. Baxter would recognize whether or not she was sick. She hadn't made any complaints to friends or family members or set up any doctor's appointments. She then left home in her car and ran off the road and hit a tree. Based on this scenario, can you tell me what caused her death?"

"All right," the pathologist said. "Based on that, I'd say the cause of death was traumatic. The trauma from the accident aggravated an underlying condition that had been lying dormant."

"You mean the accident triggered some kind of a respiratory attack that killed her?"

"I would say yes."

"So, that means Calpurnia Baxter would still be alive if not for the accident?"

"That's right."

"Then, wouldn't it be fair to say this was an accidental death?"

"If the accident triggered the underlying condition, then that's a fair statement."

I turned my smile toward Mike Barrett. His face was tilted up toward the ceiling and his hands clutched the hair on the back of his head.

End transcription

I reached out to Mr. Mike Barrett by phone today, and I will now transcribe some of his quotes that I jotted down in a separate notebook.

"Underlying condition, huh? The only underlying condition she had was being married to a man who put a pillow over her face while she was trying to sleep."

Clearly the loss of that case affected him as he grew quite agitated as we spoke.

"The judge didn't even follow the law," he said. "The Supreme Court of Alabama held that a health issue occurring in conjunction with an accident does not constitute an accidental death. When I pointed that out to the judge, he brushed me off several times and then threatened to hold me in contempt."

"Why would he do that?" I asked.

"The fix was in," he said. "Melvin helped get that judge elected, for Christ's sake." The line went silent for a moment before he added. "That part's off the record by the way."

"Did you say anything to Melvin?"

"I confronted him after the trial was over, but he just called me a sore loser."

Mike and his coworkers at the insurance company appealed the decision to the Alabama Court of Civil Appeals, who reaffirmed the prior decision and thereby established res judicata, a legal term meaning final judgement had been rendered. Even if new evidence was discovered, Calpurnia's death had been ruled an accident in the courts, and so the Reverend could not be charged with her murder. And, as Melvin would later tell me, "It was no trouble collecting the insurance money after that."

"Some people might say you were manipulating the justice system to collect blood money."

Melvin looked shocked when I said those words. "That's impossible," he said. "My clients are ALWAYS not guilty."

Transcription to follow

Melvin

It's true, though, that I wasn't popular in all quarters of town. People who used to stop and talk to me when I passed them on the streets now hurried off with their faces pointed in the opposite direction, and whereas I used to receive friendly smiles everywhere I went, now some of the expressions were overtly hostile. More than one person asked me, "What's wrong with you, Melvin? How can you defend that man?" To which I always replied, "In America, we have a constitution that says everyone has rights and everyone is entitled to a good defense. I love America."

People will always talk, though, and talk they did. Following Calpurnia's death, the police received an unusually high number of voodoo-related reports. Suddenly everyone was talking about blood-stained doorways, headless chickens hanging from trees, and homemade pin-cushion dolls found on doorsteps and in mailboxes, all supposedly indicating the Reverend's future victims.

Two wives dying under mysterious and suspicious circumstances plus the voodoo rumors, led the Reverend's church to expel him from the pulpit. He still had his pulpwood business though. He had himself a truck and crew of sawyers to cut down small trees to send to the paper mill. Even out in the woods, even on the most blistering days of summer, he always dressed in the black suit, and carried a small bible in his pocket.

End Transcription

While the Reverend was focused on his business, folks in Jackson City were busy gossiping about a few other mysterious deaths that were linked to him. These deaths seemed natural at first but raised suspicions in hindsight.

Back when Reverend Baxter was awaiting trial for the murder of his first wife, his future second wife's first husband died following a mysterious ailment that left him confined to a wheelchair. Fred Murphy's condition grew progressively worse until he was admitted to the hospital, where he died soon afterwards from organ failure.

I spoke with Calpurnia's aunt, though she requested that her name be withheld from any writings. She lived not far away and visited her niece almost every week. She recalled a Sunday morning when she stopped by the house on the way to church. Fred was no longer physically able to get to the sanctuary, but Calpurnia still wanted to go, and she had asked for a ride.

As the woman waited for Calpurnia to finish getting ready, she heard a knock on the door. When she opened it, Reverend Baxter was standing there holding a newspaper and a steaming mug of coffee.

She let out a scream and left him standing there. She ran into the bedroom to tell Calpurnia who was darkening her doorstep. "What's he doing here? I thought Fred hated Will Baxter."

"They're all made up now," Calpurnia said as she went to let Baxter into the house. "He brings Fred coffee almost every morning."

Fred liked his coffee sweet. I heard speculation that the coffee Reverend Baxter brought his dear neighbor was spiked with antifreeze. The body can't process antifreeze, and so it accumulates in the system over time until it reaches a toxic level. It's also said to carry a sweet taste that animals like, which is why it is sometimes used to kill nuisance critters like raccoons, possums, stray dogs and cats, and people married to a woman Reverend Baxter desperately needed to seduce.

At the end of the evening, following dessert and several glasses of wine, Melvin showed me to his study. He unlocked a cabinet made of tiger maple and removed a large leather briefcase that soon clapped down on a desk that matched the cabinet. In fact, I realized, all the furniture in the room was made of tiger maple.

My mind spun possibilities about what this might reveal about him as a person. Naturally, I asked him what he thought it meant, and he said he just liked the way it looked. It made him think of hunting, a pastime he enjoyed.

I reached for the briefcase, but he kept it covered with his left hand and shook my outstretched hand as if that had been my intention all along.

"Ms. Harper, I hope you don't mind my asking this, but have you, by chance, decided how you're going to write this story?" He continued to shake my hand.

"The usual way," I said, pulling free. "With my Olivetti typewriter."

"A book like this will need a heroic protagonist, will it not?" He struck the pose of a Shakespearean actor.

"At this point, I'm testing various narrative threads."

"Every story has to have a hero," he insisted. "Without a hero, the villain wins."

"Do you have someone in mind?" I asked.

"Well there's one obvious choice, but his part was too small to carry the story." His expression suddenly lit up. "It's you, Ms. Harper. "You're the only one it could be."

"Absolutely not," I said shaking my head with force and determination. "I am not a participant in this story. I'm an observer. I record what I see and hear. If I'm lucky, I'll draw a few conclusions."

"In that case, Ms. Harper, for your protagonist you might want to consider a clever country lawyer who believes in social justice and stands up for people regardless of race."

"You're definitely in the running, Melvin," I said amiably. "But the facts will determine who the heroes and villains are, and I haven't got them all sorted out just yet."

Tears welled up in Melvin's eyes. "Ms. Harper, I am honored that you would even consider me." He pushed the briefcase across the desk toward me.

"Goddamnit, Melvin. You're liable to make me start crying." Clearly, we had had a few too many drinks over the course of the evening, but I hadn't realized it until just then.

I swiped the briefcase up by the handle and then plopped down in one of the client chairs, where I proceeded to rifle through its contents.

"You know, I just had a great idea," Melvin said. "Don't feel pressured to use it or anything. I'm willing to defer to your authorial instincts on the matter, but I thought of a good way for you to begin the story."

"Do tell," I said. I was already thumbing through the contents of a manila folder.

"Picture this. We open on the bedroom of a mild-mannered attorney and his wife…"

"Mild-mannered, you say?"

"Suddenly, the telephone rings…"

"That is exciting."

"On the other end of the phone is the Reverend. He's been accused of killing his first wife. I'm half-asleep—I mean, the lawyer is half asleep—but he swiftly negotiates an agreement that is fair to both parties.

After that, I thought you might delve into my Scottish heritage. You know, show the reader some insight into what made me—my character, I mean—into the person I am today."

"That's very interesting Melvin," I said as flipped through paperwork. "There must be at least fifty insurance policies here."

"I never counted," he said.

"Did you collect on all of these?"

"Not the full amount. Some only paid fifty cents on the dollar."

I held a stack of polices in the air. "This is motive."

He laughed awkwardly. "It's not illegal to take out insurance on your loved ones."

"How much money did you make on all this?"

"Telling you that would violate attorney-client privilege."

"Look at all these policies."

"Now that I think about it, I probably shouldn't be showing you all this now either."

I stuffed the papers back into their folder and dropped it into the briefcase.

"As his lawyer, I should point out that my client has never been convicted of a crime. He always told me he was innocent."

"But if he did kill all those people, then he committed insurance fraud in order to collect the money. You helped him do it. You could have denied him the incentive by not taking his case."

"How could I do that? I was the man's lawyer. It was my duty to represent his interests. If it wasn't me, he would have just gone to some other lawyer."

"Then those people's deaths would be on that other lawyer's conscience instead of yours."

"Now, listen, Louella, I never witnessed any criminal acts committed by my client, and he always told me he was innocent. In America, everybody has a right to the best defense they can afford."

"Oh Lord, now you're going to start singing the Star-Spangled Banner."

He laughed nervously. "I think maybe we're both looking at this story from the wrong perspective. You don't have to decide on everything right now. I'm sure a lot of ideas will come to you. A good story is all in the way you tell it.

"What if we start the book at that last funeral, with everybody running around like crazy trying to get out of there? I heard some fat lady tried to crawl out a window and got stuck." He started laughing. "It would be hilarious."

I stood to go. "Melvin, I appreciate your time. I think this has been more enlightening than either of us intended."

He waved the file at me as I departed his office. He was sweating, and his tie was loose. He looked like a man who wasn't sure if he had dodged a bullet.

Chrissy

Once I knew where Louella Harper lived, I took a special interest in the comings and goings of building eleven. Whenever I walked between apartments, I looked for the black Mercedes. On two occasions, I saw the woman with the salt-and-pepper hair emerge from the driver's seat wearing a designer skirt-and-jacket combination and carrying a posh leather briefcase.

The only other person I ever saw entering or leaving Louella's apartment was a nurse's aide named Summer. Summer was six or seven years younger than me—which made her twenty-three or maybe twenty-four years old. She was plain-looking, with pale blue eyes, swollen cheeks, and dirty-blonde hair pulled back in a ponytail. She was constantly listening to music through a pair of earbuds, although if she enjoyed it, you couldn't tell from her blank expression. Unlike the rest of us, Summer was allowed to ditch the standard-issue medical scrubs in favor of professional attire.

"How come Summer only has to work with one guest?" I asked Dorothy one morning as we passed Summer on morning rounds. "And how come she gets to dress up nice?"

"Special assignment," Dorothy said. "She's more like a personal assistant than a nurse's aide."

"What does that mean?"

We paused on the sidewalk near the hedgerow separating the buildings. "She's a glorified gopher. She does whatever the old woman wants her to do. She doesn't even have to do restroom duty since Harper is still potty-trained."

"Harper?"

"You never heard of Louella Harper. Girl, you need to get some literature in your life."

"That's a good idea."

We continued on our path.

"I know what you're thinking," Dorothy said, "but it's not like it sounds. I'd rather give sponge baths to Mr. Melbourne than put up with that woman."

"She can't be that bad."

"Fine. Don't believe me."

"Okay, I won't," I said.

This was a very emotional time for me.

The first emotion was excitement. The first time I saw Louella I wanted to run up to her. "Louella! It's me Chrissy Hope. I'm a huge fan of your book. I'm also trying to solve the mystery of what happened to your lost true crime manuscript. Could you tell me what happened?"

But how much information would such an approach elicit? Probably not much. And there was a 100% chance that I would be fired, and I wouldn't get to see Louella anymore.

I couldn't go down that road. Not when I was so close to solving the mystery.

Time was of the essence. In two weeks, my training period ended, and I would be transferred to the night shift. It could take months, even years, to get back on a regular schedule.

My focus shifted to Summer.

Every morning, before heading to Louella's apartment for the day, she popped into Building One to sign in. She usually headed straight for the coffee and donuts table. I noticed she drank her coffee with three packets of Splenda and extra creamer, and if there was a cruller in the donut box, she always took it. Afterwards, she always went to the bathroom.

Once or twice, I followed her. I peed in the stall next to where she was peeing and when she was done, we both came out of the stall and washed hands together. She wore her earbuds, so it was all but impossible to start a conversation. When she turned to look at me, I gave her a big smile, which she did not reciprocate. Instead, she slowly rolled her eyes and face back to the mirror. It seemed very rude.

Then it was time for shift meeting. Even though none of the information applied to her, Nurse K still required her to attend. I started sitting in her vicinity. Over the course of a week, I moved closer and closer until Friday, when I got within two seats with no one sitting between us.

This might be my only opportunity to talk to Summer without her earbuds, I thought. As soon as the nurse finished making announcements, I turned to Summer.

"So, I heard you work for Louella Harper? What's that like?"

Summer grabbed her backpack and blew a jet of air through her lips that wiggled the hair pulled loose from her ponytail as she stood up. "You don't even want to know," she said.

"Oh, she can't be that bad."

"You don't want her. Trust me." Then, she was gone.

I caught up with Dorothy outside the meeting room. She was talking to Nurse K. Someone had called to say they couldn't work the Saturday night shift, and Nurse K wanted Dorothy to cover the shift.

"You know how hard it is for me to change schedules," Dorothy said. She had four children all under the age of thirteen.

"I can do it," I said.

Both women turned to look at me.

"I know I'm a newbie to Lake View, but I did this work for years back in Atlanta, and I don't mind."

Nurse K thought for a moment. "It's against policy, but I guess it won't hurt anything. You'll be babysitting Mr. Melbourne."

"I don't understand why that man is still here," Dorothy said. "He needs to be transferred somewhere he can get the help he needs."

"We're working on that," Nurse K said.

I was glad for the opportunity to help my coworkers, and I never minded working with Mr. Melbourne even though he always pointed his finger at me and called me the devil in his quivering old-man voice.

"You devil you."

A week later, I found myself working with Mr. Melbourne again. I was starting my last week of training and I was still no closer to meeting Louella than the first day I saw her in the parking lot.

It was October, and the weather was finally cool enough to spend a little time outdoors.

About ten o'clock in the morning, I took him to the bathroom as usually, but rather than taking him back to his chair to watch the weather channel, I decided to do something different. "Let's go out on the porch, Mr. Melbourne," I said. "It's a beautiful day."

"You devil you." Mr. Melbourne said as I helped him put on his windbreaker.

"I know you'd rather be in your chair, but some fresh air will do you good."

Mr. Melbourne scowled but allowed me to take his arm. He shuffled alongside me to the porch. With my support, he carefully lowered himself into a rocking chair.

Poor architectural planning had resulted in some of the porches facing the parking lot between the buildings, and it just so happened that Mr. Melbourne's terrace was located directly across from building eleven. *What a coincidence.*

Was it a deliberate decision on my part to relocate Mr. Melbourne to the one place I could get a view of Louella Harper's apartment? To that question, I can only say that I never moved guests to their porches during extreme weather or if I did not think there was at least a chance of them enjoying their time outside. Was I a bit more insistent with guests who lived in apartments adjacent to building eleven? It's possible. Was I hoping for a Louella sighting? Okay, I admit it. That was the main reason I'd moved down from Atlanta.

For once, I would not be disappointed.

"What kind of drink would you like, Mr. Melbourne?" I asked. "Tea or lemonade?"

"You devil you," said Mr. M.

"Lemonade it is."

I was about to head to the kitchen when I detected movement across the parking lot. Someone was opening the front door of Louella's apartment. There were noises coming from inside. It sounded like the squawking of an exotic bird, but I gradually realized it was a woman screaming, not in pain but in anger. Then I saw Summer come storming out of the apartment.

"That's it," she shouted at the parking lot. "I'm through."

"I'll be right back Mr. Melbourne," I said before rushing back into the apartment and around to the front door.

Behind me, I could hear Mr. Melbourne calling after me, "You devil you."

I met Summer as she paced the sidewalk in front of building eleven. She was smoking a cigarette, which is a huge no-no when done in view of the residents.

"Summer, are you crazy?" I asked as I pulled on my jacket. "Put out the smoke."

Summer barely looked at me. "I am so sick of dealing with that woman. I can't do it anymore."

"You have to watch yourself," I said, "or a client like that will spiral you into crazy bitch mode."

"Thief!" I heard the accusation before I knew where it was coming from.

Summer's eyes rolled up to the sky and she blew a plume of smoke into the air as she turned to face her accuser. The old woman stood in the doorway of her apartment.

"I told you already I did not steal your stupid brooch!"

"Then, where is it?" asked the old woman, who proved to be none other than Louella Harper.

Under my jacket and scrubs, my heart was beating a mile a minute.

"How the hell should I know?" Summer asked. "It's probably in your jewelry box."

"I looked there."

"Then look somewhere else!" Summer screamed. She was becoming unhinged.

"You stole it," said Louella Harper.

"Fuck this job," Summer said as she flicked her cigarette into the grass. "I quit." She marched down the sidewalk, I assumed, to Building One to gather her things.

I looked at Louella, who was reentering her home. I turned to check that Mr. Melbourne was still gently rocking in the chair where I had left him. He'll be okay, I thought, before rushing after Louella.

"I'll help you find your brooch," I said.

Louella held the door. Judging by her scowl, she was considering slamming it in my face. "Who are you?" she snapped.

"My name is Chrissy. I work for Lake View." Rather than giving her an opportunity to close the door, I slipped past her into the apartment. "Where did you see it last?"

"She had no right to talk to me that way." Louella closed the front door and began a slow, arthritic amble toward the living room. She was apparently too upset with Summer to care that I had barged into her home.

The apartment was very messy. No wonder Louella wasn't happy with Summer—the girl never helped clean up. Much of the furniture—tables, chairs, an old china cabinet—were antiques in need of polish, which I only discovered after wading through the piles of clutter that buried every available surface. As I drifted through the apartment, I saw tables and countertops littered with unread mail and assorted knick-knacks. The bookcases lining the walls were stuffed beyond capacity. There were four more stacks of books behind her chair, and I spotted two more in another corner of the living room.

"No wonder you can't find anything," I said, but in my head, I was doing cartwheels. *I can't believe I'm in Louella Harper's apartment!*

Either Louella hadn't heard me, or she hadn't cared to reply. I watched her ease herself into her recliner.

I poked through stacks of mail cluttering the dining room table. "Do you mind if I check the other rooms?" I asked.

"You might as well," Louella barked. "Why not help yourself to some of my jewelry. Everyone else does."

"I would never do that," I said in a hurt voice, and then—changing my tone and the subject—"What does the brooch look like?"

Louella put on her reading glasses and then reached for an electronic tablet. "It looks like a brooch."

It was clear that she was no longer concerned with what I did, so I wandered back down the hallway, headed toward a room I had passed by on the way in. "What's down here?" I asked, but Louella was no longer listening.

The walls held a combination of black-and-white and color photographs on the wall. Some featured famous faces. One picture showed a youngish Louella clinking cocktail glasses with Truman Capote at his black-and-white ball. Another showed her laughing with John Cheever. The editor Gordon Lish looked mopey and sour as he sat behind a desk, smoking a cigarette, but Jackie Kennedy was the epitome of elegance as she gestured toward a portrait on the wall of the Lincoln bedroom, while Louella looked on impassively.

They were the accumulated treasures of an extraordinary life, a life I could only dream about as my finger trailed along the base of a silver frame.

One book opened all these doors for her. One day she was a struggling writer, the next she was rich and famous. She went from weekly trips to the grocery store to receiving honorary degrees from ivy league universities, going to parties thrown by famous writers and entertainers, and lunching at the White House.

When I came to the end of the hallway, I found a door cracked open a sliver. I called to Louella, "What's in this room?"

"That's my office. That's where I left the brooch—sitting right there beside my typewriter."

I pressed my fingertips against the door and gave it a gentle push. The door creaked open. "Someone needs to oil these hinges," I said, but if Louella heard me, she didn't answer.

I found myself staring at a manual typewriter centered on a wheat oak desk. On either side of the desk stood two large metal file cabinets. My heart pounded against my chest. *This is it. This is where the magic happens.*

I know it sounds melodramatic, but I felt like I was about to enter a sacred space. That typewriter was the tool she used to transform a vision in her mind's eye into the greatest novel the world has ever known. On that very typewriter, she wrote *Murder of Innocence*.

I peeked to my right to be sure she wasn't following me down the hall, but I could see her feet extended in the recliner, so I stepped inside.

The room was cramped and just as disordered as the rest of the apartment, with papers strewn about the desk and stacked haphazardly on a wooden table on the opposite end of the room. There were loaded cardboard boxes everywhere, as if Louella had never bothered to unpack after moving in. Pictures and other decorations leaned against the wall, waiting for someone to come along and hang them.

"You really need someone to help you get organized," I called. Once again, Louella did not respond.

My fingers slid over the keys of her Olivetti as I drifted over to one of the file cabinets. My hand closed around the cold drawer handle. The apartment was silent but for the sound of my heartbeat. *If I open this drawer, will she hear the sound?* My thumb clicked the side lever and the drawer rolled along metal tracks. It's terrible to say, but I prayed that Louella had lost some of her hearing.

My excitement level immediately rocketed into the stratosphere. Through some magnificent stroke of luck, the very first tab I arrived at was labeled "unfinished novels." Imagine striking oil in the first hole you ever dug—that's what it felt like. I thumbed past titles such as, "Melanie's Walk," "The View from the Hills," and "Mercy." Then, about three-quarters of the way through the drawer, I found a tab labeled, "The Reverend," I stopped what I was doing, checked to make sure the drawer would not close when I let go, and then tiptoed across the office. At the end of the hallway, I could see that Louella's feet were still propped up her chair's most reclined position.

Back at the file cabinet, I removed the hanging file folder containing three manila folders packed with papers. One folder was labeled Prewriting. One was labeled completed Chapters, and one was labeled Journal Entries, which I assumed—and this was later confirmed—contained information relevant to the story.

What I did next will likely condemn me in the eyes of honest people. What I did was not honest. What I did was selfish. It was almost certainly illegal. Looking back on it now, I can see that I was hurtling down a pretty dark path, but at the time all I could think was *come to mama*. I closed the file drawer as gently as possible and stuffed the entire file folder into the waistband of my purple scrub pants. I covered the resulting lump with my shirt and then zipped up my windbreaker. When I stood and turned around, I saw Louella Harper standing in the doorway looking at me.

"Well?" she said.

"Oh hi. I didn't see you there." My voice was about three registers too high.

"Is there something you want to tell me?"

That's it. I'm going to jail.

What had compelled me to take that file? What did I think I was going to do with it? If I was just borrowing it, as I later claimed, how was I planning to return it later? These are some of the questions that have been put to me by various people after the fact.

"No," I said in my high voice. "I can't think of anything."

What a fool I had been. Of course, I was going to get caught. I deserved to get caught because I was a terrible person. What kind of person steals from a sweet old lady? What kind of person steals from her hero?

"You didn't find the brooch?"

"Nope," I answered stupidly. "I thought maybe it fell on the floor under the desk, but..."

"Like I said before, Blondie stole it."

I nodded, not because I believed her, but because I was at a loss for words.

Louella hadn't noticed anything out of the ordinary. She went back to her chair, and I walked straight out the door with her manuscript stuffed down the front of my pants.

"Bye," I called as I walked out the door. "My name is Chrissy by the way. It was nice meeting you." I said that even though, technically, she hadn't introduced herself to me at all.

I lingered in the foyer a moment, hoping she would call out my name. Down the hallway, I could see her feet at the end of her chair move through positions from least to most reclined. Seconds later, I was waddling across the street to Mr. Melbourne's apartment, where I was able to transfer Louella's file to my work bag.

I found Mr. Melbourne in his rocking chair where I had left him.

"I'm so sorry, Mr. Melbourne. I completely forgot about you." I bent down to tie his shoe, which took much longer than it should have because I kept looking over my shoulder at the parking lot to see if anyone was watching me. No one was. Only Mr. Melbourne paid me any attention whatsoever. He looked me dead in the eye and scowled at me harder than any old man has ever scowled before. "You devil you," he said.

For the first time, I almost believed him.

The Reverend
by Louella Harper

Chapter Three

1976

"The beauty of pulpwooding," says 34-year-old Lester Woods of Jackson's Gorge, Alabama, "is spending all that time alone in the woods."

Mr. Woods is a veteran of the conflict in Vietnam. He served in the army rangers and saw action at Khe Sanh and Dak To, where he was awarded a purple heart.

"Nobody hassles you. Nobody tries to hurry you up. Nobody tells you anything you don't want to hear. It's just you in the woods with a chainsaw and the trees small enough to handle by yourself."

- Quote taken from an article on the pulpwood industry that appeared in the Jackson City Sentinel

In the dim light of an early morning in February, twelve shivering men—sawyers by trade—stood waiting at the edge of the woods to receive their cut locations and quotas for the day. They wore work boots, most of them, and their most durable pair of pants, which were stained and smelly from overuse.

They wore long-sleeve shirts over sleeveless cotton tees or else over their bare skin. Nine wore coats to help them withstand the elements: the cold and rain and flying woodchips. Two wore sweatshirts rejected by the Carmichael Corporation for retail distribution but sold at a steep discount at the outlet store; they were cheap but offered a certain amount of protection. One wore nothing on his arms and neck but an old army t-shirt because he'd forgotten it was Winter.

It was forty degrees outside, but Lester considered that freezing cold. He shifted his weight from one foot to the other and rubbed his bare arms while keeping an eye on the man in the log skidder.

The Reverend was demonstrating to a man on the ground how to operate the big yellow machine—a control seat centered between four 18" tread bar tires, with a chain winch in back capable of dragging whole trees out of the woods.

The skidder's job was to bring the tree to another machine that would shear off the limbs. The logs could then be picked up by a front-end loader and put on the back of a tandem truck that would carry them off to the lumber yard.

There was a time when all that work—carrying, delimbing, loading—would be done exclusively by people like Lester: poor blacks and whites willing to do dangerous, backbreaking work for next to nothing in payment, and sometimes less. Back then, all you needed to become a pulpwood producer was a chainsaw and a truck, but those days were on the way out. Lester could see that well enough. The business was changing.

The Reverend still needed sawyers though. For now anyway. And Lester would become one just as soon as Taylor showed up with his chainsaw.

But, where was Taylor? That was always the question. And why was it so damned cold?

The crew was thinning out. Lester counted five less men than showed up last Thursday morning, when Lester ate a bad egg for breakfast and had to run home from the lumberyard, lurching into the woods every ten feet or so to deposit the waste coming out of his body from both ends.

Just after he'd doubled over with those first pains in his stomach, Taylor had run up to him and asked to borrow his chainsaw. He said he'd lost his in a poker game the night before after betting a full house against four twos. Come to think of it, Taylor was the one who'd given him the bad egg. Only Taylor could go and do something so stupid, and then turn around and do something even more stupid just to make it worse.

Where is he? Lester thought. *Where's my chainsaw?*

Then he saw it, only it wasn't Taylor carrying it, but the Reverend. Why was the Reverend carrying his chainsaw? He was walking toward the men swinging the saw by his side.

One by one, the men walked up to the boss man and listened as he pointed them in the direction he wanted them to go and told them how much wood they were allowed to cut. Once they had their orders, they walked behind wheelbarrows and timber carts lightly loaded with gear and set off into the woods in all directions.

Lester heard the clank of bottles and a jostling of equipment. "I'm here," a voice said. "I made it."

He was greeted by a round of laughter mixed with scattered jeers. Lester turned to find Taylor sidling next to him while wrestling with a six-foot-long tandem handsaw with handles on both ends.

Lester covered his eyes with his hand, but there was no hiding the fact that the other end of that handsaw was intended for him.

"Lester, here's your coat. You left it in my car last week."

Lester put it on, jammed his hands into the pockets, and pulled it tight against his body. "What's that?" he asked. He tilted his head toward the handsaw. "Why does the Reverend have my chainsaw?"

"Sorry, man. I must have left it in the woods on Friday. He must have picked it up."

"You left my chainsaw? In the woods?"

"Sorry about that, Brother. I had a lot on my mind."

Lester still couldn't bring himself to look at the man.

"Don't worry," Taylor said. "I'll go talk to him."

"Yeah, you go talk to him."

Taylor went off to face his uncle and came back a few minutes later. "He says he won't give it to me."

"What do you mean he won't give it to you?"

"He said he won't give it back to me. He said he found it on his property and it belongs to him now. He wants to sell it back to us by knocking down the price he pays us per cord."

"He wants to sell me my own chainsaw?" Lester looked up to see the Reverend walking away with forty dollars' worth of equipment swinging by his side.

"I'll get it back for you," Taylor said.

"How?"

"I don't know," he said. "I'll think of something. Now, come on. I'll show you where we can cut."

"What are we supposed to cut with, Taylor?"

Taylor put one end of saw handle into Lester's reluctant hand, then bent down to pick up the other end. Together they carried it into the woods. They also carried hatchets in their belts, taps and bottles for collecting pine resin tucked in leather haversacks, and gallon-sized jugs filled with drinking water.

Normally they would have wheeled that stuff out in a timber cart, but Taylor had left that out in the same place where he'd left Lester's chainsaw. It was normal to leave supplies at a cut location, in order to save energy when it was time to push a load of wood back to the loader, but Taylor had been in such a hurry to get to the bars Friday night, he left the cart in the woods half-loaded. He said he thought it would give him a jump start the next morning, but then he woke up hungover and decided to skip work.

"It ain't right," Lester said.

"I said I'm sorry."

"I'm not talking about you. I'm talking about him."

"Since when does my uncle care about right and wrong?" He nodded up the hill. "It's this way." Taylor moved to the front, letting the saw and Lester trail behind him.

"How does that man get away with it?"

"Stealing your chainsaw? He knows we won't do nothing about it."

"I ain't talking about that. I'm talking about everything. Why ain't the man in jail?"

"He's a good producer," Taylor said.

"What's that got to do with anything?"

"Man, don't you even know how this business works?"

"Yeah," Lester said. "You cut down trees. You sell them to the mill."

"No, the dealer sells to the Mill. The dealer is Tim Perkins."

"The man that owns the lumber yard."

"That's right. The producer sells to him, and then he turns around and sells to the mill."

"That sounds right."

"Anyway, during peak demand, the mill wants as much wood as it can get, and for a while, my uncle was putting out two hundred and fifty cords a week when most folks couldn't raise a hundred."

"He runs a tight operation."

"Hell yeah, he does. People are afraid of him. And they should be. Ain't many men get caught in bed with another man's wife, shoot the husband, and get away with it."

Lester went quiet at the mention of his sister and her ex.

"Perkins protected him."

"When the mill needs wood, they go to the dealer and the dealer goes to the producer. I told you, my uncle is a good producer."

"It didn't help him get away with killing Mary Anne."

"You don't know what happened with Mary Anne." They arrived at the grove with the abandoned timber cart. They dropped their things on the ground beside it.

"So, what happened with Mary Anne?"

"Everything was going fine. The Reverend was ready to buy a new truck to increase his haul. Perkins was more than happy to offer financing to be deducted from his cord count, but then my uncle got greedy. He tried to sell to another dealer to avoid the loss. Perkins found out about it, and all of a sudden, my uncle can't sell to nobody."

"What did he do?"

"He killed his wife and used the insurance money to pay off the truck." Taylor pulled on his work gloves. "The dealer was happy because the Reverend paid him the full amount on the truck and he got a good producer back at a time when the Mill was asking for lumber."

"Everybody's working to feed that mill," Lester said.

"But if the mill ain't hungry, none of us eat. And there still ain't no way around the dealer. So, the Reverend decided to boost production to make himself even more valuable to Perkins. He started talking to his next-door neighbors. They owned some land that had been passed down from the woman's father. My uncle told them he would strip the pulpwood, sell it, and give them half the money. They said that would be fine, so he rounded up another crew, bought himself some more equipment, and guess what happens?"

Lester shook his head.

"By then, the mill had plenty of wood. Perkins put the Reverend on a quota. It don't matter how many cords you produce when there ain't no place to sell it, and Perkins was the only game in town."

"That was after he bought the front-end loader?" Lester asked. He picked up his axe and carried it over to a tree to start the undercut. He fired a chop into a waist-high strike zone.

"That was when he killed his brother."

"I thought that was just a rumor."

"Just because it's a rumor don't mean it ain't true," Taylor said.

"You really think he killed his brother?"

"I think he had somebody else do it. If they hadn't done it, he would have."

"Between the money from his brother and Calpurnia, you'd think he'd have enough." A triangular-shaped notch had appeared in the side of the tree. Lester moved to the other side to start the top cut.

"Nothing is enough for my uncle," Taylor said. He took a swig from the jug of water and continued to watch Lester work. "Now, he owns a lot of expensive equipment outright. He holds timber rights. If they let him, he could deliver almost four hundred cords of wood per week. He just needs to be able to sell it."

"Sounds like Perkins has him under his thumb."

"Ain't that always the way."

When Lester finished the cut, he tossed the ax on the ground. The two men picked up the handsaw.

Six feet long, mostly blade, with jagged metal teeth and wooden handles on each end, the saw was an instrument of forced cooperation. One man pushed. The other pulled. They worked into a familiar rhythm until their muscles strained and moisture glistened on their skin.

They worked without talking. Only the saw made a sound, and even the screaming of nearby chainsaws faded with the intensity of their focus and exertion.

Once the tree fell down the gentle slope, Taylor stumbled over to the spot where he'd stowed his gear and reached for the water jug.

"It's too soon for a break," Lester said. He took his hatchet over to the felled tree and began hacking off limbs.

"I got to stop," Taylor said. "I drank too much beer last night.

"You drink too much beer every night."

Taylor offered the jug to Lester, who shook his head. "

You still got that gun you used to have?" Taylor asked.

"Yeah. Why?"

"Let me see it."

"I don't have it on me."

"What good is having a gun if you don't carry it anywhere?"

"I'd carry it if I needed it. I don't need it," Lester said.

"Well, I need it."

"What are you talking about?"

"He's coming for me, Lester."

Lester had the hatchet raised above his right shoulder, when he stopped to look at his friend.

"The work is drying up again."

"It can't be that bad."

"You don't get it, Lester. I know the signs. It's either going to be me or your sister, and she can do things for him that I won't do."

"Cassandra's been with him for almost two years now."

"More like six."

"All I'm saying is If he wanted to, he could've done it by now."

"You don't understand my uncle," Taylor said. "As long as you work for his interests, you got a chance. It's when you ain't worth nothing to him no more that you got to watch out. I'm telling you, he's going to kill me. I'm next on the list."

"How do you know?"

"Because I know my family. You're about to become family too, now that your sister is marrying him. You need to know what you're in for."

They heard a rustling of leaves and the crack of a fallen branch, and the Reverend appeared on the rising hill. Taylor was still standing there watching Lester work.

"Hey, Uncle Will," Taylor said. "What brings you to this neck of the woods?"

The Reverend ignored his nephew completely. He kept his focus on Lester, who had finished stripping the tree of its branches and was about to chop it into sections.

"I thought you might need this," the Reverend said as he set down the chainsaw in front of Lester.

"How much?"

The Reverend laughed. "It's your saw, and I know you'll use it. I like to reward hard work."

"What about me, Uncle Will? Are you gonna reward me?"

"You have value," the Reverend said without taking his eyes off of Lester. "But not here. You might as well go home. There's no more work for you today."

"We ain't done yet. We ain't even hardly started."

"And now you're done," the Reverend said. "Lester can take it from here."

Taylor was already gathering his things. When he had them in hand, he stared at Lester and his look said it all.

"You're crazy," Lester said.

Taylor looked at him with smoldering eyes and slowly moved his head from side to side. The Reverend put his arm around his shoulder and escorted him down the hill.

"You'll be okay," Lester shouted after him. "I'll see you at the bar tonight."

He watched the two men separate. Taylor went out front, with the Reverend following on his trail. Lester watched them vanish into the trees and then resumed his work.

*   *   *

When Lester got to the bar, it was already hopping. Women on the dance floor. Cheap beer flowing from the taps. No way Taylor was going to miss a night like this—the closest thing to heaven on Earth.

For Lester, it was the opposite. He hated crowds and had to keep his back to the wall at all times. That would be difficult, even impossible, in a place like this.

He angled through the crowd toward the bar. A live band was covering "Do it," by the B.T. Express, but there was no point in even trying to get into the rhythm of the music. Not until he found his own space.

He asked the bartender for a double whisky, and then headed to the back of the room. He sat behind a round table in a section that was empty and dark. There were no speakers in the room, though the music was plenty loud enough.

Waiting. Taylor was always late.

Lester nursed his drink until around 10:30, when a scuffle broke out at the bar. His hand fell instinctively to the lump in his jacket pocket. He sat watching two men bumping chests. Their voices rose above the music now coming from the jukebox. The band had gone on break.

A man approached Lester from his blind side. He spun around to find a heavy-set man with a large afro standing beside him. Lester's hand slipped into his pocket.

The man with the afro gestured toward the patch on the shoulder of Lester's green military jacket. "You Marines?" The man asked, oblivious to the scuffle taking place a few feet away.

Lester looked down at his patch: an ivy leaf enveloped in gold. "Army," he said, "but I served with a bunch of Marines."

"You see action?"

"Yeah," Lester said.

The owner of the bar had come out of the back and was lecturing the men at the bar. The drunker of the two men mouthed off at him, and the owner grabbed him by the ear and pulled him out of the bar like a mother leading a disobedient child.

"Oh shit," the man next to Lester said, finally noticing the commotion and enjoying what he saw. He laughed and followed the men outside.

Lester went to the bar and ordered another drink. "Damn you Taylor."

*   *   *

One week later, in neighboring Butler County, a man walking his dog discovered Taylor's car in a ditch. The vehicle was partially concealed by bushes and invisible from the road. Authorities arrived shortly thereafter and were the first to find Taylor's decomposing body behind the steering wheel.

Fact Checking Melvin's Story

Transcript of Interview with Melvin Little Conducted by Chris Hope July 2, 2009

Melvin

The trial for the nephew found its way to the docket in the Fall of 1976. I remember calling Calvin Whitehead, the state toxicologist, to the stand and really letting him have it.

"Dr. Whitehead, you tested the remains of Taylor Bennett. Is that right?"

"That's right."

"And what caused Mr. Bennett's death?"

Silence.

"Go on, Dr. Whitehead. What did Mr. Bennett die of?"

"Well..." He looked to the DA for help, but Henry Russell was hunched over the prosecutor's table, rifling through a bunch of papers.

Whitehead finally shrugged his shoulders and said, "I don't know for sure."

Transcript of Melvin Little interview conducted by Louella Harper 6/15/1977

Melvin

That's what was so funny about that case. I asked the toxicologist, "What did the guy die of?"

He said, "Well, I'm not sure." (laughter)

I said, "What do you mean you're not sure? You have the report, don't you? You have all the resources of the state of Alabama at your disposal. You even have a lab up there in Auburn with all that fancy new equipment. Now, you're gonna sit there and tell me you don't know what killed this man?"

He said, "I guess so."

I looked at the judge and the judge looked at him and said, "Cal, you've been determining cause of death for fifteen years. Just tell us what killed this man."

He said, "Judge, all I can tell you…" He reached into his pocket. "I can tell you what the black folks are saying."

I moved to strike that. The judge granted my motion.

The judge said, "Just tell us—as an officer of the court—what did he die of?"

Whitehead said, "Judge, I don't know." He held up a vial of black powder. "But this stuff was found in the car sprinkled all around the body. We've studied this at the lab. The FBI has analyzed it. We don't know what it is or if it had anything to do with his death. We've never seen anything like it."

Excerpt from the Research Journal of Louella Harper

I went to the sheriff's office and found the newly elected Sheriff Ford standing at the coffee machine gabbing with a secretary. When I interrupted, he greeted me with a smile full of yellowing teeth. He offered me a cup of coffee, though I declined.

"Do you remember the powder found at the scene around Taylor Bennett's body?" I asked.

"Which one was Taylor? The nephew?"

"Yes, that's correct. It has been said that a certain powder was found in the car with him when his body was discovered."

"Powder? You mean like cocaine?"

"No," I said. "I mean voodoo powder. Did you find any in the car or in the victim's pockets?"

"Voodoo powder?" Ford laughed and looked around for someone with whom to share the humorous nature of the comment, but the secretary was gone and no one else had taken her place. He turned back to me in all seriousness. "No ma'am. I think I'd remember something like that."

Interview Transcript 6/15/77

Melvin

I asked some of my black friends about it. I said, "What do you think killed Taylor Bennett?"

They all said, "Oh, it was voodoo. Voodoo powder killed him."

"Well, where'd he get it?"

They said, "He got it down in New Orleans."

Louella

Would you mind telling me the names of the people you asked.

Melvin

Why do you need that?

Louella

I just need to verify the information.

Melvin

Why? Don't you trust me?

Louella

Of course, I do, Melvin. It's nothing personal. I'm writing a journalistic account though, and facts have to be verified.

Melvin

Oh, well, you know, let's see. That was several years ago. I believe... I believe I talked to my old buddy Hector Caldwell about it, if I'm not mistaken. It's been several years as I said. Hector works as an automobile mechanic here in town.

Louella

Thank you. Please continue. Mr. Caldwell told you the powder came from New Orleans.

Melvin

Yeah, I'm pretty sure Hector was one of the people I talked to about that. Anyway, the toxicologist had testified late on a Friday afternoon. The judge ordered a recess until Monday. Since I had the weekend off anyway, I decided to make a trip to New Orleans.

Excerpt from the Research Journal of Louella Harper

I found Hector Caldwell at a downtown body shop underneath a wood-paneled station wagon. He rolled out from under the car on a mechanic's dolly and sat up, staring and blinking at the middle-aged woman standing above him holding a notepad. He wore a blue jumpsuit smeared with axle grease and held a large monkey wrench in his hand. The garage was filled with the overpowering scent of motor oil.

"Are you friends with Melvin Little?" I asked.

Hector recoiled at the mention of Melvin's name. After climbing to his feet, he glanced nervously over both shoulders and lowered his voice.

"I know Melvin," he said. "He represented me once a long time ago. I'm not the same person I was back then."

"I'm not interested in your felonious past, Mr. Caldwell." I fished a pencil from behind my ear and started writing. "Did you know Taylor Bennett?"

"Yeah, I knew Taylor. Why are you asking me about him? You think I had something to do with his death?"

"No one suspects you of any involvement, Mr. Caldwell. I'm attempting to verify someone else's story."

Hector sighed. "I knew Taylor a little bit. He was a year behind me in school."

"How do you think he died?"

Hector blinked at me for a moment as if trying to determine whether or not I was mentally ill "I think Willie Baxter killed him."

"Alright," I said. "And how do you think he did it?"

"I'm not sure exactly. I heard he drugged him and then suffocated him with a pillow."

"What about voodoo?"

"What about it?"

"Did you hear anything about voodoo or voodoo powder?"

"Well, I heard rumors that he stuck dolls with pins. That sort of thing."

"Thank you for your time, Mr. Caldwell."

Interview Transcript 6/15/77

Melvin

I went down to the French Quarter and I paid a visit to the Voodoo Shop. There was a lady dressed in African garb standing at the counter. I showed her the vial of powder.

I said, "Do you sell this stuff?"

Louella

How'd you come to have the powder? Wasn't that evidence?

Melvin

Oh, I told the judge the defense needed to have the stuff analyzed independently.

Louella

I wouldn't have thought they would just hand over evidence to the defense lawyer to take home with him.

Melvin

Well, you see the powder was never formally entered into evidence.

                    Louella
I see.

                    Melvin
Anyway, I showed the stuff to the woman at the Voodoo Shop. I said, "Do you sell this stuff?"

She said, "Oh yeah, that's voodoo powder. It's made in Africa."

I said, "What's in it?"

She said it included parts of sixteen different animals: zebra hooves, elephant tusks... crocodile shit. They crushed it all up into a powder and blessed it with some mumbo jumbo at a special ceremony. She told me it was powerful stuff. Black magic.

I said, "Did you ever sell this powder to a preacher from Alabama?"

She goes, "Do you mean Reverend Baxter? Oh yeah, he used to come in here all the time. How's he doing?"

                    Louella
Do you remember the woman's name?

                    Melvin
What woman?

                    Louella
The woman at the voodoo shop.

                    Melvin
Why do you need her name?

                    Louella
I'd like to talk with her.

Melvin

I didn't think to get her name.

Louella

I see. And the name of the place was The Voodoo Shop?

Melvin

Hell, I'm not even sure it had a name. It was on Bourbon Street, I think. Or maybe it was Canal.

Louella

I see.

Excerpt from the Research Journal of Louella Harper

I met the District Attorney at a diner called the City Café. It was within walking distance of the courthouse, and I judged from the appearance of the clientele that it was popular with lawyers and government employees.

Henry Russell was a barrel-chested man with hair as white as cotton. He wore a cream-colored suit and hunched over his tray as if his food might try to escape from the trap set by his meaty forearms.

Of the food, he said. "It's not good, but at least you get a lot of it." He added, "If you can finish a second plate, they'll give it to you for free."

I ordered a grilled chicken salad and made small talk until the food came, at which point, we got down to business. "Do you remember the Taylor Bennett case?" I asked.

"Dismissed for lack of evidence," Russell said before shoveling a forkful of turnip greens into his mouth. He wiped his face with a large paper napkin and then let it fall beside his plate. He scowled as he scanned the tray of condiments in the center of the table. "Hey," he barked to no one in particular. "Need some pepper sauce over here!"

"I was told that the toxicologist found voodoo powder around Mr. Bennett's body, and that it was an issue at trial. I've searched for a transcript of the trial, but no one seems to have a copy."

"Smells like a load of crap," Russell said. I had to assume he wasn't talking about his turnip greens.

A female server whisked by the table, dropping off a clear bottle filled with vinegar and yellow tabasco peppers. The prosecutor took it without comment and proceeded to douse his plate. His turnips, fried okra, and country fried steak all received a heavy soaking. He left his mash potatoes alone as they were already swimming in gravy.

"What do you mean?" I asked.

"All that voodoo stuff," the prosecutor said. "It's all a load of crap."

"Baxter wasn't a voodoo man?"

"Southern Baptist." A glob of congealed gravy hung at the corner of his mouth. "Just like everybody else."

"He was just a garden variety murderer then."

Russell's were glued to his mashed potatoes. "He was always a gentleman around me. He paid off his debts. The man had excellent credit."

"Well, I can see why you let him get away with murdering all of his relatives."

That got his attention. "Hey, I treated this case just like any other." A clump of mashed potatoes flew out of his mouth and across the table. It missed me, but his pointer finger was aimed in my direction. "When I had the evidence, I prosecuted. The evidence wasn't there."

"What about all the witnesses who came forward saying the Reverend tried to hire them to help commit the murders?"

"People came forward initially, but none wanted to testify in open court."

"Let me ask you this. If Baxter was a white man murdering members of his own family for insurance money, and all the evidence was the same, do you honestly believe it would've taken five victims to get him locked up?"

The term pregnant pause was invented in the time it took the DA to finally spit out an answer. "Yeah," he said, "All things being equal. I think I would."

"All things aren't equal."

"That's true. Sometime the guilty party marries the lead witness against him. Sometimes the jury won't indict. Sometimes the case gets botched by the boys in lab coats. Sometimes the judge has it in for you." He threw his napkin into his plate. "Damnit, Lady. You're making me lose my appetite. And I was thinking about going for the second plate today."

"Why would someone start the voodoo rumor?"

"Why do any rumors start? To get people stirred up."

"That's what I thought." I puffed out my lips and frowned. I had yet to take a bite of salad. "Or maybe just to distract them from what you're doing in broad daylight."

Interview Transcript 6/15/77

Melvin
Monday morning, I was back in court.

Louella
Did you tell the judge what you'd learned in New Orleans?

Melvin
Nope. I let them stew in their juices. It's not my job to give evidence against my own client. I'd never get another one. Hell, I might even get disbarred.

Louella
What happened?

Melvin
The judge said to the DA, "Mr. Russell, let's proceed," and Mr. Russell said, "Judge, we can't do it. We can't figure out what killed him."

The guy had to have died of something, you see, and since they couldn't prove it was murder, the judge dismissed the case.

As usual the insurance company didn't want to pay, but I started taking depositions, one after another, hour after hour, and the insurance lawyer finally said, "Just stop. Please stop."

I said, "What if I don't wanna stop?"

He said, "If you stop now, we'll give you fifty cents on the dollar."

That sounded okay to me. The Reverend and I made about $200,000 each.

BLOOD CRIES

From the Diary of Louella Harper

Every weekend, it was another party. I went to cocktail parties, dinner parties, fondue parties; there was even talk of something called a key party, though I never found out what that meant, and whenever I mentioned it, people snickered. I guess my invitation got lost in the mail. That was fine with me; I already had so many invitations, I needed a whole wardrobe worth of new outfits. Everyone wanted to meet me at least once.

People are always so excited to meet a famous person until they realize we're just normal people. "You're so elegant," one woman told me at a Friday night party back when I was still pulling clothes out of my suitcase. I got the impression her husband would have preferred meeting Farah Fawcett Majors.

It helped my cause that some folks were a little star struck. Most were curious, if not outright happy, to meet me. We'd make small talk while our host or hostesses brought us matching drinks: a ginger ale for me to match the scotch and water of the person I was talking to; a glass of water to match a gin and tonic; a Coca-Cola to match a double bourbon. Within an hour I would know everything the person had ever known or heard about the Reverend.

Cecil and I used the same system back in Kansas, only Cecil matched every drink with a triple martini. You tend to pick up a lot of gossip in this manner, but there is often a little pebble of truth buried in the word soup. It seemed to me that every individual I encountered was in possession of one of those pebbles. My job was to dig it out and put it in my pocket for later.

Gradually, a portrait of the Reverend began to emerge. Here was a man who preached the word of God and was universally acknowledged for his charisma in the pulpit, but who went home and lived a life devoted to his own carnal pleasure. He was a man who had girlfriends to supplement his wives, and he viewed them all as dispensable and replaceable. Reverend Baxter was completely unconcerned with emotional attachments and unencumbered by respect for the rights of other individuals.

He had been expelled from his church and made to feel unwelcome in all the other churches where he had sometimes spoken as a guest before the suspicious deaths of three of his family members turned him into a pariah and led him to become devoted fully to the Church of Will Baxter.

In my experience, churches aren't buildings, though they may conduct services in them. A church is a community of people with common beliefs and common interests. It is a group of people who agree to look out for one another, to help each other, and to treat each other as they would want to be treated.

But that wasn't the way of the Church of Baxter. That church was devoted solely to the glorification, enrichment, and gratification of his own self. To this end, he required the assistance of only one man: his attorney.

This put me in something of a sticky situation, since I bumped into Melvin and Miriam every time I turned around. At dinner parties, it has long been my custom to adjourn with the menfolk to a porch or parlor to drink scotch, smoke cigars, and discuss politics, history, and sports. Under normal circumstances, mutual interest in these subjects would have bound Melvin and me together in friendship. Clearly, Melvin believed we were friends, but I wasn't sure it was in my best interest to be his friend.

One evening, at the tail end of a Friday night cocktail party, I squirreled myself away in an unused formal living room and reflected on this potential conflict of interest.

The walls were painted bright red for reasons I may never understand. Miriam Little entered the room through open French doors, looking perky and pretty in a pink chiffon dress. I could see people behind her picking their way around a buffet table.

"What's wrong, Louella? Why aren't you drinking?"

"I need to think more than I need to drink," I said.

"I think you've got it backwards." She took a seat on the cushion next to mine.

I shook my head.

"Isn't the book going well?"

"I haven't started," I said. "I've been too busy going to parties."

"That's the fun part." Miriam tilted back her glass until the ice cubes rattled.

"I guess I just haven't figured out how to get a handle on this story."

Miriam fussed with the frill of her dress. "I know. It's so dark."

"What if your husband doesn't like how he is depicted?" I asked. I wanted to be as upfront about that as possible. I watched her profile carefully. Her face was smooth and impassive, without so much as a clenched jaw muscle.

"He's too busy to worry about that right now, what with the trial coming up. He thinks everything rests on the outcome of this trial." She smiled at me through bright red lipstick. "He says that about every trial, but this time he's bouncing off the walls more than usual."

"He may be right this time. This may be the biggest one of all."

Miriam frowned. "Why wouldn't he like the way he's depicted?"

"Well, if he was paid from the insurance money and the insurance was the motive for murder, then..."

Miriam wagged a finger. "He was never convicted."

"Did Melvin have any qualms about taking a share of the insurance money?" I asked

"Why should he? He works hard for his clients, and he is very good at his job. He deserves to be paid well."

"I imagine he charged the Reverend a hefty percentage of the insurance claim to make it worth his while."

Miriam nodded. "Fifty percent."

That raised my eyebrows. "Fifty percent? Of Every policy?"

"I know it sounds like a lot. It was a lot. But Melvin deserved that money. He earned it."

"It sounds like Melvin and the Reverend were equal partners in a business venture that hinged on the death of innocent people."

Miriam stuck out her bottom lip as she considered this comment, but I urged her mind to move on to something else by continuing to speak.

"Let me ask you something, Miriam. After the third or fourth time your husband collected insurance money on one of the Reverend's dead relatives, did he ever start to suspect that maybe his client was guilty?"

"He thought it was just a strange coincidence at first. He said it wasn't his job to think about that, but I could tell it bothered him, especially after that young nephew was found. That made him real nervous."

I noticed people lingering in the doorway, and I realized I was treading on dangerous ground. "I would think so."

Miriam slumped against a decorative pillow. "Melvin did what he was supposed to do," she said in an exasperated voice. "He did what the law allowed."

"You know," I said, leaning toward her conspiratorially. "It may not be in Melvin's best interest for me to write this book."

Miriam poked out her bottom lip. "Oh, I hope not. It means so much to him that you're writing it."

"He may change his mind after he sees what I write."

Miriam grasped my wrist and looked deep into my eyes. "Louella Harper, you listen to me. Melvin is a good person. He'd do anything to help someone in need. I know this in my heart to be true. When you finish writing this book, everyone else is going to know it too."

"I'm sure you're right," I said. I wasn't going to argue.

Chrissy

By the time I got home, I was shaking so badly I dropped my key three times before finally stabbing it into the lock. Entering my basement apartment, I hurried to my bedroom and hid the file under my bed. I then scampered back to the front door and spied through the peephole to see if anyone had followed me. Of course, there was no one there, but my anxiety level had been rising all day and I was tingling with guilt. I paced the room, shaking my head, and thinking the same two words over and over again.

Oh shit. Oh shit. Oh shit. Oh shit. Oh shit.

Back in the bedroom, I removed the contraband from beneath the bed and cradled it in my arms while I scanned the room for a safer hiding place. The manila folder was thick with papers held in place by a rubber band I'd found in one of Mr. Melbourne's kitchen drawers.

Now, where can I put this?

It was something of a miracle that I'd managed to smuggle it out of Lake View in the first place. All afternoon, I'd walked from building to building with the file stuffed down the front of my bulky purple scrubs. Even with additional camouflage provided by my over-sized windbreaker, the giant rectangular-shaped lump flattened against my lower abdomen felt pretty conspicuous.

In order to complete my duties, I had to put it somewhere, so I wedged it into my bag of supplies between a box of rubber gloves and a package of disposable underwear. It made me nervous to flaunt the stolen property, but it's not like Mr. Melbourne was asking any questions. None of the guests even noticed it. At the end of my shift, I stuffed the folder down my scrubs again and made the awkward shuffle back to the main building to sign out for the day. I went straight to my locker and transferred the file to my purse. No one noticed.

Now that I'd made it home, the guilt I felt was kicking into overdrive.

Oh shit Oh shit Oh shit. I am such a terrible person! I stole something! Something valuable! Priceless! From an old woman! I'm going to Hell!!!

I hid the file behind a tile in the drop ceiling, then I took a shower to wash away my sins. After drying off, I wrapped my wet hair in a towel and went through my nightly routine to try to forget what I had done. I put on a pair of pajamas and then ate a cup of noodles on the couch, all while obsessing about the file. It was sitting up there in the ceiling accusing me like the Tell-Tale Heart.

The sound of my cellphone ringing snapped me out of my trance. I looked down at the display and saw that it was James. This was the first time I'd heard from him in months. It was a call I had been hoping for, but at that moment, I couldn't bring myself to answer. Instead, I stuffed the phone between two couch cushions, jumped up, and paced the room while trying to think of a plan. But all I could think about was how stupid I was.

How am I going to fix this?

I plopped back down on the sofa, ferreted my phone out of the cushions, and checked my voicemail. I really needed to hear James's voice.

"Hi, it's me," he said. "I've been thinking about everything, what we said, how we left things, and... I don't know. I haven't felt right about anything since you left. Give me a call if you want to."

Aww. Jamesie.

My heart melted into a puddle. I wanted to call him back, but I knew I would immediately blab everything that I'd done, and I knew James—so high-minded and judgmental—would never forgive me. It was too much to think about, so I tossed the phone aside and paced the room some more.

Oh, screw it. I'm in it this far. I might as well read the thing.

Back in my room, I stood on the bed and removed the file from the ceiling. Leaving it on a pillow, I ran back to the front door and checked the peephole once more to make sure no one was lurking in the driveway. What can I say? I was paranoid. I expected the police to come breaking down my door at any moment. If I was to be arrested, I wanted to at least know what it was I'd stolen.

I laid the file folder on the nightstand while I made my bed. That file had been sitting in a cabinet for something like thirty years. I worried about dust particles and little bits of ancient paper tearing off and contaminating my sheets. In a way, I made my bed, so I wouldn't have to lie in it. Literally.

The file just sat there, judging me.

You have no right to judge me. Also, you have no ability to judge me. You're just a file.

I plopped down on the comforter and sat and sat crisscross applesauce. My moment of truth had finally arrived: I was about to read an unpublished manuscript by Louella Harper!

Within the green folder, I found four stacks of paper, each more than an inch thick. One stack consisted of Louella's personal notes about the case. One featured journal entries. Another consisted of interview transcripts. And the last one contained ten chapters of a book called *The Reverend*. All total, the entire portfolio weighed in at just over two-hundred typed double-spaced pages.

I picked up the first chapter and began to read. For the next hour, I was transported back to Jackson City, Alabama circa the 1970s. While some of the names and places were familiar to me from my early childhood, it was a side of my hometown I had never seen before. And although it was an early, unedited draft, I recognized glimpses of the voice of the author I had loved so much growing up.

I read a dozen pages of notes and the first chapter of the manuscript before my growling tummy told me I needed more sustenance than one small cup of noodles had to offer. I went to the kitchen and munched tuna salad on crackers and thought about what I'd read.

Then, I called James.

It was getting late by then, and I could tell by his voice that he had been sleeping. To his credit, James listened patiently and without judgement while I told him the whole story.

"I don't see the big deal," he said after I finished.

"Really?"

"It's just an old story, right? It's not like you stole a diamond brooch like that other girl. It's a stack of papers she probably hasn't thought about in years. I doubt she'll even notice it's gone."

This was not the response I had expected. "It's not just an old story, James. It's a story written by Louella Harper. It could be worth millions."

"Really? Wow. I guess you better put it back."

"Ya think?!" Sometimes James can be really dense. Of course, I was going to put it back. But how? It's not like I could just walk into Louella's apartment whenever I wanted.

"Maybe you could slip it under the door."

"I can't! It's four inches thick. And I wouldn't feel comfortable leaving it by the door. I'll have to give it to her myself and then tell the truth about what I did."

"You're going to get fired. You know that, right?"

My face and shoulders drooped. "Yes."

"All that work. Moving down to Florentine. Leaving your wonderfully gorgeous boyfriend behind. It will all have been for nothing."

"Yeah, but, don't you think I should tell the truth?"

"Under most circumstances, yes. But in this case, you've already lied so much that... well..."

"I haven't lied-lied."

"You completely misrepresented yourself."

"We've been over this, James. The only way to get this close was to cover up a few facts about myself."

"Well, you're screwed now."

It was great to hear James's voice and all, but this conversation was going down the tubes fast. The call ended with nothing resolved. I still had no idea what I was going to do with the stolen file and I still had no idea whether James and I were getting back together. On the plus side, at least I had reestablished some kind of relationship with him. If nothing else, we were still friends.

That's something!

The next day I showed up to work with the manuscript tucked into the middle pocket of the largest purse I owned. I clutched it by my side as I went into Nurse K's office to clock in. Every time I passed someone in the lobby or in the hallway, I could feel their eyes bearing down on me. It's ridiculous, I know, but I felt like I somehow advertised my guilt and that people around me would know what I'd done. I prayed Nurse K would be in the bathroom when I came in, so I wouldn't have to see her, but of course she was sitting behind her desk, staring at her monitor, and tapping away at her keyboard.

I tried to slip in quietly and clock in using the computer console mounted on a counter beside her desk and then slip out again before she noticed I was there.

"I need to talk to you," she said without looking up.

"Huh? What? Okay. Sure," I said in the most guilty-sounding stupid way possible.

In my short time at Lake View Estates, I had never known Nurse K to engage in small talk, and I immediately began experiencing heart palpitations.

"Have a seat," she said, motioning to a lone chair in front of her desk.

As soon as I sat down, she asked, "Were you in Louella Harper's apartment yesterday?"

Nurse K had an air of confidence and gravitas I found intimidating under the best of circumstances. My whole body went into a tremor that I felt certain would be discernable to anyone within a hundred feet, but if she noticed me trembling she let it pass without comment.

"Um, yes." I admitted. I cradled my purse in my arms like a baby. This is it. Better get it over with quickly. Like ripping off a Band-Aid.

"And where was Mr. Melbourne during this time?" Nurse K wasn't going to make this easy on me. It was going to be like a trial. She would lay out all the damning evidence against me and convict me on one charge after another.

"It was only for five minutes, but yes I did leave him alone. I'm sorry." In my defense, my duties only brought me into contact with Mr. M. for a few hours a day, but he was spiraling into dementia so fast, he needed around-the-clock care, and everyone knew it. His family was in the process of having him moved to a full-time care facility.

"So, you are aware Summer will no longer be working here at Lake View Estates?"

"I am. Yes. I mean, I got that impression." My natural inclination was to continue rambling incoherently, but in the back of my mind I could hear the Miranda rights being read to me by an imaginary detective, so I knew anything I said could and would be used against me in a court of law.

"And apparently you made quite an impression on Ms. Harper."

I hugged my purse tightly. "What did she say?"

"She said you were annoying, but that at least you tried to be helpful. She suggested you as Summer's replacement for a trial period. You'll have a few days to prove yourself before she decides whether or not to keep you."

My jaw dropped into my lap. "She requested me?"

"The truth is, I'm running out of people to send her."

"Am I being reassigned?"

"Is that a problem?" Nurse K handed me my assignment sheet, but this time, instead of five or six residents on my list of rounds, there was only one: Louella Harper.

Any thoughts of confessing my crime vanished instantly. At least for now, I was still in the clear. And since I would now be working exclusively in building eleven, I could return the stolen file whenever I wanted. My whole body seemed to lighten as the weight of impending doom lifted off of me.

"Anything else?" Nurse K asked.

"No, that's it. I mean, thank you. I'm going now." Nurse K had already moved on to some other pressing business and wasn't paying me any attention.

As I walked out of her office I relaxed my grip on my purse. No one had x-ray vision. No one could see what was inside. I slung it over my shoulder and let out a huge sigh. I felt like I had just gotten away with the perfect crime.

I could not have been more wrong.

The Reverend
by Louella Harper

Chapter Four

In the early morning darkness of June 11, 1977, Sheriff Maddox wheeled his patrol car around a bend in a dirt road. Up ahead, twin circles of headlight eased across a row of tree trunks. As the road straightened, the sheriff let the steering wheel slip through his hands and return to its natural position. The scent of pine trees rode the wind into the open window where his left arm rested on the doorframe. In the distance, flashing blue lights reflected against the treetops.

In less than a minute, the sheriff was parked about twenty feet behind the crime scene. He sat for a moment watching his deputies setting up a light rig. A cigarette ember glowed in front of his lips. Smoke spiraled into his eyes.

He took two more drags and then crushed the cigarette into the ashtray.

Deputy Ford met him at the perimeter of police tape. "Hey Sheriff, you ain't gonna believe this."

Located at the center of the crime scene was the car: a brown Ford Torino the Sheriff knew to be registered to William James Baxter. "Christ," he said.

"I know, Sheriff. I couldn't believe it myself. I mean, I could believe it—look at who we're dealing with—but dang. Are you kidding me?"

It was, without a doubt, the most ill-conceived crime scene Maddox had ever seen. The front tire on the passenger side lay punctured in the grass a few feet beyond the car. The spare lay beside it, stretching out of the grass onto the dusty road. An overturned jack lay beside the victim, who protruded from underneath the vehicle at a ninety-degree angle. Her face was obscured by the exposed rotor that had come crashing down upon her now crushed neck.

Maddox was soon presented with his first description of the victim: a black female, approximately sixteen years old, dressed in white short pants, an orange-striped halter top, plain white tennis shoes, and bobby socks. No identification had been found on her person or in the vehicle.

"Sheriff, you ever seen anyone go up under the car like that to change a tire?"

Maddox reached into his pants pocket and removed a handkerchief. "No."

It was a muggy night. Eighty-six degrees and climbing. Maddox covered his nose and mouth as he bent down to examine the girl's injuries. It was all a ruse, he thought, to cover up the strangle marks.

The radio squawked in a nearby cruiser. "I got it," Ford said. He ducked into his car and pulled the handset to his mouth. A few seconds later he called out to the sheriff, who was shining his flashlight on the punctured tire.

"That was Tommy. He said he's got the girl's parents down the road. They want to see her."

"How the hell are they here already? I just got here for Christ's sake!"

"Apparently, they were out looking for the girl and stopped by the station. Sheila told them we had her out here."

"Did Sheila tell them the girl was dead?"

"Tommy didn't say."

Maddox ducked under the police tape. "If Baxter is here, the son of a bitch may well intend to contaminate his own crime scene."

Ford held the handset to his chest as he waited for a definitive answer.

Maddox headed for his car. "Tell Tommy I'll be down there in a minute."

It was a perfect location to dump a body—a little-used road surrounded by forest. Only one person lived in the area. Milton Hendricks was driving home from a fishing trip around 11:45 p.m. when he came upon what he thought was a wayward motorist in distress. When the tragic nature of his discovery became clear, he hurried home to call the police.

Maddox received the call at 12:03 a.m. Stirred from his bed and half asleep, he barked the necessary orders into the phone. By now, the routine was familiar, almost expected. Everyone knew what to do. He told his wife to go back to sleep—she needed her rest—and then he made himself a cup of coffee, showered, and pressed his uniform just in case there were news cameras. He had taken his time, knowing he was in for a long night. Now, driving down the road, he cursed himself for dawdling.

He found Tommy at the entrance to the road, sitting on the hood of his car, cleaning his fingernails with a pocket knife. Another vehicle was angled toward his, and Tommy appeared to be using the car's headlights to aid him in his task.

When he saw the sheriff, Tommy hopped down and folded up his knife.

Maddox looked from his deputy to the darkened windshield of a black Crown Victoria. He could just make out the face of the Reverend sitting in the driver's seat. The girl's foster mother, Cassandra Baxter, sat beside him.

Maddox focused his flashlight beam on the driver. "She can come with me," he said. "You stay in the car."

The Reverend leaned out of his window. "She's my wife. I should be with her."

"This doesn't concern you."

The third Mrs. Baxter shuffled out of the passenger's seat and over to the sheriff.

"There is no cause to treat me this way," the Reverend said. "If any harm has come to that girl, then I am a victim too."

"If you're a victim, then I'm the king of the ocean." Maddox took Cassandra's arm in his, patted her on the hand, and escorted her to his car.

*   *   *

Behind Tommy's cruiser, a van skidded to a stop, sending up a cloud of dust. "Take the Money and Run" by the Steve Miller Band was audible as Jim Easton jumped out and jogged up to the deputy.

"Hey, Tommy. Thanks for the tip. Who is it this time?"

Tommy, whose attention had returned to his fingernails, tilted his head in the direction of the Reverend.

"Holy macaroni," Jim said. "Is that who I think it is?"

"How should I know? I'm no mind reader."

Jim turned his back to the Reverend's headlights. He lowered his voice to a whisper. "What's he doing here?"

"Waiting for his wife to identify the body of her little girl."

"Lucy?" Jim asked. "Jesus, when will it end?"

Tommy shrugged.

"I wonder if he'd give me an interview," Jim said.

"Yeah, after he commits murder, I bet there's nothing he likes to do more than talking about it with a reporter from the newspaper."

"Or is she his stepdaughter? I can't remember." Jim said. "I know her real dad died in a car wreck."

"Too bad. He'd probably go after the Reverend with a buzz saw."

"I think I'll go ask him if he'll give me that interview."

"It's your funeral."

* * *

Maddox deliberately parked the car a hundred feet away from the spot where Lucy Mae Woods lay dead beneath Reverend Baxter's Ford, allowing him additional time to elicit information from the girl's foster mother prior to her having to identify the body.

"Did one of the deputies tell you what to expect, Mrs. Baxter?"

"The deputies?" Cassandra asked. Her voice possessed a dreamlike quality, like she wasn't sure any of this was real.

"Did they tell you about Lucy?"

She shook her head and smiled. "Lucy's been with me since she was three years old. Her mother was too sick to take care of her, so I took her in and raised her like she was my own child."

"Can you tell me where you were today?" the sheriff asked.

"We drove out to my sister's house this morning. We spent the day there. We came back around seven, but then Lucy said she wanted to go out again. I said, 'Forget it. It's too late.' I went to the den to watch television, and a little while later, I heard the car start up. I went to the window to look for her, but she was gone. She thinks she's all grown up. She thinks she can do anything she wants to do."

"Where was your husband during all this?"

"You know Will. He had business. He came home while I was making a report to the police. He drove me around looking for her. We drove back out to my sister's house, but Lucy wasn't there. We drove all over the county. Everywhere we could think of. We stopped by the police station on the way home. They said you had her here." She shook her head again, still smiling. "You can't tell that girl anything. She won't listen to me. Won't listen to Will. Sometimes I feel like she's not our little girl anymore."

"Mrs. Baxter, Lucy's gone. You're going to need to prepare yourself for that."

"Lucy's not gone. You have her here. The deputy told me."

"If you have information about who did this, now's the time to say so. It's too late for Lucy, but it's not too late for you. If your husband hurt her, you need to tell me."

"Why would Will want to hurt Lucy? She's his daughter too."

"Mrs. Baxter," Maddox said, but she had gone on ahead. Ford—after a nod from the sheriff—lifted the police tape, allowing her to pass.

Maddox watched her circle Lucy's body. She looked down the whole time. Her lips moved, and Maddox believed she was mumbling to herself until he stepped forward and heard that she was actually talking to Lucy. She was admonishing the dead girl for all the trouble she'd put her through. Then, as she was reminded of how miserable she was, her lip began to quiver, and a tear slid down her cheek. She dropped to her knees beside the girl and started to scream.

* * *

The reason the press conference would be held on the courthouse steps, Jim was told, was because there wasn't enough room inside to accommodate all of the journalists and media people who wanted to ask questions. After Lucy's body was discovered, someone at one of the Montgomery papers had written a piece that was picked up by the wire services. The story went national, fueled by a single word: voodoo. News agencies from all over the country sent representatives to wring out the lurid details.

Jim recognized faces from the *Montgomery Advertiser*, the *Alabama Journal*, and *WSFA-TV*. He spotted press badges from the *Miami Herald*, the *Atlanta Constitution*, and the *Washington Post*. Photographers were rumored to be on site from *People Magazine*, *Life*, and *Jet*. They milled about the town square, suffering in the ninety-degree heat, and waiting for someone to emerge from the courthouse and provide them with some little tidbit of information they could print or a nice bit of monologue they could show on television.

The presence of TV cameras in the town square summoned the curious townspeople. Ordinary citizens emerged from their houses and braved the heat to see what all the fuss was about. Vendors appeared from nowhere, selling hot dogs and balloons to an otherwise untapped market. Someone set up outdoor speakers that blared the WHHY radio station throughout the square. A festival atmosphere ensued.

Jim tried to gauge the pulse of the community and found the reactions mixed. Young people were excited to be part of the hullabaloo. Older people bemoaned the fact that traffic was heavier than usual, and they resented all the negative attention the town was getting. "Why aren't you reporting on all the good things people are doing at the churches, the high school 4-H club, and the new junior college?" one woman wanted to know. Jim tactfully pointed out that his paper had covered all of those things.

After garnishing a few quotes for a possible article, and not wanting to be marginalized from his own story, Jim made his way toward the courthouse and elbowed his way to the front of the crowd, stopping only long enough to eavesdrop on the idle chatter coming from the other reporters.

"Who's running things here?" he heard someone ask.

"The ABI. Guy named Victor Ellis."

"What happened to the Sheriff?"

"He's out. As of this morning."

"He had enough chances to catch this guy, I guess. What do you know about Ellis?"

"Usual bureau type."

On cue, Victor Ellis and his entourage spilled out of the courthouse and headed down the steps toward an out-of-place lectern affixed with several large microphones.

Ellis looked to be in his mid-fifties, but other than his age, only a pair of wire-rimmed glasses distinguished him from every other man in the bureau. He had the same square jaw, wore the same square haircut, the same square clothes.

Among the men and women shuffling down the steps after him, Jim made note of the mayor and the chief of police. Representatives of the sheriff's department were conspicuously absent.

"Can everyone hear me?" the agent began. He paused a moment while someone adjusted the sound, then he started again.

"I'm Agent Ellis from the Alabama Bureau of Investigation. I have a few details to share with you." He looked down at his prepared notes. "In the case of Lucy Mae Woods, an autopsy was conducted yesterday, June 12, which lasted over eight hours.

"I have in my hand the coroner's report. As you know, Miss Woods was found dead underneath a 1974 Ford Torino. It has been determined by our esteemed doctors that this young woman expired prior to the vehicle collapsing upon her neck. Consequently, the ABI is treating the matter as a homicide. As of yet, no arrests have been made, but our investigators are gathering evidence and I can assure you all, just as I want to assure the people of Jackson City and its surrounding areas, that the person who committed this crime will be caught and brought to justice. I'll now take a few questions."

"Has the actual cause of death been determined?"

"We believe the evidence will show that she was strangled."

"When are you going to arrest Baxter?"

"That's not something I can comment on at this time. I can tell you that we have a suspect, and we expect to make an arrest very soon. Next question."

"Did you find any evidence of voodoo at the scene of the crime?"

Murmuring and laughter passed through the throng of reporters.

"This is an ongoing investigation. I'm not going to confirm or deny any specific details about the crime scene."

"I heard he has a room in his house where he stores shrunken heads."

"Can you confirm that a doll filled with pins was found on the girl's body?"

"I heard the doll was pinned to her body."

As Ellis proceeded to not answer questions, Jim began easing his way toward the back of the crowd. Another man sidled up beside him. "Hey, are you Easton?" the man asked. "I'm Dave Everett from the Birmingham News. I've been following your coverage in the Sentinel. It's good stuff. Say, after the press conference, maybe I could buy you a cup of coffee. I'd like to pick your brain."

"Maybe another time," Jim said. "I'm late for an appointment."

"Is it about the story? Mind if I tag along?"

"No, this is personal," Jim said. "I'll catch up with you later."

As soon as he broke free from the crowd, he glanced over his shoulder and saw that the man Everett was still looking at him but was making no effort to follow. That was good. It was very important that no one follow him.

CHRIS HOPE

From an Interview with Melvin Little

Melvin

The last one was that poor little girl. How stupid could he be? The Reverend came to me—usually he came in through the front door, but this time he came in through the back—and said, "Mr. Little, you've got to help me. Now they're accusing me of killing my own daughter."

It wasn't his blood daughter, but I knew what he meant.

I said, "Reverend, you say you didn't kill this girl." He always told me he was innocent of the crimes of which he was accused. I said, "You're my client, so I have to believe you, but I'm afraid I can't defend you anymore."

Louella

How did he take your decision?

Melvin

Well, he was unhappy, but what could he do? I had to draw the line somewhere. He begged and begged, but I wouldn't relent. I told him to get out of my office.

Louella

Why did it take you so long to fire him as a client?

Melvin

The girl was the last straw.

The Reverend
by Louella Harper

Chapter Five

Jim stood on the doorstep of the Reverend's cottage, looking around at the surrounding area. Mostly he saw trees, but he noticed a man at the house next door rocking in a porch swing. Jim waved, but the man only nodded, or perhaps he was only rocking forward; it was hard to tell.

In the window beside him, a curtain peeled back, and then, behind the front door, a chain lock rattled. The door swung open and the Reverend appeared, beckoning him inside.

He was a large man, with the added meat of middle age packed around his face and mid-section. A warm smile stretched beneath his mustache. "Come on in," he said as he gestured toward his den.

The room was well-lived in with no particular style of decoration. There was a yellow cloth couch with brown paisley print and heavy wear on both arms, but also a brand-new leather reclining chair angled toward a 32-inch color television set. Vacuum tracks were visible on the light green carpet. The walls were bare. The scent of cooking pot roast drifted in from the kitchen.

"Tell me something," the Reverend said as he gestured toward the couch. "Why is the news media trying to destroy me?"

"I think my newspaper has been fair." Jim said as he sat down on the sofa and unexpectedly sank almost to the floor.

"The others are much worse," Baxter agreed. He sat down in his recliner. "That's why I'm talking to you."

"I appreciate that," Jim said. He struggled out of the sinkhole until he could balance his weight on the part of the cushion supported by the couch frame. He removed a tape recorder from his satchel "If it's okay with you, I'd like to go through each case one by one."

"Fine," the Reverend said. "I have nothing to hide. I'm glad to have the opportunity to dispel the rumors people have been spreading. I think that after you hear my story, you will discover that I am as much of a victim as anyone."

"You've lost a lot of relatives."

"I've lost five relatives," the Reverend corrected. "Imagine how you'd feel if you lost five members of your close family."

"It would be devastating."

"You have no idea."

Jim looked for signs of genuine sadness. The Reverend's eyes were downcast, but his cheeks remained dry. "Do you understand why people think these deaths were more than just a coincidence?"

"I do, and I agree with them," the Reverend said. "The odds against so many suspicious deaths happening around one man must be astronomical."

"Let's start with your first wife, Mary Anne."

"I believe she was murdered and placed in her car, and that it was made to look like an accident."

"You collected a good bit of insurance money after her passing."

"I was the beneficiary, but I wasn't the ones taking out the policies."

"Then who was?"

"My wives and I had policies on each other. I always believed it was the sensible thing to do. If something should happen to me I wanted Mary Anne, and later Calpurnia, to be taken care of, and they felt the same way about me. But Melvin Little was the one who handled all of the details. I just signed my name. And I never asked him to take out policies on any other member of my family. I have come to learn that someone did, and they signed my name."

"To frame you?"

"I believe so."

"But you took the money."

"I didn't want it. I even instructed my attorney not to take it, but he reminded me of my mounting legal fees and burial expenses. I paid for every funeral. I didn't know it at the time, but by paying those burial expenses," the Reverend hesitated as if deciding whether or not to finish his sentence, "I was actually paying the person who committed the murders."

"The funeral director? Are you talking about Ernie Smith?"

"I never said his name, and if you print it in the paper I will deny it. If I live long enough."

"You're saying Ernie Smith killed Mary Anne? Why?"

"He was jealous. They used to see each other, but when she got to know him she didn't like him. He said he would kill any woman who tried to leave him. Then one day she attended a church service with a friend, and I happened to be the guest preacher. After the service, she came up to me and we started talking. I could tell immediately there was a spark between us and that she felt the same way. I asked her to have dinner with me that night, and she agreed. By the end of the meal, we both knew we were meant to be together. After that, she almost never left my side, not that I wanted her to. We knew Ernie would be angry, but we thought the fact that I was a preacher would protect her. It seemed to work at first. Ernie went on with his life and never spoke of her again as far as I know. She called me her knight in shining armor. Little did we know, he was only biding his time."

"It's hard to imagine someone holding on to a grudge that long."

"You don't know Ernie Smith. He doesn't let anything go. He always has to be in control, and he always has to win. He believes his sole purpose in life is to dominate his competition. I didn't realize it at the time, but he thought I was his competition."

"So, he killed Mary Anne for leaving him and to show dominance over you?"

"And to receive a nice payment as well."

"Because he owned the funeral home."

"And the cemetery where most of Mary Anne's family is buried."

"I think I might have buried her in my backyard before I gave him my business."

The Reverend offered a grim smile. "I don't think the backyard was a viable option for the person the police suspected of killing her, though I never would have considered such a thing. I believe people should be buried near their family, and Mary Anne's family—and mine as well—are all buried at Locust Grove. I didn't know then Ernie was responsible for their deaths. I only pieced that together much later."

"After Calpurnia?"

"I was very suspicious after Calpurnia. Calpurnia was the person I turned to for comfort in my time of grief. She had lost her first husband around the same time I lost Mary Anne, and I suppose the fact that we were both recently widowed bound us together. Each of us was the only person in the world who knew what the other one was going through. But then one day, she left the house and never came home again. When I found out that she was dead, I became paranoid. I thought I was going crazy. How could this have happened to me again? Eventually I convinced myself that it was all a strange coincidence. The medical expert even testified in court that it was the accident that killed her."

"The police seemed to think you did it," Jim said.

"The authorities decided that I was guilty right from the start, and so they never even considered anyone else. Especially after people in the news media turned me into a witch doctor. I suppose I can't blame them all for suspecting me."

"Your brother died shortly before Calpurnia, is that correct?"

"Yes, but J Christopher was a drunk. He struggled with that demon all his life. I never had reason to think anything else played a role in his death—other than the sudden appearance of a life insurance policy taken out in my name."

"And you think Ernie, or someone, did that to frame you?"

"I believe so," the Reverend said.

"But, once again, you took the money."

"My mind was reeling from one calamity stacked on top of another. I felt that God was testing me like Job."

"Was your nephew's death also a test for you?"

"By the time Taylor was killed, I understood that someone was out to get me and that my family members were in danger. More insurance policies turned up naming me beneficiary. Clearly the person who was setting me up was establishing a motive. I just didn't know who was behind it.

"Then, shortly before Taylor was found dead, I ran into Ernie Smith on the street in front of the pharmacy. He asked me if I expected to give him some more business any time soon, and then he smiled in a very sinister way. I thought it was just a sick joke and I pushed it out of my mind.

A few weeks later, I accompanied my sister to the funeral home to pick out a casket for her son. She became so overcome with grief she begged me to handle the details for her and then went to the car to wait for me. I found myself alone with Ernie in front of a display of caskets. 'That's some run of bad luck you're having, Reverend. Pretty soon you won't have any relatives left.' He laughed as if he'd just said something humorous. Suddenly, it all made sense to me. I looked at him and said, 'You did this.' I don't know what I expected him to do or say. I guess I thought he would deny it, but he didn't. He looked me straight in the eye and then he winked at me. Then, he walked away."

"I can't wrap my head around why he would kill every member of your family just because you stole his girlfriend."

"I think he wanted to teach me a lesson. In his mind, I thought I was better than him. And the truth is, I did think I was better than him. He was a terrible person who had treated my wife badly. Shortly after Mary Anne, many of my sermons contained veiled allusions to Ernie and people of his ilk. I used them as examples of how not to act. This would have gotten back to him. I suppose he wanted to knock me off my pedestal. And, he did. He made my life a living hell."

"Why didn't you go to the police?"

"I told my attorney to do just that. 'With what evidence?' he asked. 'A wink and a smile?' But Melvin had another reason to dissuade me from going to the police, which I didn't know until recently: Melvin represented us both."

"Seems like a conflict of interest."

"I believe Melvin may have used his power of attorney to take out those other insurance policies in my name. If you were to hire a handwriting expert, I believe you would find that it was either Melvin or Ernie who signed my name. It was quite a little operation they had going—they still have going. Melvin gets half the insurance. Ernie gets most of the rest. All of the suspicion falls upon me, and I'll be the one who ends up in jail."

"And now Lucy."

The Reverend stared at the floor. He was silent for a while. This time, Jim could see the tears sliding down his cheeks.

"I can't talk about that," The Reverend said after a while. "But I want to ask you a question. Do you think I am a stupid man?"

"No," Jim said. "I don't."

"Then, do you really think I would be so stupid or so arrogant as to think such a ridiculous set-up would not immediately be seen for what it was, a coverup for murder."

"I guess not."

"Ernie Smith is not a stupid man either. He is evil, but he isn't stupid. He knew how it would look. And he knew I would be blamed. He must have lured Lucy somehow, talked her into stealing my car and then..." He trailed off.

"Wow," Jim said, shaking his head. "That's quite a story, but without evidence or someone to corroborate any of it, I don't think my paper is likely to take it to print."

"I don't expect them to. Ernie would sue us all for defamation. At this point, I have no options. I've lost almost everything. I have Cassandra, but for how long? If I don't end up in prison, she will probably be killed next. I need help."

Jim sat staring at the Reverend for a long time. "That's why you brought me here? You want me to help you?"

"It occurred to me that you might direct some of your investigative skills toward the man responsible for murdering at least five people. If you turn up any evidence, and put it in the newspaper, the police would be forced to follow it through."

Jim made an exasperated sound with his lips. "This is not what I was expecting." He turned off the recorder. "I tell you what. I'll make a few inquiries. If your story checks out, I'll see what I can dig up on Ernie Smith."

"That's all I ask."

Jim smiled. "There's one more thing I want to ask you about. It's ridiculous, but I have to ask. Would you mind... showing me your voodoo room?"

The Reverend dabbed at his eyes with a handkerchief. He returned Jim's smile. "I would be happy to show you my voodoo room."

Jim pushed himself up from the couch and followed Baxter to the center of the house, to a plain wooden door that opened to reveal a stairway descending under the house.

"I have to apologize," the Reverend said. "The bulb is out."

Jim took the first step onto a creaky wooden plank and descended into a world of blackness. He grasped for a handrail, but he felt nothing but the splintered, peeling texture of unfinished wood. Using his foot like the cane of a blind person, he inched his way down the stairs. He thought about what the

Reverend had told him. It made a certain amount of sense, but could it true? Ernie Smith was not a man to be trifled with—he knew that much.

The Reverend's boots landed heavily on the steps behind him. Jim felt the hairs on the back of his neck stand on end. If the Reverend really was a murderer, it would be easy enough for him to end Jim's life by pushing him down the stairs. He hadn't even bothered to tell his editor where he would be today. That probably would have been a good idea, he thought.

He wanted to move quickly down the stairs, but the steps were shorter than the length of his foot, and it was a steep decline, so he had no choice but to go at a snail's pace. He could feel the temperature drop as he descended below ground-level. He was unprepared when his foot finally landed on the concrete floor. Below his outstretched arm, a hand brushed against his side. He jumped away from it just as light flooded the room. The Reverend's finger was pressed against the underside of the light switch.

"Well, what do you think?" he asked.

Jim stood clutching his heart. He lowered his hand and followed the Reverend's gaze until he understood what he was meant to see. "I like it," he said. Instead of a wall of shrunken heads and shelves lined with jars and potions, he saw wicker furniture surrounded by masks and carvings, a tropical beach mural, and a black velvet painting of a hula girl. Reverend Baxter had his own tiki room.

Chrissy

On the first day of my dream job, I stood on the front step of building eleven and waited. And waited. Finally, I heard someone fumbling with the chain lock, the door creaked open, and there was Louella. She wore a pair of navy slacks, a white golf shirt, and a scowl.

"Well, are you just going to stand there, or are you coming inside?"

This is going to be great!

I still worked for Lake View, but thanks to a special arrangement, I was now the exclusive property of Louella Harper. Plus, I was liberated from bathroom duty, since Louella was still firmly in control in that area. On the con side, I wasn't exactly sure what my new duties were going to be.

"You can start in the kitchen," Louella said by way of clarification.

"Okay," I said as I trailed her down the hallway. "Start what?"

"Cleaning."

"But... but... I'm not the maid."

Louella slowly turned to look at me. My anxiety level rose in inverse proportion to the furrowing of her brow. "I thought you wanted to help me?"

"I do," I said.

"Well, I need help cleaning the kitchen."

In Louella's mind, a home health aide was basically a personal servant, someone to keep her mouth shut and do whatever she wanted done. This conflicted with my own rosy outlook of my newfound career. Whereas I saw myself as more of a private secretary, she saw me as someone who could clean the toilet. It turned out, we were both right. Over the next few weeks, I would clean her house, organize her clutter, run errands for her, fix her meals, and bring her refreshments. I sorted her mail and took possession of her personal calendar, scheduling and reminding her about appointments.

At first, I could not ascertain why one of the best-selling authors in the world needed to take advantage of a home health aide making twelve bucks an hour plus benefits, but I developed a few theories:

1) Louella was as frugal as she was pragmatic. She believed in using the resources at her disposal. To do otherwise was borderline sinful.

2) Assistants contracted from Lake View ensured a measure of privacy. On our date of hire, we were required to sign a document stating that we would not divulge anything about the facility's guests without their expressed written consent. Louella was VERY concerned about her privacy.

3) After going through a series of professional assistants—who got tired of being snapped at and made to clean the toilet—Louella turned to Lake View to provide a steady supply of new recruits.

4) A combination of all of the above.

The truth, I eventually discovered, was that Lake View was financed and overseen by a group of investors who all happened to be close personal friends who would do just about anything to keep her happy.

By ten a.m. my first day, I had cleaned the kitchen five or six times, and it was immaculate. Confident my efforts would meet Louella's lofty expectations, I was ready to track her down and ask her for my next assignment. I found her in the den, sitting in her recliner, working a crossword puzzle. After three solid minutes of her failing to notice me standing in the middle of the room, I moved to another spot. I cleared my throat several times before she finally looked up and said, "I'll take my tea now."

"Great," I said. "I'll have some too." Without waiting for her to answer, I amscrayed into the kitchen, leaving her sitting in a cloud of stunned silence. I was living out a fantasy; I figured I might as well have fun with it.

A few minutes later, we sat at the dining table and drank our tea in silence. I tried to think of something awesome to say, but I drew a blank. What do you say to one of the greatest writers who ever lived? Louella apparently couldn't think of anything to say to me either, so we just sat there not looking at each other. I'm not going to lie—it was a little awkward.

I started to get nervous. My leg did that bouncy thing under the table. I had to think of something to say, and I had to do it fast. If I didn't establish a rapport, I would never impress her, which meant she wouldn't want to hang out with me and tell me everything there was to know about what happened in Jackson City and why she never published another book, and we would never become best friends.

I was under a lot of pressure.

"So," I said once the lack of conversation became maddening, which in retrospect was probably only a few seconds. "How long have you lived at Lake View Estates?"

"What a banal question," Louella observed as she raised and lowered her teabag into the hot water.

I felt like I'd been shot in the neck with a poison dart. "And what's the banal answer?"

"About three years."

I was ready to fall out of my chair and die, but then I heard the front door open.

"Hey Lou Lou," a woman called.

Such familiarity raised my jealousy level. I sat up straight and sipped my tea.

Louella's expression never changed. "In here," she said. She swept a few stray grains of artificial sweetener into her napkin.

"I brought you some papers to sign," the woman said as she entered the room. She dropped a manila folder in front of Louella. It was the woman I had seen driving her around that first day.

"Well, who do we have here?"

"This is the new aide they sent me," Louella said.

"Does she have a name?"

"They usually do."

I stood and held out my hand like any young go-getter would. "Hi, I'm Chrissy."

The woman took my hand in her limp grip and faked a smile.

"My friends call me Chrissy," I added weakly.

Inwardly, I shuddered as it suddenly occurred to me that I had made a fatal mistake. I'd sent that stupid letter asking about the Reverend. I knew Louella had read the letter because she answered it, but she was an old lady who had probably forgotten all about it. What if Melissa Taggert read it too? I'd signed with my first and last name. That letter was like a trail of bread crumbs leading straight to me.

Who knew living a lie could be so stressful?!

"This is Melissa Taggert, my attorney," Louella said.

"A pleasure to meet you."

"Do you always have tea with your employers?" Melissa Taggert asked tartly. I hated her so much.

"Every chance I get," I said.

She stared at me a few moments before I took the cue.

"Oh. Sorry. Would you like a cup?" I jumped up out of my seat.

"With Lemon and sugar," she said and then took my place at the table.

When I returned from the kitchen, Louella was going through the papers in front of her. She looked at me and snapped her fingers in the direction of the living room until I realized she wanted me to go get her reading glasses. It was humiliating. I fetched the glasses and then began clearing the table while Melissa and Louella proceeded to forget I existed.

Other than the one complete and utter humiliation, the rest of the day went pretty well. I spent most of it tidying up and fetching things Louella needed. We didn't have any meaningful conversations, but it was still nice getting to be a fly on the wall of a famous writer. And the best part? She spent two hours in the afternoon locked in her office, typing away on the antique Olivetti typewriter rising from the heap of papers on her desk. For ten glorious minutes, I stood in the hallway outside her closed door savoring that wonderful sound.

"Do you know what that means?" I asked James that night on the phone.

"She needs a computer?"

"She's still writing! Who knows how many more books she may have written!"

"Why doesn't she publish them?"

"Maybe she doesn't want to publish them. It's not like she needs the money."

"Too bad."

"No, don't you see? I might get a chance to read them! Can you imagine? I could be the only person in the world, other than maybe her lawyer, who is in a position to read the latest book by Louella Harper."

"Aren't you getting ahead of yourself?"

"Wouldn't it be amazing if she asked me to give her my impressions of her plots and characters..."

"I take that back. You're going off the deep end."

"James!" I shouted, but honestly, I was having too much fun imagining new scenarios to get upset.

"Did you at least put the manuscript back where you got it?"

"No, but I will," I assured him, "just as soon as I finish reading it."

"Chrissy," he said in that stern voice that reminded me so much of my mother. My mother, by the way, also did not approve of what I was doing.

Oh my gosh. I'm dating my mother! Wait. Are we still dating?

For all I knew, he was seeing other people.

Don't think about that! Give yourself a pat on the back. You just achieved one of your main goals which everyone else thought was impossible. You just got a job working for Louella Harper. Don't blow it!

BLOOD CRIES

The Reverend
by Louella Harper

Chapter Six

Lester stared bleary-eyed through a dead bug and bird shit-covered windshield, listening to the incessant thunderous groan of his big rig eating up asphalt, slurping up the never-ending yellow lines of highway that slid between headlamp beams and disappeared beneath the body of a beast he sometimes struggled to control.

An empty thermos lay beside him on the seat along with a half-eaten stick of beef jerky. Crumpled potato chip packages littered the floorboard. His stomach rattled with indigestion.

Leaning forward, he tightened his grip on the steering wheel. As the truck lurched onto an uneven section of interstate, he bounced in his spring-supported seat. It had been eighteen hours since his last four-hour stretch of shut-eye, and there were sixty more miles until the next rest stop. Until then, there was nothing to do but watch the road.

The CB radio squawked his call sign, snapping him out of the trance. He pulled the hand-held transmitter to his mouth. 'I'm here."

"Your wife is trying to get ahold of you," the dispatcher said.
"Why?" he asked.
"Don't know, but she said it's urgent."

At the next exit, Lester steered his eighteen-wheeler a quarter of a mile down a county highway before he located a gas station with a payphone. At four a.m. the sky was still black with night and there was no one around as he hopped out of his cab and jogged across the parking lot to the phonebooth.

The metal door folded in, and he stepped inside. He patted down his pockets for dimes before he remembered he wouldn't have enough for a long-distance call anyway. He spun the rotary dial for the operator and placed the call collect. The phone rang four, five, six, seven times. Just as he was about to slam down the phone, he heard his wife's voice on the other end of the line.

"Yes, Operator. I'll accept the charges."

"Jan, it's me." He cracked open the door of the phonebooth to let in a breeze. "What's going on?"

He heard her take in a breath. "Lucy's dead."

It took a minute to process the words. Slowly, he lowered his forehead against the cold glass door. He watched a stray dog scamper up to the gas pumps and sniff at one of the tin garbage bins situated there.

"They found her on the side of the road," Jan said.

It had been almost a year since Lester had quit the pulpwood business, driven out of the forest by fits of panic made worse by Taylor's death. It was like Vietnam had followed him home. One day he was drinking with his buddy and the next he was gone forever. Only now, the enemy was the same man handing out the duty assignments. Lester told himself he would either have to frag the son of a bitch or get another job.

Lester's uncle Heywood was the manager of a small trucking company. With Heywood's help, Lester got his CDL, and pretty soon he was making short runs to and from the lumber mill in Prattville. At first, he worried his new job would bring him into close contact with the Reverend, but Baxter ran a small operation. During Lester's first six months behind the wheel, he only made two pick-ups at locations where the Reverend held the timber rights, and only on one of these occasions did Lester actually see him in person. The timber had already been secured to the trailer, and Lester was sitting in the cab, completing the paperwork, when he noticed the Reverend standing there talking to a lumber dealer.

Lester felt a sudden uncontrollable need to get on the road. In his haste, he forced the transmission, botched the double clutch, and caused a loud grinding noise that pulled the attention of the ground crew in his direction. Out of the corner of his eye, he saw the Reverend watching him. He tilted his head back in laughter. The muscles in Lester's jaw clenched, but there was nothing else to do but get in gear. The truck lurched forward, peeling a layer of dirt from the road as it rumbled away.

Six months later, Lester was making long hauls as far as Kentucky and Ohio. He had just completed a delivery of sweet potatoes to a regional distributer in Toledo and was returning with a load of heavy machinery when he received the message to call his wife and learned the news about Lucy.

"The wake is this afternoon," Jan told him as he mashed his face against the glass of the phone booth. "It's at our house."

He scratched at the peeling plastic cover that had once held a phonebook before someone ripped it out. It hung from the side of the booth by a strip of metal. "Our house? Why's it got to be at our house?"

"It was either here or at the Reverend's house," Jan said.

A moment of silence followed. "Jesus Christ, not Lucy... Why did it have to be Lucy?"

"Are you coming home?"

Lester balled one hand into a fist and pressed his knuckles against the glass of the phonebooth with restrained pressure. He could smash the thing, free himself from the box he was in, send the shards raining down, and probably cut up himself up, but what good would that do?

"Yeah," he said. "I'm coming."

The road became a blur of trees and tears and highway signs, coffee and caffeine pills, and a never-ending stream of memories.

He remembered going to his brother Robert's house that first time after they brought home his baby girl from the hospital. Lester bought her a stuffed panda bear as a gift. "That thing's bigger than she is," Robert said. Lester didn't believe it at first until they put it next to the baby and sure enough it was almost twice as big as Lucy. They took a picture, and throughout the next year, whenever Lester visited, they always photographed the baby next to the panda bear to mark her growth.

He remembered birthday parties, barbecues, and watching football games on television while the little girl played with her dollies on the floor. "This is Amanda. She likes to sing in the Thanksgiving Day parade."

"That's beautiful, Darlin'. Tell me all about her during the commercial."

Lester was in a helicopter over Da Nang the same night Robert died in a car wreck. He learned the news in a hole in the Kim Son Valley while the rain came down on the poncho he had tented over him—it sounded like popcorn popping.

According to the letter he received from Jan, Lucy's mother was in no condition to take care of a child, and so Lester's sister, Cassandra, had agreed to take her in.

Lester wrote back, wanting to know, why Cassandra? Hannah was more reliable.

Jan responded that Hannah was struggling to put food on the table since her husband abandoned her, and besides she had problems enough with her own daughter. Cassandra was married to a good man who could at least provide a stable environment.

Nobody knew that within six months, Cassandra's husband would divorce her after he caught her sleeping with the man whom she would eventually remarry, the man everyone referred to as the Reverend.

After Lester's deployment ended, the first person he saw when he got home was Lucy. He threw open the front door and tossed his duffle bag to the floor. He looked around for someone to hug, and there she was, sitting on the couch, reading a magazine. She turned toward him, and her face lit up. "Uncle Les!" she said as she jumped up and ran to greet him.

"Look at you," he said. "I can't believe how much you've grown."

She jumped into his arms and squeezed his neck. "I missed you, Uncle Les. I'm so glad you're home."

He had wanted Lucy to come and live with them. He knew all the stories about the Reverend—after Taylor was killed, there could be no doubt about his guilt—but Cassandra refused to let her go as long as there were relief checks coming in, and anyway Lester was still struggling to adjust to normal life.

Keeping a job proved more difficult than he could have imagined. Every day was a struggle just to leave the house. Then there were the nightmares that woke him up screaming and frightened Jan so much she sometimes slept on the couch. It didn't make sense to bring a child into that environment. Looking back, he realized it might have been the one thing that would have kept her alive.

He drove into a rainstorm outside of Nashville. Drops splashed down on the windshield so fast the wipers couldn't keep up with them, and the road dissolved in a watery blur. His muscles tensed, and his hands ached from gripping the steering wheel as he barreled down the highway at 80 mph.

It was the thought of Lucy that saved him from a major collision. He realized he would be no better than the Reverend if he drove his rig through the back end of a station wagon moving at half his speed. He downshifted, decelerated to sixty just as a string of taillights lit up in front of him. Traffic had come to a standstill. He slammed brakes and came within centimeters of tapping the bumper of the car in front of him.

Four hours later, he arrived at his home to find his driveway overflowing with cars. He had to park up the street and walk.

When he opened the front door, he saw a crowd of people dressed in their Sunday clothes milling about his home, chatting and sampling casseroles. No one even noticed him enter.

It was all a little too festive for Lester's liking. People were eating and talking, even laughing. What in the world could anyone be laughing about at a time like this?

He froze when he saw the girl. She was sitting in the same place where Lucy had been sitting the day he came home from Vietnam. For a moment, he thought it was Lucy, and that was enough to erase the misery of the ten-hour drive. Then she looked up, and he saw another girl's face and the misery came back on him all at once. It was Hannah's girl, Laverne.

It felt like Lucy had been killed all over again.

He moved through the crowded living room in a stupor. A line of people formed in front of him, offering greetings, shaking hands, nodding, and mumbling short phrases. The house was so thick with people he couldn't even get to his bedroom to change out of his road clothes.

Everywhere, people were talking and laughing as if this was merely another social occasion, an opportunity to get together and exchange pictures of their kids, as if a young girl's life hadn't been stolen away.

The dining room table was piled with casserole dishes. A line of acquaintances, extended family members, and other people he only saw at weddings and funerals circled the table. They held plates in one hand and used the other to scoop up heaps of green bean casserole and squash. They stabbed their forks into slices of pork loin and babbled on about church gossip or the end of the basketball season. Lester hadn't eaten in no telling how many hours, but the thought of food revolted him.

He felt a hand on his shoulder, and there was Hannah leaning in for a hug. This was a woman who smiled her way through even the most trying of circumstances, as if she could will away the misery of others through the force of her own cheerfulness. Not today. Today her face sagged under the weight of her grief. Without saying anything, she released him and went back to the flurry of activity that would keep her mind from dwelling on the tragedy. She dropped a bowl of fresh coleslaw on the table and scooped up an empty casserole dish, and then skidded off to the kitchen.

Lester stood there, trying to make sense of what was happening, and then, realizing there was no sense to be made, he squeezed his way through the crowd, heading for his bedroom. He needed to get away, to find a place where he could become himself, maybe lie down for a while, but he found that his bedroom, like the rest of his house, had been confiscated.

Jan ran up to him, wrapped her arms around his body. "I'm so glad you made it home." She pulled back, looked at him. "It's been crazy."

Lester looked past her at the room. "I can see that." But what he really saw was Cassandra in the vanity chair, gazing solemnly at her reflection. "What's she doing in my bedroom?" he asked.

"I'm sorry. She was driving everyone insane. I had to get her away and this was the only place I could take her."

He could tell by the way her head was angled that she could see him in the mirror. He walked up behind her. "Cassandra," he said.

Her shoulders sagged dramatically. She sighed. "What am I going to do, Lester?"

"Where is your husband?" Lester asked.

"He went to see his lawyer," she said. "Wouldn't even stay with his own wife during her time of need."

Lester shook his head in disbelief. He went down to one knee, so they were on the same level and looked at her reflection in the vanity mirror. He squeezed her shoulder.

"Do you understand what's happened, Cassandra? Don't you know what's going to happen next? That man doesn't care about you. He doesn't care about anyone but himself. The rest of us don't mean anything. We're all just pieces of trash to him."

Cassandra smiled beneath her smearing makeup. "He always told me he loves me. I think he does in a way."

"He doesn't Cassandra. That man ain't capable of love. He's coming for you next."

The tears were streaming down her face now, driving away dark streaks of makeup down her face. "Don't you think I know that, Lester? Do you think I wouldn't stay here if I didn't have to?"

"You don't have to. Why do you have to?"

"He said if I ever left him, he'd come for me. He'd find me wherever I was in the world. He said, 'There ain't no hiding from me.' It's not like I have anywhere else to go. Everyone I know is here, and he's got control of all my money."

"You can stay here. I can protect you."

"You don't get it, Lester. He's the one who's protected. He'll find me. He'll always find me. He'll wait until you're gone driving and then he'll show up here. There's no way to stop him."

BLOOD CRIES

From the Journal of Louella Harper

Lorrie Braswell has worked in Melvin Little's office for seven years, ever since she graduated from the Dadeville Community College secretarial program. She is a plump, congenial woman who wears her auburn hair pulled back in a tight bun and speaks in a high-pitched, almost sing-song voice. The interview took place at Melvin's office on October 14, 1977. Transcript to follow:

Lorrie Braswell

People in Jackson City love themselves some drama. They may say they hate this group or make fun of that group, but when they get to know each other, they don't care about people's color, or religion, or if they voted for so-and-so instead of what's-his-name. On a one-to-one personal level, they like each other. That's what made the Reverend so different. He wasn't like good, normal people, and he had no desire to become one of us.

I came to work one morning after Lucy Woods died. The whole town was talking about it—how the Reverend killed her and put her underneath that car. Of course, I couldn't say a thing about it to anyone on account of Melvin makes us all sign a bunch of papers saying we will not discuss any of the clients who come into this office with anybody under any circumstances. "Not even your preacher or Jesus Christ himself." That's what Melvin always says. I don't think it's actually in the contract.

That's why when he said it was okay to speak on the record, I said, "Oh no you don't, Melvin Little! I won't say a single word unless you have me sign another piece of paper cancelling out that other piece of paper that says I can't do it."

He said, "Come on, Darlin'. If I say, it's okay, it's okay. You go ahead and talk to that nice lady. She's the famous writer who's gonna tell my story to the world." He kept going on and on, and I never did sign that other piece of paper, but I guess it's okay. Nobody knows the law better than Melvin.

Louella

You were saying something about the morning after Lucy died.

Lorrie

Oh, that's right. I came in one morning after Lucy Woods died, and the first thing I noticed was that a light was on in Melvin's office. I thought about how strange that was because I'm usually the first to arrive, and sometimes Melvin doesn't show up until almost noon. Anyway, I didn't shout "good morning" to him right at first because I had to go to the bathroom, and I didn't want to call attention to that. Instead I put my stuff down on my desk and started the coffee pot brewing because I knew if he was up that early he would be ornery until he had his cup of Maxwell House.

Once that was going, I went ahead into the bathroom. I won't tell you about that, but after I came out of the stall and was washing my hands, I heard this banging sound coming from the backside of the building.

It took me a minute to figure out that someone was banging on the back door. Nobody ever comes in through the back door. That door is for emergency purposes only. When I came out of the bathroom, I heard voices coming from Melvin's office.

I know I shouldn't have done it. I try not to eavesdrop, but sometimes I do it without even realizing that's what I'm doing, although on this occasion, I knew what I was doing. That's what makes it wrong, I guess.

Louella
What did you hear?

Lorrie
Well, I sort of tiptoed up to the door of Melvin's office, and stood just to the side, so I could hear what was being said around the corner. I heard Melvin say, "Now, Reverend just calm down. Everything will work out just like it always does."

My stars, when I heard that it was the Reverend in there, my heart just started beating so fast it was like it was trying to jump out of my chest and punch me in the face. I'd seen the Reverend around the office maybe a half-dozen times, but that was when I thought he was just a regular client. I never knew what all he was accused of until after Lucy's death made the news. Like I said, we don't ever talk about our clients. By this time, though, I knew everything. You couldn't help but hear everything. People were talking about it at church and the grocery store and just about everywhere else you went. I was scared.

Louella
What did the Reverend say to Melvin?

Lorrie
He was arguing. He said, "They will believe it. They'll believe whatever I tell them. They'll believe whatever I tell you to tell them." He was talking to Melvin, you see.

Melvin said, "Not this time, Reverend. I'm afraid they're going to make you pay for this one. I don't see how I can stop it."

The Reverend started going on about the journalists, how they kept hounding him for interviews, and how he was trying to get them to shift the attention onto someone else, but it wasn't working.

Louella

That's what he said? He wanted to shift the focus to someone else?

Lorrie

Yes, ma'am. Well, Melvin said, "It's just not as easy as you make it sound." And the Reverend said, "It is that simple. It's just as simple as saying, "Look over there."

"Now Reverend," Melvin said, "You don't want to start nothing with Ernie. You and him are friends."

"His value is all used up."

Melvin said, "That may be, but Ernie Smith is one of my clients and a dangerous one at that."

Then Reverend Baxter started yelling, "You think Ernie Smith is dangerous? Do you know who I am?"

I have never been so frightened in my life. I stood there beside the open door with my back flat against the wall, and, well, let's just say it's a good thing I had already went to the bathroom. I knew Melvin was scared too because I heard him stuttering, "N-n-now Reverend, let's just talk about this." I heard him back up his rolling chair until it banged into the wall, and I could tell the Reverend was moving closer because I could hear the floorboards creaking underneath his footsteps.

I thought to myself: Oh... my... stars!

I knew I had to do something. I didn't know what I was going to do, but I knew it had to be something, so I tiptoed away from there as fast as I could tiptoe, all the way back to the front door, where I pulled an umbrella out of the umbrella stand, and I don't know what I thought I was going to do with it, but I had it in my hands.

Then, I decided I needed to make some noise to distract the Reverend from doing whatever he was doing to Melvin, so I opened the front door real fast, and slammed it shut. Did you notice the bell above the door? That wasn't there before. Before that, it was a lot easier to sneak in if you were running late for work. Anyway, nobody made more noise coming in than I did right then. I hollered, "Good morning, Melvin! We're here!" Even though it was only me and my little umbrella. I almost shook to pieces.

When I got to that coffee maker right there, I realized it wasn't raining in Melvin's office, and that umbrella wouldn't do me a bit of good, so I swapped it for a mug of hot coffee. I figured if I poured hot coffee in his face, that would get me enough time to run screaming out of the building.

By then though, I was so scared, I couldn't even move. I was just standing there outside Melvin's office, when the Reverend rounded the doorway. If I'd had any liquid in my body I would have literally peed all over myself.

I said to myself, "This is it Lorrie. Get ready to throw that hot coffee in his face," but all I could do was just sort of hold it up like I was offering it to him.

"Lady," he said. "If you don't get out of my way, I'll run over you."

So, I just sort of shuffled over to one side and out of the way. And when he was gone, I just started praying and thanking Jesus. I felt like I had just gone face to face with a wild tiger, who gave me a sniff and then decided I wasn't worth eating.

I was still shaking when Melvin came out of the office still holding up his cup of coffee. He grabbed it without giving me a second look. "Thank you, Darlin'" he said, and then turned around and went right back into his office.

CHRIS HOPE

The Reverend
by Louella Harper

Chapter Seven

The offices of the *Jackson City Sentinel* are located in a squat brick building downtown. The small, dark room in back is where they keep bound copies of every issue printed since the early 1900s. It was there that Jim Easton and his editor, Arnold Rosenbush went looking for background material to fill out the articles they were writing about the latest suspicious death tied to Reverend Baxter.

"What year was the trial where the woman changed her testimony?" Rosenbush asked. The heels of his boots rested on a long, rectangular table while the giant book containing a year's worth of newspapers rested flat against his thighs. He casually turned pages while puffing on a cigar. "1970, right?"

"I believe so," Jim said. He moved down the line of newspaper-sized books that filled three shelves along two walls.

"Well we covered the Jaycees and the goddamned girl scout convention. Where the hell's the coverage of the most interesting trial in the town's history." Arnold was only two years older than Jim. He had long red hair and wore circular-framed glasses, bell-bottom jeans, and an Aerosmith t-shirt. But he was also a seasoned professional who knew the newspaper business inside and out, which is why Ms. Pat had hired him to be the editor.

"I told you already. It isn't here. We didn't cover it." Jim pulled another volume from the shelve and eased it onto the end of the table opposite Arnold's feet. He began flipping through pages. "I couldn't find anything on Calpurnia's death either, or the brother, or the nephew. None of it made the paper."

"Apparently, my predecessor didn't know the difference between a good story and the hole in his ass."

"Not so fast; he was also corrupt. I'm sure he would've reported on all of the murders if only someone had slipped him twenty bucks."

"Well, I'm editor now," Arnold said. "And it looks to me like we're on to a hell of a story."

"I just wish we could confirm Ernie Smith's involvement."

"Don't worry. We'll get him eventually."

"I haven't seen Ernie lately. I heard he went on vacation."

"Who's running the funeral home?"

"A guy named Kevin Summers."

"So," Arnold said, as he twisted the cigar in his mouth and covered the end in a dark patch of saliva. "The girl dies, and he suddenly goes on vacation."

"Supposedly, the vacation has been planned for months."

"What does your source in the sheriff's department say?"

"Tommy? He said Ernie is a world-class son of a bitch, but nobody is looking at him for these murders. The Sheriff is operating under the assumption that the Reverend acted alone."

"You'll need to verify everything the Reverend told you," Arnold said. "Somebody will be able to tell you if his relationship with his first two wives was as lovey-dovey as he claims. Maybe you can talk to some of the family members at the funeral home."

"You're sending me to cover Lucy's funeral?"

"Of course. All the relatives will be gathered in one place. It's the perfect opportunity to talk to them."

"I can't think of a better way to ensure that none of them will ever talk to me than by asking a bunch of prying questions at a young girl's funeral?"

"So, don't pry. You'll go. See what you overhear. Engage when you can, and if so, steer the conversation to the Reverend's first wives. You're a reporter, Jim. I shouldn't have to tell you this stuff."

Jim rubbed his hands through his hair. "Fine. I'll see what I can do."

"I wonder if you should bring a camera."

"I should definitely not do that. I'm going to stick out enough as it is."

"Your probably right. It's not as if the funeral itself is front-page news, but if anything happens, give me a call. I'll be there in five minutes."

"It's a funeral service. What do you think will happen?"

"You never know."

Jim was a few minutes late arriving to the service. Most people had already taken their seats. When he pushed through the chapel doors, it felt as if two hundred people simultaneously turned their heads to stare at him. He already felt out of place—his would be the only white face in a sea of mourners—and now he was coming in late. To make matters worse, he wore a bulky leather haversack around his neck containing a Nikon camera, which only added to his feelings of self-consciousness.

Trying his best to ignore the blatant stares, he scooted through the crowd looking for a place to sit. Every pew in the chapel was jammed with people and folding chairs set up where the pews ended. The back of the room—where Jim found himself—was standing room only.

Spotting an empty space along the back wall, he pinned the bulky haversack against his hip with his hand and slid through little openings in the crowd until he landed in a small patch of floor he could call his own. It was just beneath a stained-glass image of the archangel Gabriel.

Was it really this hot, or was it just him? Outside was bad enough, but inside it was like a brick furnace. Or Hell. Water beaded on his forehead and sweat stains expanded in the pits of his shirt. He had to wipe the sweat from his eyes with the sleeve of his jacket just to see in front of him.

Jim was lucky to be tall. For the most part, he could see over the people in front of him. The pulpit stood on a podium on the right side of the room facing him. On the far-left side was the organ, where some invisible organist sat behind a pew screen playing the introductory music. In between, placed on high in the center of the back wall, hung a large wooden cross. Below that, was the casket, where a line of people had come to pay their respects.

Starting at the front of the line, a plaintive wail filled the chapel. People in the pews craned their necks to see who was responsible for the commotion. Jim had already homed in on her. A woman wearing a wide-brimmed hat and sunglasses was crying into the open coffin. "My baby! My poor baby!" She then attempted to climb into the coffin with her baby. It was only through careful intervention by other mourners that she was extracted from the coffin and escorted away. The hysterical woman, Jim realized, was Cassandra Baxter, mother of the deceased.

Within a few minutes, the viewing line disappeared, and Reverend Pilgrim began the speaking portion of the service. Jim slipped his hand into the inside pocket of his jacket and retrieved a small notebook and pencil. He began jotting down a few notes despite a disapproving glance from the man standing next to him. When he was done, he scanned the room looking for Reverend Baxter, but it was too crowded to see if he had actually been brave enough to make an appearance.

As the sermon wound down, Jim decided he had seen enough. He would wait outside where he could take off his jacket and stand in the shade and least there was a chance of a breeze. Hopefully he could pull a few good quotes from the people who gathered there after the service ended.

He awkwardly made his way through the crowd, causing a ripple in the mass of bodies, but only those directly affected by him paid him any attention. Out of the corner of his eye, he saw Reverend Pilgrim make a sign with his hand, and Jim thought it strange that a protestant minister would make the sign of the cross. He didn't dwell on it though, focusing instead on making it to the promised land.

As he pushed open the chapel door, he felt a warm breeze. The door closed behind him and he stumbled a few steps and then paused to loosen his tie. That's when he heard something that sounded like a scream. A great clamor erupted from behind the closed doors: more voices, more screams. There was a quick succession of sounds like firecrackers—clap clap clap—and the doors burst open and people came spilling out into the daylight and ran in all directions.

Jim's instincts worked in the opposite direction. As soon as space was made available, he lowered his head and waded through a wave of panic-stricken mourners, screaming and jostling for position. For a brief moment, he feared he would be crushed in the melee.

The chapel was evacuated in less than a minute. A pair of uniformed officers elbowed past him, charging inside with pistols drawn. Jim's hand slid into his haversack. It seemed as if he might need that camera after all.

Chrissy

For the first few weeks of my employment, Louella Harper had no idea what my name was and elected to call me by several variations of the phrase, "Hey You."

"I can't find my reading glasses," she would say as she snapped her fingers at me. "You there. How about checking under the papers on that end table?"

"My head is killing me! Bring me an aspirin, would you Sis?"

"You'll have to excuse me Miss Lady, but I happen to prefer bath water that doesn't scald the skin off of the bottom of my feet!"

Most of the time, she wouldn't even bother to honor me with a proper designation and instead referred to me in the generalized form.

"I've never seen *someone* take so long to set a table!"

"This tastes awful. You'd think *a person your age* would know how to fix a cup of coffee!"

"How does *a person like you* find employment as a home health aide without learning how to fold a fitted sheet?"

I remember the exact moment she finally broke down and asked me to tell her my name again. She had decided to donate some of her books to a local library, and I was helping her sort through them to decide which ones to keep and which to throw away. I spotted a John Irving book in the "to donate" pile.

"Do you mind if I take this? I haven't read it yet."

"By all means. Have the Pat Conroy too."

"Thank you so much, Ms. Harper. I will treasure them."

"I had no idea I had employed a reader."

"You never know about a person until you talk to them," I said. I was full of wisdom that day.

"I'm sorry. I seem to have forgotten your name."

"Chrissy is fine. Some people call me Chris."

The words were no sooner out of my mouth when I realized I had made a huge mistake. All I could think about was that stupid letter I wrote. I couldn't remember what I'd written exactly, but in hindsight, it looked something like this:

Dear Miss Harper,
My name is Chrissy, but some people call me Chris. I'm planning to track you down and steal a book you wrote called the Reverend. I might even get a job working for you under false pretenses. See you soon!
Your Pal, Chrissy (Chris) Hope

"Someone else went by Chris and Chrissy," Louella said. "It's going to bother me until I think of who it was." She placed Zora Neale Hurston in the "to keep" pile.

Rather than giving her the opportunity to remember that it was me, I decided to change the subject. "You're some kind of famous author, right?"

Louella considered the statement. "I was. Maybe I still am."

"Are you writing anything now?"

"Mostly I write about the world as I see it."

"That sounds interesting."

"It isn't. It's just a way for me to try to make sense of the world and my place in it. Sometimes I do it to motivate me towards some kind of action, like why I need to make a casserole to bring a covered dish to a sick congregant of my church. I write down all the times people reached out to me and made my life better, and that inspires me to do the same for others. Sometimes I write down things I did or said, and I don't like the person who did or said them. It motivates me to do something different the next time. Maybe I do it to remind myself how to stay connected to the human race."

"That's beautiful," I said. "It sounds exactly like the kind of thing I'd like to read."

"Well, don't get your hopes up."

Time and familiarity helped me see Louella for the down-to-earth person she was. Our awkward silences morphed into small talk and, eventually, comfortable banter. And by simply showing up to work every day I became a fixture of Louella's home, someone she counted on to assist her with the mundane details of her life.

Then, I went and pushed my luck too far. I was late bringing in the groceries one morning, and found Louella sitting in the dining room, drumming her fingers on the table, and waiting for her tea.

I dropped full grocery bags all along the kitchen countertop—everywhere I could find space—and got a tea pot going. Then, I got out Louella's favorite mug, a bag of English tea, and then went searching through the bags for the box of Sweet N Low.

"I can tell you were born in the South," Louella said. "Because you sure don't seem to be in a hurry."

"Jackson City, Alabama," I said and then shrank into my skin almost as soon as the words were out of my mouth. That's when I realized I had just led her one step closer to remembering the letter I'd written and my true motive for being there. Maybe a part of me wanted her to find out where I was from as a way of forcing myself to tell her the truth. This would be my opportunity to confess everything and start over from an honest perspective. Mentioning my hometown might even be my best shot at getting her to open up about her time in Jackson City. That is, if she didn't fire me on the spot.

Louella raised an eyebrow.

"Do you know the town?" I asked cautiously.

"I spent some time there years ago," she said.

I found the box of artificial sweetener and set it down beside her cup of tea. I emptied grocery bags on the table while waiting for her to continue. When she sipped her tea instead I offered a gentle prod.

"What were you doing in Jackson City?"

"Wasting my time as it turned out." She shook a tiny bag of sweetener and then tore it cleanly across the top. "I thought I was working on a best seller." She emptied the contents of the bag into her cup of Earl Grey.

"A book set in Jackson City? I just can't believe it."

Louella's eyes shifted from her tea to me. I could feel the scrutiny, so I sat down at the table and separated canned fruits from canned vegetables.

"Haven't you ever heard of the voodoo preacher?"

"Voodoo preacher. Hmm, that sounds familiar." I was going for an Academy Award with this one.

"It's an old story," Louella said. "I don't suppose it holds much interest to people these days."

"I'm interested."

"Well, you are from the area."

"Are you kidding? I bet a lot of people would be interested reading about a voodoo preacher."

"Well, they are out of luck," she said. She examined a crack in the china. "Oh dear, I suppose it's time to replace my tea service."

"Why are they out of luck?" I asked. My head was trembling, imperceptibly I hoped. It was all I could do to keep my voice level.

This is it. She's going to tell me everything.

"I couldn't write the book. There was nothing good in it, no heroes for people to root for."

"What about Lester Woods?" *Whoops.*

She looked at me with sudden, penetrating interest.

"I just remembered the story," I said. "I think my mother told me all about it when I was little."

There's nothing like the truth to help cover up a lie. She seemed to accept the explanation. I was hoping to return to the topic, but the telephone rang.

"Aren't you going to answer that?" Louella asked.

"Oh yes, of course." I meandered toward the phone. "You were saying something about Lester Woods."

"Really, Chrissy, please hurry. Before it goes to voicemail.

Ugh. It was Melissa Taggert. Melissa had a way of popping up whenever I didn't want her around, which was pretty much all of the time. She came by every day! I mean, really, how much time does a lawyer really need to spend with her client?! I wanted to shout the question whenever I saw her—literally every day—but instead I did what I always did when she came over. I went into another room to do some light cleaning.

Dusting was my preferred activity because it was quiet and if I listened closely I might pick up snippets of conversation in the next room, depending on my location. If they were in the dining room, I would arrange picture frames in the hallway around the corner. If they visited in the den, I would go to the kitchen to rearrange coffee mugs or something.

As usual, James was my conscience. "Spying on them just makes you look more suspicious," he'd tell me when I called him that night.

"I know," I'd say in a voice just a bit whiny, "but I'm so close to learning the truth! As soon as I do, I swear I'll fess up about everything and come home."

"And then what, Chrissy? What are you even going to do with this information once you get it?"

"I've been writing," I announced happily. "It's pretty much all I do when I'm not working. It's not like there's anything else to do around here."

"Oh... okay, well, that's great," James said, trying to be supportive. "I mean, I still think you should have been honest from the start but..."

"I never would have been in a position to write the story if I'd been honest," I said. "Look, James, I know you don't approve. I understand that, and I love that you are so honest and think everyone else should be too, but in this case, I had to lie!"

"I don't know about that, Chrissy."

"You don't have to know about it, James. Just please trust me. I know what I'm doing."

Okay, that was also a lie. I had no idea what I was doing, but my impassioned plea seemed to pacify him, at least for the moment. What I was doing was hard enough without receiving pressure from the home front.

Now, I just had to figure out what to do about Melissa Taggert. I was starting to get the feeling the woman didn't trust me. I came to that conclusion after she told me outright that she didn't trust me. I was dusting in Louella's office, just minding my own business, keeping Louella's Olivetti free from particles, when I suddenly heard her voice behind me.

"And just what do you think you're doing?"

"You scared me," I said after wheeling around to face the woman who had somehow slipped into the room without making the door creak.

Melissa Taggert wore a fake smile. "Louella told me you're from Jackson City."

"Born and raised. For a little while, at least. I mean, I moved away when I was eight."

"And you were asking her about the voodoo preacher?"

"Yeah, well, he came up." I didn't like where this was going.

"And the manuscript she wrote?"

"I guess so." Uh oh.

"Isn't that interesting?"

"I... don't know. I guess so."

"And here you are sneaking around her office."

"I'm not sneaking. I'm cleaning. Louella asked me to help organize her office."

Melissa stared at me for several seconds before she spoke again. "Do you know what I think? I think you're up to something, and you can bet your sweet bippy, I'm going to find out what it is."

Bippy? My feather duster hung at my side. My mouth dropped open in a look of utter astonishment. But what I was thinking was, *Oh shit oh shit oh shit! This is it. Maybe the time to put the manuscript back in the file cabinet would have been any time before this conversation started.*

I honestly thought she was going to pat me down right then and there. Lucky for me, the stolen manuscript was back at my apartment, hidden in the drop ceiling. Unlucky for me, she was right about everything. It was all I could do to summon the self-righteous indignation needed to maintain my innocence. "I'm sorry, ma'am, I just don't know what you're talking about."

"I want to be perfectly clear, so you understand me. My job is to protect Louella. Period. People are always coming out of the woodwork trying to take advantage of her, and when they do, they find me. And, I'm the last person in the world they want to find."

Of that, I was certain. "I don't understand why you're telling me all of this. Are you accusing me of something? What did I do?"

"I'm not accusing you of anything. I'm promising you. If you step out of line, you're going to wish you were never born."

"I'll have you know that I haven't done anything wrong," I said. "You go do your background check or whatever you need to do, but I'd appreciate it if you would leave me alone from now on. I have a job to do."

With that, I threw my feather duster over my shoulder and marched out of the room. I gathered my things and left for the day, all the while, maintaining the demeanor of the falsely accused victim. I made it as far as the staff bathroom before I melted into a puddle.

Oh shit oh shit oh shit. What am I going to do?

CHRIS HOPE

From the Journal of Louella Harper

When the phone rang, I expected it to be Maris. She was still mad at me for not staying with her at the lake, but I made a promise to myself not to disrupt her household. I had a whole speech prepared. Only it wasn't Maris on the line, but Melvin Little.

"I know how I'm gonna do it, Ms. Harper. I know how to make it right."

"If this is about the dinner party the other night, please tell Miriam I am sorry. I must have gotten carried away. You don't owe me any promises or explanations."

"You have to understand, I never meant to... I never even made a connection..."

"Are you saying you didn't knowingly partner with a killer? That it never occurred to you that every time you got that man off the hook for murder and then halved the insurance settlement with him, that you were in fact setting the man up to do it all again?"

"No, of course not. I never thought of it like that. You see, I had a duty to my client..."

"Some might say you have a duty to your community as well."

"Ms. Harper. That's not fair."

"I'm sorry, Melvin, but I'm not comfortable writing about a morally ambivalent protagonist."

"It's not true, Ms. Harper. I am a moral person. I'm a deacon at my church."

"It ain't enough to go to the building, Melvin. You have to live by the principles. I may have to approach this story from a different angle. I hope you understand. I have my audience to think about."

"I understand, Ms. Harper," he said in a wounded voice. "I really do. I'm sorry I let you down. I'm sorry. I let everybody down. I never meant to do it."

I took an audible breath and held it. I could think of nothing else to say.

"Ms. Harper," he said, when it had been made clear that I wasn't going to let him off the hook. "I won't you to know. It ain't over yet."

"I don't know, Melvin," I said. "I don't know how you could possibly make things right at this point."

"Well, maybe I can't make it right," he said, "but I may be able to make things better than they are now."

CHRIS HOPE

The Reverend
by Louella Harper

Chapter Eight

In his bright green three-piece suit, Lester Woods stood out among the mourners crowding the small chapel known as the Temple of the Smith, though he behaved like a man who wished to remain invisible. He sat hunched in the front-row pew, his elbows propped on his knees, and his face buried in his hands as if to avoid the gaze of the preacher towering above him in the pulpit.

His wife Jan reached out and touched his shoulder, but he made no movement or sign to acknowledge the gesture, and so she pulled her hand away again.

His niece, Laverne, sat on his other side, nearer to the center aisle, looking around the room at foreign faces and muttering her judgments. With her arms crossed over her chest and her chin extended, she resembled a coiled snake.

"Look at all these people. They never even knew Lucy."

"This is a good turnout," Jan said across Lester's back. "They came to pay their respects."

Laverne blew a puff of air threw her lips. "That's not why they came."

A great mournful howl pulled their attention to the viewing line extending through the center aisle to the front of the chapel.

"Oh Lord," Jan said.

Two men held Cassandra back from clawing her way into the open coffin. "My baby. Oh, my poor baby," she wailed. "I can't let you go."

Lester lifted his head and watched as his sister broke free and tried to climb into the arms of the deceased. Her legs kicked in the air until the men recovered their balance and pulled her out again.

"No, I won't go. I won't go," Cassandra cried. "I have to stay with my baby girl."

Jan ran over and helped coax her out of the box. She wrapped her arm around her shoulders and soothed her with quiet words, and then led her back to the pews and deposited her in the row behind where she and Lester and Laverne were sitting.

Lester observed the commotion without expression. He had already paid his official respects to Lucy. He'd looked down at the little girl's face, swollen with death and whatever chemicals Ernie's people had used to preserve her for viewing. He'd reached into the coffin to caress the purple scarf Jan had given her last Christmas, now used to camouflage the bruises on her neck, and an image passed through his mind—the rotor coming down on her neck—and he felt anger welling up inside him. He gripped the side of the coffin so hard he thought he might snap it to pieces. Beyond the open coffin lid, the true object of his rage came into focus.

The Reverend was sitting at the end of the second pew, dabbing his forehead with a cotton handkerchief. The man had travelled no viewing lines, he'd paid no respects. He flaunted his crime and his ability to escape justice. He'd come for one reason and one reason only: to tell everybody that the Reverend could kill as he pleased and remain immune from prosecution.

Lester's eyes locked on to him as he made his way back to his seat, almost directly in front of the Reverend. He watched him dab the side of his face with the handkerchief and some part of Lester hoped it was more than just the temperature that made him sweat. He hoped it was the raving panic of a a rat trapped by a pack of hounds. Could he feel the eyes of his neighbors bearing down on him? Did he know how much he was despised by his own family, or by the people who made him believe they were his friends?

Sadly, there was nothing in the Reverend's eyes that indicated fear. He was just hot. And bored. And he knew that there was nothing and no one in the chapel who could, or would, touch him.

As Lester sat down, he could feel the man's evil presence burning through the back of his suit jacket. It was the reason he leaned forward, rested his elbows on his knees, and stared at the floor. He tried to keep himself together for Lucy's sake.

The minister, Reverend Pilgrim, rose in the pulpit to deliver the eulogy, staring down at the man in green as the last notes of organ music washed over the sweating congregation.

"Good morning," he began.

The congregation murmured hello.

"Today is a sad day," Reverend Pilgrim said. "Nothing can be as sad as the death of a child, but we must remember that we are here not only to mourn her passing, but to celebrate the life of Lucy Mae Woods, and to be jubilant in the knowledge that she is going to meet the Lord."

"Amen," said the congregation.

Reverend Pilgrim proceeded to tick off a list of Lucy's virtues and sing the praises of her short life, but each little offering of the life cut short sank into Lester's belly like a dagger, and when the preacher repeated that the Lord had called Lucy to be with Him, he found only reminders of the joy robbed from his life.

"It wasn't the Lord that sent Lucy to Heaven," Laverne hissed.

"Quiet girl," said her mother, Hanna, who was sitting to her left.

"How can I stay quiet when he's sitting in this room? Sitting in the pew right behind us?" She looked at Lester. "At the end of the pew."

"You're interrupting the sermon," Hannah whispered.

Lester tilted his head to the right, tried to see the Reverend with his peripheral vision. He could see the man was wearing a little smile on his face. His right arm stretched across the back of the pew and around his sobbing wife. He looked as relaxed as a man could be. Lester tried to shift his focus back to the preacher in the pulpit, but all he could think about was the Reverend sitting behind him.

"You know I struggled to come up with the right words to speak to you today," Reverend Pilgrim continued. "Like all of you, I read the news, I follow the gossip, and my mind keeps going back to a lesson from Genesis. We are all familiar with the story of Cain and Abel..."

An uncomfortable restlessness passed through the congregation as individuals looked around at neighbors and shifted in the pews.

"We know that both Cain and Abel had delivered offerings unto the Lord. Cain had offered a share of his crops and Abel offered the firstborn from his flock, and we know that Cain became very jealous when the Lord preferred Abel's offering. The Lord saw this and said to Cain, 'Why are you angry? If you only do what is right, will you not be accepted? Sin is crouching at your door; it desires to have you, but you must rule over it." Reverend Pilgrim paused to allow the last sentence to sink in before he repeated it. "Sin desires to have you, but you must rule over it."

Lester glanced over and saw Laverne mumbling her argument under her breath. He could see the muscle movement behind her jaw and beneath her lower lip as she leveled her eyes on the man in the pulpit. If Pilgrim hoped to influence her, then she was having none of it.

"But we know how Cain responded. He was a petty and jealous man, who wanted the Lord's attention all to himself, so he invited Abel to the fields and murdered him. Then the Lord said to Cain, 'Where is Abel?' and Cain replied, 'I do not know, Lord. Am I my brother's keeper?'" Reverend Pilgrim gazed down at the second pew, where another reverend was sitting.

Lester turned his face and peeked back behind him. He knew he couldn't look at the man directly, but he had to see the reaction on Baxter's face when he was called out in the sermon. But Baxter only sat there, comforting his wife and occasionally dabbing the handkerchief against his forehead.

"The Lord said, 'What have you done? Your brother's blood cries out to me from the ground. Now you are under a curse and driven from the ground, which opened its mouth to receive your brother's blood from your hand. The ground will no longer yield your crops and you will be a restless wanderer on the earth.'

"Now Cain could not bear this punishment. He was scared. He begged the Lord to let him stay. He thought people would seek revenge and come and kill him. But the Lord said to him, 'You are safe. Anyone who kills Cain will suffer vengeance seven times over,' and he put a mark on Cain so that no one who found him would kill him."

Reverend Pilgrim reached out into the air, directing his hand at Reverend Baxter it seemed. He made an x in the air with the pad of his thumb, delivering the mark of Cain unto the Reverend.

"So that's the way it has to be," he continued. "That's the way it always has to be. Any man who kills his brother will be made to suffer, but it is not man's judgement to give but God's. God will deliver his judgement."

"That's not good enough," Laverne hissed.

As Reverend Pilgrim moved on to the benediction and said his final prayer. Laverne shook with fury. People were standing to leave when she whipped around to face the Reverend. She pointed at him from across the pew and screamed with rage, "You!"

The Reverend glanced up wearing an expression of mild curiosity. He fanned himself with a memorial bulletin.

Cassandra lifted her head off his shoulder to see what her niece was making such a fuss about.

"Will Baxter!" Her finger jabbed forward like a spear point as she spoke. "You killed my sister, and you're going to pay for it."

Cassandra peeled away from her husband and folded her arms in disapproval, but the Reverend never even flinched. He remained in the same position as before with one arm stretched across the pew and the other waving a fan. The only change was the murderous look in his eyes and the little smile that crept across his face.

Other than Laverne, he never saw anything else. Maybe a flash of movement, the blur of Lester's green jacket, the glint of gun metal, and then, nothing. The first bullet passed through his brain before sound could travel to his ears, and he was already dead when the next two rounds entered his body. He never saw his blood spatter against his wife's face or heard the sound of her screaming.

CHRIS HOPE

Selected Interviews Conducted by Louella Harper
9/23/77 - 11/11/77

Hannah

Tea?

       Louella

No thank you.

Hannah pours some for herself

       Louella

Can you tell me what happened?

       Hannah

Well, we were sitting in our pew and then Lester shot Will. That's about all I know.

       Louella

Was there any indication beforehand that Lester might take matters into his own hands?

       Hannah

He was sad of course, but he certainly never said anything about it to me. I was as surprised as anyone. Are you sure you won't have a cup?

Reverend Pilgrim

Louella
Did you know Lester Woods was going to shoot Reverend Baxter at the funeral?

Pilgrim
If I had known, I would have told the police.

Louella
It's strange. Your eulogy was more about the Reverend than it was about the girl.

Pilgrim
I wanted to celebrate Lucy's short life and mourn her death, but in my mind, funerals are for the living. They are about offering comfort and, in this case, soothing angry spirits. I knew people would be angry. People get angry when someone close to them dies, especially a young person. Some lash out. I'd heard rumors over the years (about the Reverend). I knew he was being blamed. It did not take a genius to realize that someone might be tempted to seek retribution.

Louella
Is that why you picked the story of Cain and Abel?

Pilgrim
It seemed appropriate. Unfortunately, the moral of the parable was lost on certain members of the congregation.

Louella
Did you think you were absolving Will Baxter as God absolved Cain?

Pilgrim
God didn't absolve Cain. He forgave him.

Jan

Louella
Did your husband plan to murder the Reverend?

Jan
Lester wasn't acting. He can be a very emotional man, especially since the war. He just got carried away in the moment.

Louella
He brought a gun to the funeral home.

Jan
That doesn't prove anything.

Laverne

Do I need my lawyer?

Louella
I'm a writer, not a prosecutor. I just want to know the truth about what happened. My readers will want to know the truth about what happened.

Laverne
I don't know what happened.

Louella
I thought from your vantage point, directly beside your uncle, you might have seen something.

Laverne
I don't remember.

Louella
Did you know ahead of time that Lester was bringing the gun to the funeral home?

Laverne
I'm not answering any more questions.

Mary Alice Waverly (Friend of the Family)
I almost went to that funeral. I thought they were going to kill him at the cemetery.

The Reverend
by Louella Harper

Chapter Nine

A camera flashed as Arnold Rosenbush captured Reverend Baxter's final repose. There was nothing in the image to suggest feelings of anxiety or urgency at the moment of his death. He appeared completely at ease. His arm still rested across the back of the pew, but he had slumped down somewhat, and his chin rested on the right side of his chest. It might even be said that he had the look of a man who was only sleeping, but for the blood trickling out of the hole in his cheek.

The blood collected in the dimple on his chin before falling in drops into an ever-widening dark stain on the lapel of his suit jacket. On his chest, two red splotches slowly expanded beyond the visible portion of his white button-down shirt.

"What are you going to do with that?" Jim asked his editor. "You'll never get it published."

"You never know," Arnold said.

The church doors opened, and a horde of uniformed officers swarmed the aisles, followed by a couple of paramedics carrying a stretcher. "A little late, aren't you, boys," Arnold said. Turning to Jim, he added, "I told you I would get here fast."

"It offers me no comfort that you beat the ambulance," Jim said.

The police cordoned off the area and ordered the two reporters to vacate the premises.

"Yeah, yeah, yeah," Arnold said. "We got what we came for, right Jim?"

"What? Oh, yeah, of course," Jim said, though he still wasn't sure why Arnold had wanted to photograph the body.

They walked together in the general direction of their respective cars. The hadn't gotten far when they spotted the police cruiser. Two officers sat in the front seat. The driver was writing on a clipboard balanced on the steering wheel, while the other man leaned over the back of his seat talking to someone.

Jim shifted his gaze from the police officers to the man they had in custody, Lester Woods.

Jim slapped his editor on the shoulder. "That's the shooter," he said. "They haven't taken him to jail yet."

"Let's see if we can get an interview. Do you want to talk to the cops or should I?"

"You go ahead."

"Alright, take the camera. See if you can snap a decent picture." He handed over the camera, but as he approached the vehicle, the officers noticed him and drove away before he could ask them any questions.

* * *

As Lester sat in the squad car, his mind replayed the shooting.

He remembered leaning forward in the pew, chin on the backs of his hands, elbows touching knees. He rocked back and forth a few times and, psychically, he was projected back to Vietnam. The conflict had taught him a lot about survival.

In Vietnam, in order to survive, you focused on your enemy. You entered a zone, a kill-or-be-killed mentality that required laser-tight focus of the type where time slows down to the millisecond. He knew in that moment that he had the advantage.

The service was over. All around him, people were standing up, slowly making their way out of the pews and down the aisle toward their cars. The slow mass exodus was a perfect form of camouflage and provided the perfect opportunity to launch a surprise attack. The target would be confused. He wouldn't know where the danger was coming from.

Then came the distraction. Laverne stood and shouted—it didn't really matter what it was she shouted, just so long as it caught the Reverend's attention and pulled it away from Lester. Laverne performed her role perfectly. While she confronted the Reverend, Lester slipped his hand into his jacket pocket and pulled out his gun.

As he stood and spun around, he never saw the people running toward the exit. He never heard their screams. There was only one person he could see, and it was a dead man lying in the pew. He never even knew he was dead. He was too busy staring up at Laverne, wearing that evil smirk on his face. And then, he had some extra holes.

When Lester looked around again, he found the pews empty. Jan and several others had to pull Cassandra out kicking and screaming, but Lester never even noticed. Neither did Laverne, who remained by his side long enough to lean forward and spit on the Reverend's suit. Then, she was gone, and two policemen were running toward him.

The gun slipped out of his hand and banged down on the floor, and still he kept staring into the Reverend's lifeless eyes. He knew then he'd finally done what he'd set out to do. He felt compelled to deliver the message he'd intended to give the Reverend before he'd fired the first shot, but that had somehow gotten lost in the rush of adrenaline.

"You are done hurting my family."

BLOOD CRIES

The next thing he knew, the police had his arms pinned behind his back, and handcuffs were biting into his wrists. He fixed his stare on the dead man in the pew as they marched him away. His head swiveled around as he walked, watching him all the way to the chapel door.

He walked out into the heat of the day with his two police escorts toward their waiting cruiser. A few people were still running around on the lawn like they didn't know where to go, like they didn't know what to do. So, they just stood there gawking at him.

Let them stare, he thought. Get a good look at the man who killed the Reverend.

"What about the crime scene?" One of the officers spoke for the first time. "We can't leave the body unattended, can we?"

"Get him in the car while I call it in," the other man said. "Then I'll go back and guard the body until the cavalry comes."

The officer who spoke first helped Lester into the back of the waiting vehicle. It wasn't like the other times he had been thrown into the back of a police car. The last time, he'd been beaten bloody after he was in cuffs and the cop deliberately smashed his head against the roof of the car before he was pushed into the back seat. This time, the guy handled him as gently as a baby. He even put his hand over his head to make sure he didn't bump his head. Looks like I'm getting the star treatment, he thought.

The door shut, and he was alone with his thoughts, but only for a moment. The officer climbed into the driver's seat and Lester could hear him talking into his radio set, and then he turned to Lester. "You okay back there?"

Lester shrugged. "Cuffs are a little tight."

"Turn around. I'll loosen them for you."

Lester looked up in surprise but did as he was told. He saw for the first time the face of the man who had him in custody.

"Hey Ellis, I didn't recognize you. How are you?"

The officer smiled. "Better than you, I suppose. Listen, I'm going to leave these cuffs off for now, but I'll have to put them back on when we get to the station.

"Okay," Lester said. He rubbed his wrists. "Thanks."

"What happened back there, Lester?"

"Shit. I guess I shot the Reverend." He heard sirens in the distance.

"Yeah," Ellis said. "You shot him alright. You're gonna need a lawyer."

"I shot him in the face." Lester grabbed the back of the seat and pulled himself forward. "And, do you know what, Ellis? I'm glad I killed him. If I had it to do over, I'd shoot him again."

From an Interview of Melvin Little
Interview Conducted by Chrissy Hope on July 2, 2009

Melvin

I met Lester in the same holding cell where I'd met so many of my other clients, the same room where I'd first met with the Reverend Baxter on several occasions and Ernie Smith before that.

The cage door opened, and Lester shuffled in wearing chains and an orange jump suit. He wore a look of resignation and more creases than should appear on the face of a thirty-six-year-old man. He took a seat across the table from me, saying nothing even after the guard removed his handcuffs and left the room.

"Aren't you gonna say something?" I asked.

"Ain't got nothing to say."

I laughed. "Those are beautiful words to hear coming from one of my clients. Too bad you already did too much talking."

He said, "I don't remember saying anything."

"That's more like it."

The problem now was defending someone who killed a man in church in front of three hundred witnesses and then bragged about it to the arresting officer.

Chrissy

Wait. I thought you were the Reverend's lawyer. How could you represent the man who shot him?

        Melvin

Lester asked me the same thing. I said, "You cleared up any conflicts of interest I had when you pulled the trigger." Let's just say I made a phone call to the bar association, and they agreed there was no conflict.

The first thing I had to do was to get that statement he made to the arresting officer thrown out of court.

I said to him, "What in the hell were you thinking talking to the police? Don't you know that's the last thing you're ever supposed to do?" I figured he ought to know that. I'd represented him before a time or two.

He said, "I don't remember what I said."

"Tell that to the head shrinker when he gets here."

"I don't want to see no psychiatrist."

I said, "Well, good because this guy doesn't have a medical degree, but if you want to stay out of jail, you might want to talk to him."

At that point, I don't think Lester cared what happened to him one way or another.

The Reverend
by Louella Harper

Chapter Ten

On the day the Reverend lay in state, a rolling thunderhead blotted out the sun. The temperature dropped ten degrees. The wind picked up as the sky darkened. Some of those who had gathered on the lawn of the funeral home to chat and smoke cigarettes before the viewing turned their faces skyward. Women held the tops of their heads to prevent their hats from blowing away. Others commented on the sudden change in weather.

Most had made the pilgrimage out of a morbid sense of curiosity. Others were young people, friends or acquaintances of Lucy Woods. Some wanted to pay their respects to the Reverend. Some just wanted to be sure he was dead.

A sudden flash of lightning followed by an explosion produced a startled cry from the mourners on the lawn. They turned their heads toward an ancient pecan tree across the street. The tree swayed in the wind, and then, with a cracking sound, it dropped a heavy top branch into the layer of limbs beneath. The limbs seemed to want to catch their fallen comrade but sagged under the heavy weight and dropped it once more onto the layer below. This happened again and again, and the broken limb slowly dropped to the ground, where it jackknifed and rolled into the street.

While a contingency of menfolk climbed down the embankment to clear the road, one man who remained on the lawn told a circle of people, "The Reverend did that."

The tension released in a burst of laughter.

One woman maintained her concerned look. "You joke," she said, "but that was no coincidence. That was a sign. You all saw it." A few heads nodded while they watched the men clear the road.

"It was just a freak occurrence," said the first man. "Lightning strikes sometimes."

"Do you think something like this just happens by accident on the day they bury..." the woman's voice dropped to a whisper, "the Reverend?"

The first speaker's eyes widened in comic exaggeration. He grabbed the lapels of his friend standing next to him. "She said his name! She said his name! Now he's going to come for us too!" The sky continued to darken, and the wind whipped at dresses and hair.

There was more laughter among the young people, but the woman looked worried. The first drops of rain drove everyone inside.

The funeral took place the next day at Locust Grove Baptist Church—Reverend Baxter's former church, presided over by Reverend Martin, the man who had replaced him in the pulpit.

A sense of excitement permeated the church as men and women filed in dressed in their finest mourning wear, with hair freshly cut or coifed just in case they happened to enter the shot of one of several photojournalists documenting the event.

Television crews set up at the edge of a cemetery across the street from the church and filmed people walking inside. Newspaper journalists fanned out and took positions both inside and outside the building. Meanwhile, the sheriff's department made its presence felt both in the streets directing traffic and in the parking lot where they smoked cigarettes while leaning against their vehicles.

Inside the church, a packed congregation sat and watched as Reverend Martin began his eulogy with a question. "Who was Will Baxter? I believe I knew him as well as anybody, but I still don't know the answer to that question. I still don't know what made him do the things he did. I could stand here and state a list of characteristics about the man: dedicated to business, charismatic inside and outside the pulpit, a killer with the ladies." There was an audible moan and then a murmur rippled through the crowd.

Sitting on the front row, underneath a black veil, his third wife Cassandra wailed, "Oh no, it's not true."

Reverend Martin cleared his throat and continued. "He was also..." He paused, as if considering whether or not he wanted to continue, "... a personal friend of mine."

The pews creaked under the weight of a shifting congregation. Cassandra cried, "No no no."

"I know I'm not supposed to say that. I am supposed to disavow this man, to condemn him with evidence I do not possess, to sacrifice the loyalty I feel to a brother because of rumors and gossip."

"I know that's right," said a woman's voice from among the congregation.

"I believe God worked through Reverend Baxter, that God made use of Reverend Baxter in some way we may not even be able to fathom. No matter what else we think, we have to know that God has a plan, and we are all instruments in His hands."

"Amen."

"Moses himself was a murderer, forced to flee after killing an Egyptian who had been mistreating one of his people. His own people judged him. They said, 'Who are you to lead us? Are you going to kill us like you killed that Egyptian?' And maybe they had a right to ask that question, but God still had a purpose for Moses. Moses was an instrument in God's hand."

"Amen."

"Now I don't know if everything they said about Reverend Baxter was true..."

"No No No," Cassandra cried.

"I don't know whether he did everything people said he did, and you don't know if he did all those things. We may never know the truth about all of it. That's the way the world is. We don't always get to know." Reverend Martin smiled. "But that's okay. That's okay because God knows what He is doing. And that's all we really need to know."

"Amen."

Chrissy

After my confrontation with Melissa Taggert, I went straight to my apartment and called James in a panic. I needed him to tell me that everything was going to be okay, that Melissa had no proof that I had taken Louella's manuscript, and I could simply return it the next day, and then move on with my life as if it never happened.

"Wait," James said. "You still have the manuscript?"

"Um. Maybe." I was sitting cross-legged on my couch with the phone cradled between my ear and shoulder, while my hands were occupied by a pint of ice cream.

"I thought you put that back weeks ago."

"Well, I didn't know I was under suspicion."

"Did she check the file cabinet?" James asked.

"I don't know. I don't know."

"You need to know that."

"She may suspect something, but she can't prove anything. I could put it back under the label of a different story. It will look like it was misfiled."

"Or," James said, "you could put the manuscript in her mailbox, quit your job, and come home."

"James! Then everyone would think I stole the manuscript."

"You did steal the manuscript."

"Yes, but they don't know that for sure. Besides, I want to try one more time to talk to Louella about Jackson City. I think it's the last thing I need for my book."

"What book?"

"I told you about this, James. I've been writing, and I'm almost finished. But I need Louella to confirm what I've already read in her manuscript. That way I won't have to admit I stole anything. There are a couple of bombshells in there you wouldn't believe. Then, I can quit my job, come home, and put the finishing touches on the book, sell it, become a millionaire, and live happily ever after."

"What bombshells?"

"I can't tell you that, James. It's privileged information."

"What privilege? You stole the manuscript!"

"I really don't need you making me feel guilty right now. I've got enough to worry about." It was the reason I was polishing off a pint of Cherry Garcia.

"Are you really not going to tell me the bombshells?"

"I don't want to betray her confidence."

"You already betrayed her confidence when you stole her manuscript."

"Yes, James, but we already established that she has no proof. Why aren't you listening?"

"This is too much for me, Chrissy. I'm going to hang up now. Please, return the file and come home."

"Hmmm," I said, sucking on the end of my spoon.

"Why do I get the impression you're not going to do the right thing?"

"No, I will return the file. I'll do it tomorrow. I promise." I'd already photocopied the contents of the folder, so it's not like I was going to lose anything. "I'm just thinking about the problem from all angles."

After a few more minutes of bickering, I ended the call, tossed my phone on the couch beside me, and stared into my empty ice cream carton.

The next morning, I arrived at Louella's condo around nine. I noticed a light shining through the crack underneath the office door. Down the hall in the den, I could see Louella's feet propped up in her recliner. I had hoped to go immediately to the file cabinet and unburden myself of the file weighing down my bulkiest purse, but instead I stopped outside the door and listened to someone rummaging around within.

That's not good, I thought.

Hesitantly, I made my way to the den where I found Louella reading something on her electronic tablet. She was already dressed for the day in a colorful striped button-down shirt and a pair of white slacks.

"What's going on in the office?"

"Melissa has a few things to take care of before she takes me into town," Louella said without looking up."

Melissa used the office on a semi-regular basis, but it bothered me that she was using it today of all days. Oh well, I thought. I've had the manuscript this long. A few more minutes isn't going to hurt anything. And, it gives me a chance to speak with Louella in private.

I unslung my purse and dropped it on the floor at the end of the couch, where it was least likely to attract attention.

"Louella," I said. (I called her Louella now. We were on a first-name basis.) "Remember the other day when you were telling me about Jackson City?"

"Hm?" Louella turned her head slightly but remained focused on her task. I could see now that she was playing a word game.

"You were telling me why you couldn't write the book. You said there were no heroes."

Louella shook her head slightly and frowned. "A story needs a person you can root for."

"What about Lester Woods?" I asked.

"Lester would be the first to tell you he's no hero. He was a man at his breaking point, who shot another man down in cold blood."

"But he had to do it. The Reverend was killing his family."

"I wasn't there to judge him, but I wasn't going to glorify him either. I saw no reason to publish a book if no good was to come from it. When I dug into that story, all I found was narcissism and greed. From the lowliest grocery clerk to the mayor, I heard more people ask me if I was going to make them famous than I could have imagined. Not a day went by when someone didn't try to charge me for asking them basic questions. Even worse, they'd ask when the movie was coming out!" She furrowed her brow as her finger swiped across the face of the tablet. She peered at me over her reading glasses. "If there's one thing I hate, it's being used."

"I feel the same way," I said.

Even though her comment applied to me, I don't think she suspected that I'd borrowed her manuscript. Had she known that, she would have realized that I already knew why she never published her manuscript, and I knew that she was leaving out the most important details. It really irritated me was that she wouldn't tell me the whole truth. I thought we were friends!

A half-eaten bagel sat on a plate on the dining room table. I cleaned up the mess and then settled into my usual routine: cleaning the kitchen, making up her bed, straightening up her bedroom, and sorting her fan mail on the kitchen table—one stack for her to sign, one stack for her to peruse at her leisure, and one stack for the trash. I completed these tasks silently and without my usual relish. I suppose I was ruminating on our disappointing conversation. I was still finishing up when Melissa emerged from the office, carrying her briefcase.

"Ready to go?" she asked Louella.

"Ready to go where?" I asked.

As usual, Melissa ignored me. She stood beside Louella's chair, waiting for her to finish her puzzle.

"Melissa needs me to run by her office to sign some papers, and then she's taking me to lunch." Louella lifted her hand and allowed me to assist her out of her chair.

"Have fun," I said half-heartedly and then returned to the kitchen even though there was nothing left to do there.

I leaned against the counter, listening to Louella shuffling toward the door and wondering what else she had lied to me about. I waited until I heard the front door close before easing out of the kitchen and into the dining room. I peeked around the corner and down the hall where I could see that the front door was closed, and then I went over to the end of the couch and picked up my purse.

At the end of the hallway, I passed the office and gave a quick peak through the long rectangular sliver of frosted glass beside the front door. It's pretty much impossible to see anything through those things, but I detected no shadows or distorted blobs approaching the door, and I figured they were gone.

Doubling back, I entered Louella's office. There was no particular hurry. I dropped the purse on the floor and unzipped the main pouch, happy to rid myself of the evidence against me. I slid the thick file folder out of the pouch. Some of the papers were sticking out on one end, so I had to take them out and tamp them down against Louella's desk to make sure they were all lined up and straight before I put them back into the file. Then, it was a matter of opening the old metal file cabinet, listening to the sound of the drawer sliding along its tracks as it opened. I thumbed through the files until I came to the letter R. I raised the file and slid it back into its place.

That was easy.

I returned to the den and sat down in Louella's recliner, wondering how I was going to finish my book now. Should I just fess up and tell the whole truth? Could I just admit that I was a terrible person? I was still pondering my options when I heard the front door open. No more than a few minutes had passed since they had left, and I assumed Louella had forgotten something.

I climbed out of Louella's recliner and glanced down the hall. I saw that the light was on in Louella's office. I thought about going to the laundry room to fetch my feather duster, so I could pretend to work until they left again, but I didn't feel like it. Instead, I just stood there and waited until Melissa poked her head out of the office.

"Chrissy, can you come down here for a minute?"

As far as I could remember, this was the first time Melissa had ever called me by my name. An hour earlier, this would have caused alarm bells to go off in my head, but at his point, I really didn't care.

"What did you forget?" I asked when I came into the office.

"Nothing," Melissa said. She was looking down at rectangular box made of metal and plastic. She messed with it until it did whatever it was she wanted it to do, and then a smile crept across her face.

"I was just checking to make sure I got my video," she said, glancing up at me.

Video what now?

"Oh," Melissa said, with faux nonchalance, "I recorded you returning a stolen manuscript to Louella's file cabinet. You know? *The Reverend?*" She turned the screen toward me, and I watched in horror as it projected a video of me walking into the office, removing a file from my purse, and returning it to the file cabinet. "It looks like I caught you red-handed."

Shit.

The Reverend
by Louella Harper

Chapter Eleven

On September 22, 1977, in a sweltering courtroom jammed with spectators, the State of Alabama vs. Lester Woods began. Makeshift fans fluttered in front of faces, while those without cooling instruments contented themselves to sit and sweat. A constant murmur took up residence in the courtroom and maintained the dwelling throughout the trial. People who arrived late stood against the walls. Others failed to find a place in the courtroom and had to wait outside, where they strained to hear a snippet of argument.

Television cameras had been barred from the courtroom, but members of the press were given seats in a prime location, on the judge's right side, opposite the jury box. One discerning journalist jotted down conversations eavesdropped from spectators and reported them later, including some addressing recent sightings of the deceased Reverend Baxter.

"My cousin saw him down by the lake. He was driving a white Cadillac."

"He was not."

"He was. My cousin saw him."

"Black pepper," said a woman in another conversation. "That's what you have to use to ward off evil spirits."

"Pepper makes me sneeze."

Lester Woods sat quietly at his lawyer's table. His suit jacket hung on the back of his chair. He wore a button-down shirt, open at the neck, and a pair of blue jeans. His wife sat on the pew behind him.

Judge Barber sat up in his high seat—looking rather small behind an enormous wooden bench—calmly puffing a cigar while he studied the day's itinerary.

The local newspaper would later sum up the varying styles of Melvin Little and District Attorney Henry Russell with a headline, "the Peacock vs. the Bulldog." Melvin would be described as strutting around the courtroom, taking every opportunity to display his feathers while Russell was brusque and sarcastic and would attack with the tenacity of the moniker bestowed upon him.

Even before opening arguments, starting with jury selection, each of the two lawyers spewed vitriol toward the other.

The first objection from Melvin arrived the moment Russell opened his mouth to speak.

"Ladies and gentlemen," Henry Russell began. "You're going to listen to certain so-called expert witnesses..."

"I object your honor," Melvin said.

"Sustain the objection."

"These quote-unquote experts will try dubious legal maneuvers..."

"Objection, Your Honor. He's making a speech."

"Sustain the objection."

"I must have a chance to ask my question," Russell said.

"Objection, He doesn't 'must have to' do anything."

"Sustain the objection. He doesn't have to ask any."

"Now just because a person claims to be an expert, or has a fancy degree, that don't mean..."

"Objection, Your Honor. He's not asking questions. He's trying to poison the jury against the insanity defense."

"Careful, Henry. If I have to delay the trial to round up a new jury, it won't reflect well on you."

"Sorry, Your Honor. Let me just ask this one question of every juror here. Can you stand up and make up your own mind about whether something is right or wrong even if it goes against what some so-called expert says?"

The hands of every prospective juror went into the air.

"Now, it's my turn," Melvin announced as he strode in front of the pool of jurors crowded into a section of courtroom seating. "Does anyone here reject outright the insanity defense?"

No hands raised.

"Is there anyone here who will refuse to give credence to expert testimony?"

Again, no hands raised.

At the end of both rounds of questioning, the lawyers huddled over legal pads at their respective tables. After a few minutes, the judge called for them to issue their strikes—those who would automatically be removed from the pool. Within a half hour, the jury was set.

"That went well," Melvin said as he sat down beside his client.

Lester leaned over and whispered in his ear.

"What's that?" Melvin asked.

"Don't you notice anything particular about the jury?"

Melvin looked up and examined the faces of those he had helped select, most of whom he knew. There was Tim Jacobs, who owned the body shop where he sometimes took his car for repairs, and Earl Tidwell, who was a teller over at the bank, and Bill Caldwell, who ran the car wash. He scanned each row of faces. As far as he could tell, they were all good and fair-minded people. "What am I supposed to be looking at?" He asked.

"There ain't nothing but white men on the jury."

Melvin looked at the members of the jury again, but this time it was like he was seeing them for the first time. "Well, I'll be damned."

"No," Lester said. "I am."

"Gentlemen of the jury," Henry Russell began in his opening statement. "Mr. Little over there at the defense table is going to step forward in a few minutes and tell you a lot of things and use a lot of fancy words to try and convince you to release a murderer. A murder was committed in plain sight in front of three hundred witnesses, in a house of God no less." Russell turned and pointed at Lester Woods. "The defendant sat in the front pew, and in the middle of the service, he stood up and turned toward the victim, and with malice and forethought, he fired three bullets into the victim's face and chest."

Russell paced in front of the jury box, keeping silent to let his message resonate before continuing. "Three hundred witnesses saw it. I could parade those witnesses in front of you all day every day for the next month and they would all say the same thing: Lester Woods shot the Reverend down in cold blood.

"Now the defense lawyer is going to say all kinds of things to confuse the facts. He's going to put the victim on trial for murder. You wait and see. He's going to say the victim was an evil man. He's going to say, 'Look at all the bad things the victim may or may not have done,' and he's going to do it in such way that you may forget—if you are not vigilant—who it was that actually pulled out that gun and shot a man to death in the middle of a church service.

"Furthermore, he's going to parade a bunch of so-called expert witnesses to claim that the victim drove him to do it, that he was not in his right mind when he shot that man down.

"I ask you to not be fooled! Do not fall for this sleight of hand, this bit of legal trickery. Instead, I implore you to stick to the facts and remember that on the day of June 18, 1977, Lester Woods took it upon himself to take the law into his own hands, and to become a one-man lynch mob. Don't you let him get away with it! At the end of the day, I would like to be able to look at you good men eyeball to eyeball and say, 'The rule of law won the day.' I expect you men to be able to look through the shambles of make-believe and adjudicate this case based on the facts: on June 18, Lester Woods did unlawfully take a life here in Jackson City. I thank you for your attention."

As the prosecutor strode back to his table, Melvin Little turned to his client. "That was good. I didn't think Henry had it in him." Lester put his head down on the table. "Don't worry, Brother," Melvin said as he rose from his chair. He straightened his blue silk tie. "It ain't over yet." He wore his hair slicked back to reveal the smooth skin on his quarter moon-shaped face. He strutted over to the jury box.

"Wow, that was a pretty good speech Mr. Russell just made. I'm tempted to rest on my laurels and let that stand as my opening statement too." He looked at the defendant. "What do you think, Lester? I can't really argue with what he said, so maybe I should just sit down, and we can commence to calling witnesses."

Lester stared in disbelief.

"No?" Melvin said. He turned back to the men of the jury. "I suppose I've got to say something then. I suppose I should say that I too think you men have good character and that I too will look you eyeball to eyeball or whatever he said, and I too think you will make the right decision in this case even though the right decision isn't what Henry Russell says it is.

"The defense is going to show through evidence and witnesses who know the man that Lester Woods is a hard-working family man, a long-haul truck driver, a devoted husband and father, a Vietnam veteran who served bravely and brought home a combat infantry medal for his service overseas, a man who brought stray children into his house and treated them like they were of his own blood. There was one girl he even began to think of like she was his own daughter, a little girl named Lucy…"

"Your Honor," Russell stood up. "We object at this point. Mr. Little seems to be straying into a matter of little relevance to this case."

"Goes to state of mind, Your Honor," Melvin said.

"Henry," Judge Barber said, "We talked about this. The insanity defense allows a lot of leeway."

"A travesty of justice is what it is," Russell said.

"You'll have to excuse the District Attorney," Melvin said to the jury. "He seems to be getting a little hot under the collar. As I was saying, the defense will show that Lester Woods is a good man who fought for his country, who loved his family and worked to help others in the community. I admit right now that we don't know, won't know at the end of trial, and we may never know whether a man called Reverend Baxter killed his first wife, killed his second wife, killed…"

"That's it," Russell shouted, "the prosecution asks for a mistrial."

"Denied."

"Your Honor…" Russell pleaded.

"The judge has ruled, Mr. Russell," Melvin said. He leaned forward with a gloating face and then straightened up and faced the jury, holding his lapels like Perry Mason. "As I was saying, we don't know whether or not Reverend Baxter killed his first wife, killed his second wife, killed his brother, killed his nephew, or killed his little stepdaughter, but the defense will show that the people in the community believed it, and Lester Woods believed it, and we will bring in experts…"

"Your Honor," Russell said, "I repeat my request for a mistrial. The defense is trying a dead man."

"State of mind," Melvin said.

"Motion denied," said Judge Barber.

"Can we at least call a sidebar?" Russell asked.

"Denied."

"Witnesses will show," Melvin continued, "that all those murders…"

"Alleged murders," Russell said.

"Whatever you want to call them," said Melvin. "All those murders weighed heavily on the defendant's mind. Furthermore, the defense will show that the defendant was licensed to carry a concealed firearm everywhere he went. So, it was in his pocket when he went to the funeral of that sweet little girl that he looked after like she was his own daughter. He was present when some other relative of the girl—I forget how she was related—but she stood up and shouted at the Reverend, "You killed Lucy," and something snapped in Lester's brain because he stood up and shot the Reverend. We admit he shot him in the face and wherever else the prosecutor says he shot him. The defense will show that he was not in his right mind and he should therefore be treated accordingly. He should be found not guilty by reason of temporary insanity."

Melvin gave the jury a curt nod at the end of his statement and then strutted back to the defense table.

Various Accounts of the Trial

Judge Barber

I barred television cameras from the courtroom, but I allowed the front row to be filled by reporters because I thought their presence would help the attorneys behave. As it turns out I was mistaken.

Henry Russell

The spectators talked constantly, and occasionally people would laugh at something that was said. I made the crowd laugh more than a few times, and I know Melvin tried to do the same.

Melvin Little

I know for a fact I got more laughs than he did.

Judge Barber

The trial was rather unorthodox, but the fact of the matter is, the insanity defense allows a great deal of leeway for the defendant. Things that normally wouldn't be allowed become admissible.

Henry Russell

The judge essentially tied my hands behind my back. The whole trial was a sham.

Melvin Little
When I defended him, Reverend Baxter never had to face a jury. Somehow or other, the case would always fall apart. Now, with the Lester Woods trial, I had to take up some unusual tactics. I admitted right away that Lester killed the man. Never disputed any of Henry Russell's evidence. I even admitted some of his exhibits for the defense. I had to change things up a bit.

Henry Russell
Oh, he changed things around alright.

Melvin Little
One of the first things you learn as a trial lawyer is to put someone else on trial other than the defendant, so that's what I did.

Henry Russell
Reverend Baxter himself was prosecuted by his own damned lawyer at the trial of the man who killed him. It was a joke and a travesty of justice. At one point, Melvin got a guy on the stand—had nothing to do with this case whatsoever—but the judge let him up there, and the guy testified the Reverend had tried to hire him to kill his foster daughter. Had nothing to do with our case whatsoever.

Melvin
Goes to state of mind.

Alvin Thomas
I had worked for the Reverend cutting pulpwood for a month or two, and then about a year later he came up to see me. He said if I did him one favor, I'd never have to work again. He said he'd buy me a car, a house, you name it. I asked, "What is it you want me to do?" The Reverend said, "Not much. There's this girl about to run off and get married. I need her dead before she does that." I said, "I don't want to kill nobody." He said, "She'll be dead before you ever see her. Just put her in a

car for me"—he had this Ford Torino he was going to use—"and bang yourself up a bit. Give yourself a few scratches. And then run the car into a ditch. It's the easiest money you ever made." I told him I'd have to think about it. He said, "You can think, but don't talk if you know what's good for you." My wife called the police and they came down and made a report, but nothing came of it.

Melvin Little
The police had all the information they needed to help that poor girl. The DA had the police report in his files.

Henry Russell
I never received such a report.

Melvin Little
I was able to show that the statement was related to the defendant. It all went to his state of mind. Of course, I had psychologists testify to his condition. They determined that he was diseased of the mind at the time of the shooting.

Henry Russell
As far as I could tell, the tests all showed he was normal, but somehow these jokers made up a diagnosis, Transient Psychosis, or some such nonsense. One of these "psychologists" was nothing more than a glorified guidance counselor.

Dr. Albert Wexler
I have a Bachelor of Psychology degree from Florida State University, a Master of Psychology degree from the University of Texas, where I also earned a doctorate degree in abnormal psychology.

Henry Russell
They think they can learn about humans by testing little white mice.

BLOOD CRIES

>Dr. Albert Wexler
I don't have any mice.

>Henry Russell
(Shaking his head) He based his whole diagnosis on talking to the defendant twice!

>Dr. Albert Wexler
I based my diagnosis on Mr. Woods's description of event before, during, and after the shooting, my observations, and the results of his psychological examinations.

>Henry Russell
The man confessed!

>Melvin Little
Lester made a statement in the police car after he was in custody.

>Henry Russell
He said, "I'm glad I did it. If I had to do it over, I'd do it again." Sounds pretty rational to me.

>Melvin Little
The judge ruled, rightfully, that any statements made prior to Lester's receiving the Miranda were inadmissible.

>Henry Russell
I curse the day the Supreme Court handed down that decision.

>Melvin Little
Of course, that didn't stop the esteemed district attorney from trying to sneak it in, so the jury could hear.

Excerpt from Trial Transcript

> Henry Russell
> Officer Murphy, at any time while you had Lester Woods in custody, did you hear him make any statements...
>
> Melvin Little
> Now, wait just a minute, Mr. Russell. The judge has ruled—
>
> Henry Russell
> ...any statement from the defendant...
>
> Melvin Little
> Now, you wait a minute, Henry. You shut up right now!
>
> Henry Russell
> Go to hell!
>
> Melvin Little
> I probably will.
>
> Henry Russell
> Nobody tells me to shut up.

End Transcript

> Melvin Little
> I'm surprised neither one of us got thrown in jail for that exchange.
>
> Henry Russell
> My one shot at winning the case rested on the gun. He brought a loaded gun into a church service. The murder was clearly premeditated. Who brings a gun to a funeral?
>
> Melvin Little
> That was no church. It was the Temple of the Smith. Lester had a permit signed by the sheriff allowing him to carry a concealed weapon.

BLOOD CRIES

Janet Woods
(Wife of the defendant): Lester carried the gun everywhere he went. I testified to that effect. At one point the judge even looked at me and said, "Even to church?" And I said, "Everywhere."

Henry Russell
It was the character witnesses that set him free. That and the fact that the judge tied my hands. When Elizabeth Abbott got on the stand and told how she pulled Lester's name out of a pen pal program when he was over in Vietnam, and she read the letter he sent back to her in '68—right at the start of the Tet offensive, and he described life over there, routine search and destroy missions and all that, and at the time of the letter he was bracing for an attack at any minute, actually thinking he might die, and yet he said he believed in what they were doing over there—when the jury heard that, I knew it was over. There wasn't any way they were going to convict that man. I was hoping at that point for manslaughter. I didn't even get that.

Judge Barber
I sent the jury back four or five times and the last time I threatened to keep them sequestered for another week or until they reached a verdict. They came back fifteen minutes later. Not guilty due to temporary insanity. I remanded him to the state psychiatry center for evaluation.

Henry Russell
He went in one door and came right back out the other.

Melvin Little
They evaluated him for a few weeks and he was released.

Henry Russell

Of course, all the tests showed he was normal, just as they did for the first group of psychologists. The man was as sane as you or me. I now have the unhappy distinction of failing to convict a man who executed his victim in front of three hundred witnesses. I'm not sure I'll ever live that down.

Melvin Little

I was jubilant. It was a triumph of the justice system and for racial relations in the state. A black man in Alabama was exonerated by twelve white men. If it was in a story, you wouldn't believe it, but it's true. It happened.

Henry Russell

It's sad, but true. Every word.

From an Interview with Melvin Little
Conducted by Chrissy Hope on July 2, 2009

Melvin

Other than Henry Russell, everybody I talked to was satisfied with the outcome of the trial. According to the general consensus the Reverend got what he deserved. No one wanted to see Lester Woods go to prison. In fact, getting him off the hook helped cancel out the bitterness some people felt toward me for defending the Reverend all those years. Now that Justice was served, life could go back to normal.

Part of normal life for me—the town's first celebrity lawyer—was attending cocktail parties, steak clubs, and various fundraisers. In the first few weeks after the verdict was handed down, I received lots of pats on the back and messages of congratulations. For a year or more, I was regularly called upon to regale folks with stories about the Reverend, the trials, and my courtroom prowess. All that was left was for Louella Harper to immortalize my words and actions in the literary canon.

For once, a story based on a Southern town wasn't going to be all about rednecks or the Ku Klux Klan. The way we saw it, the story had nothing to do with race. If anything, it showed that the citizens of Jackson City were willing to rise above petty tribalism. An all-white panel of jurors sat down together, looked at the facts, and objectively decided that it was okay with them for a good guy to kill a bad guy. Justice was served. Hell, the city council named me Man of the Year.

It's difficult to say why Louella soured on the project. For a long time, she came to all the parties, told stories about New York and Hollywood and had the town eating out of her hand. She always carried around a glass of scotch, but it wasn't like she was drinking any more than anyone else. Then, as the year dragged on, she seemed to be drinking more and coming around less.

One night—this was a good while after the trial, maybe a year or so—my wife Miriam and I were expected at the house of Dr. Jason Miller and his wife Evelyn, but on this occasion, we were late arriving. Miriam takes two hours to get ready for anything. By the time we got to the house, everyone had already sat down to supper.

Miriam rushed on ahead to the dining room. I could hear her receiving loud, boozy greetings from the other guests. Evelyn lingered behind in the den. She gave me a knowing look and pointed toward the glass door at someone sitting out on the deck. I stopped and stared like I'd just seen a purple kangaroo.

"Is that Louella?" I asked. I hadn't seen her in weeks. "What's she doing out there by herself?"

Evelyn looked at me in a funny kind of way. "She said she isn't hungry." She made that gesture people make when someone is drinking too much.

"Well, is she okay out there?" I asked.

Evelyn shrugged. "I honestly don't have time to babysit a grown woman—I don't care if she is a famous writer—not while my house is full of guests."

"I'm not all that hungry," I said. "I'll go sit with her and let you get back to your party. All I ask in return is a glass of bourbon over ice with a splash of water." Evelyn rushed off to the liquor cabinet.

The Millers have a pretty nice setup. It's like a huge, modernized log cabin. I stepped outside and found Louella slumped in a deck chair, lying on her side, hugging a cocktail glass. The days were starting to get long. Even though it was getting close to eight o'clock, there was still a touch of light in the sky. The weather was cool without being too cool. Just the way I like it.

"Hey there, Louella," I said. "What are you doing out here by yourself?"

Louella rolled over and stared at me with one eye closed for a good ten seconds. "I'm drinkin'." She held up a glass of melting ice. "What are you doing here?"

"I suppose I wanted to appear sociable," I said, "and a drink or two sounded relaxing."

I dropped into a lawn chair beside Louella. We sat in silence for a moment before the sliding glass door opened and Evelyn stepped out carrying drinks on a silver tray.

"How are y'all doing out here?" she asked. She handed me a drink. "Bourbon for Melvin," she said. She turned and swapped a full glass for Louella's empty one. "And scotch rocks for Miss Louella Harper. You don't need any cheese or anything, do you?"

"Just keep the drinks coming," Louella said.

Evelyn shot me a look.

"No thank you, honey, we're fine," I said. Her face melted into a honey-drenched smile and then she fluttered off to her dinner party.

Turning to Louella, I asked, "How's the story coming?"

Louella stuck out her tongue and made an indelicate sound.

"Not good, huh?"

"There is no story," Louella said.

I looked at her like she was crazy. "The Reverend is nothing but story."

"The Reverend is nothing but greed and narcissism."

"They say there's nothing new under the sun, but the way you put a story together makes it new."

"No," Louella said. "I can't do it."

"Yes, you can. You just haven't done it in a while, that's all. Once you get back into practice, it'll all come back to you. Just wait and see."

"I'm not interested in your stupid motivational speech," Louella said.

I knew there was no sense arguing with a drunk person, and I figured I could always talk to her again in the sober light of day. I didn't know that would be the last time she would ever set foot in Jackson City. The next morning, she checked out of her motel.

Despite what she said, I wasn't about to give up on that story. That trial represented the highlight of my career, and I intended to read about my exploits in a book someday, or else see it played out on a movie screen. I knew she wasn't about to give up on it either. Who in their right mind would be willing to throw away a year of their life and all that work?

I gave her a call that December to wish her a Merry Christmas and to convince her to keep going with the book. "No, you're right," she said after I wore her down with argument. "And I've been working on it. It's just about finished."

Well, I waited and waited, and I didn't hear anything about a new Louella Harper novel or read about one in the papers, so a year or so later I called her up again.

"Oh, Melvin, I'm just putting the finishing touches on it this week."

And it went on like that. I'd call her up once or twice a year, and she would always say she was still working on it. "Oh, my editor asked for changes" ... "Oh my editor didn't like the changes I made. He asked for more" ... "Oh, it's finished. I'm expecting the proofs any day." It went on like that year after year. I knew she was stalling me, but I kept calling her just the same to see how long she would keep lying to me.

That would have been fine, I suppose. At least I would have maintained contact with her, but I went and did a stupid thing, something I'll regret until the end of my life. Sometimes my mouth acts independently of my brain. A man came down here a few years ago working on a biography of Louella— unauthorized of course. The man wanted to know why Louella never finished the book about the Reverend. I said something to the effect that Louella cared more about drinking than she did writing. She hasn't spoken to me since.

From the Journal of Louella Harper

Jim parked his van beside a curb and deposited me in front of a squat brick house at the end of a cul-de-sac. He offered to stay with me—practically insisted—but I would not hear of it.

"Go find a story to report."

"Looks to me like there's a great story right in front of me. What did Louella Harper uncover when she came to Jackson City?"

"You can read all about it in due time. I'll make sure to give you an advance copy."

He waved goodbye and drove away, leaving me standing on the sidewalk. After watching his van shrink from sight, I turned to a house that seemed to be sinking into its own yard. I followed the cracked sidewalk through an iron gate and down the slope to a concrete porch. Pausing at a sun-bleached door, I adjusted my hat and removed a piece of stray lint from my blouse. Once I was presentable, I took in a deep breath and lifted the dull brass knocker.

After a short wait, a young black woman opened the door. She looked to be in her mid-to-late teens and wore short white pants cut off at the thigh and a red-and-white striped t-shirt that emphasized her cleavage. I waited for a greeting, but the girl only stared at me with an expression that mixed boredom and indifference.

"Good morning. My name is Louella Harper. I spoke with Hannah Woods on the phone. I have an appointment to meet..."

The girl tilted her head slightly toward the ceiling. "Mom," she yelled. "Some woman is at the door." She spun around without another glance in my direction, leaving the door open and me still standing on the outside. Her see-sawing hips seemed to punctuate her disdain for me and, it seemed, common courtesy.

Her mother passed her in the hallway. "Laverne," she scolded her daughter. "This is Louella Harper. She's a famous author and an invited guest."

Laverne shrugged and then disappeared around a corner.

Hannah reached out to take my hand. She matched a a white blouse and gray skirt with rouged cheekbones that radiated cheeriness. "Please come in, Ms. Harper. I'm Hannah. We spoke on the phone."

"Thank you for inviting me," I said.

"You'll have to forgive Laverne. This last year has been so difficult for her, and for all of us. It's hard enough to deal with the loss of someone close to you, but to do it under such scrutiny..."

"The newspapers made it sound like she was very close to that poor young girl."

"It's true," Hannah said. "Lucy and Laverne were cousins, but they thought of each other as sisters."

"It must have been devastating for her," I said. "And for the rest of your family."

"Oh, you can't imagine. Half the family curses the Reverend's name, the other half is trying to clear it."

Hannah escorted me to the living room, offered me a seat on a plush, aquamarine sofa. "Would you like coffee or tea?"

"Coffee would be lovely."

Hannah disappeared into the kitchen, leaving me sitting in front of a remotely controlled 22-inch Zenith television set and a GE 8-track cassette player. I was trying not to sink into the couch cushions when a woman entered the room.

She wore a black dress and a black hat with a lace veil over her eyes. She gazed at the floor and sighed loudly then plopped down in a light blue wingback chair that almost matched the sofa. A gold compact mirror appeared in her hand and popped open like a switchblade knife. The woman peeled back her veil, revealing a prominent chin. She glanced at me out of the corner of her eye, making sure I was watching before returning her gaze to her own reflection.

I recognized her instantly. "You're Cassandra. Hello," I said as I worked my way out of the grip of the sofa. "I'm Louella Harper. We spoke briefly at the trial."

She touched the mirror to her chin in a moment of apparent contemplation. Slowly, the corners of her lips curled into a blushing smile. "Yes, of course. The famous Louella Harper."

"Unfortunately, that's about the size of it. Thank you for meeting with me."

"Charmed, I'm sure." She leaned forward and extended a gloved hand with her fingers pointed down to the floor. I wasn't sure if I was supposed to take her hand or kiss the back of it, so I took it, gave it a light shake, and let it go again. It was ten in the morning, and her eyes were bloodshot.

I rifled through my purse for a pencil, found one, and stuck it in my teeth until I found the notepad.

"I suppose you'll want to know how Will and I met," Cassandra said. She looked at the ceiling and smiled in a reverie. "It was like a fairy tale. The first time I saw him I was seventeen years old. He was up in the pulpit preaching, and I thought I'd never seen such a handsome man. I knew right then I was going to marry him."

I nodded. "And, at what point did you realize he was a murderer?"

Cassandra wrinkled up her nose as if she didn't like the way I smelled. "I never said anything like that."

"I know you never said it. That's why I'm asking you now. You're not a fool. You must have known the man was a killer. I just want to know when you knew."

Cassandra shook her head. "That's wrong. Just because a person was accused of a thing..."

"The fact that you continue to defend him after his demise suggests to me that either you were complicit in his crimes or in denial about them. Which should I suppose it is?"

"I don't like what you're saying."

"I'm sorry if I offended you," I said. "I'll move on. You had been married prior to Reverend Baxter, is that correct?"

"I was divorced," Cassandra said. "It's not a crime."

Hannah entered the room carrying the coffee set on a plastic tray. "So, how is everyone doing?" she asked in a singsong voice. She placed the tray on a glass-top table and began pouring cups from a stainless-steel coffee pot. "Cream and sugar?"

"No thank you," I said. I took the cup of coffee and held it over my lap as I glanced at my notebook, now balanced on the sofa's armrest.

Hannah finished pouring the coffee and took a seat in one of two white upholstered chairs. "Don't mind me," she said. "You won't even know I'm here."

"And is it true your first husband caught you in bed with the Reverend?"

Hannah stood up again. "Excuse me," she said and exited the room again.

"Just because a person is accused of doing one thing doesn't make them guilty of something else," Cassandra said.

"Maybe you could tell me a little bit about Lucy and what happened the day she went missing."

"She took the car and left. She didn't want to be with us anymore."

"Did your husband have a life insurance policy on her?"

"That has never been proven."

"You were Lucy's foster mother. Is that correct?"

"I looked after that girl her whole life."

"And you received a stipend from the state to provide care?"

"A pittance," Cassandra said. "After food, clothes, and expenses, there was barely anything left over."

"So, she was worth much more to you dead than alive?"
"I never said that."
"Feel free to explain yourself..." I trailed off as I became distracted by a hissing sound coming from the foyer. I looked around and saw Hannah standing in the doorway, motioning me to follow her down a hallway.

I nodded at Cassandra. "Excuse me," I said.

"I don't know if I can," she said, following a moment of stunned silence.

I followed Hannah down the hall. She walked with her head down and purpose in her stride. She came to a bedroom door, then hesitated. Her hand rested on the knob.

"You can't push her like that," she whispered. She opened the door, and we entered a tidy bedroom with a stained hardwood floor and a four-poster bed with white curtains.

"You are referring to your sister?"

Hannah stood facing the bed. "Will had her head all mixed up."

"I don't know if I can accept that excuse."

Hannah got down on her hands and knees and removed a briefcase from underneath the bed. She carried it over to an antique vanity with mirror attached and set it down on the marble top. "I found this in the Reverend's den when I was helping Cassandra move in with me," she said. "I thought it might be something you'd like to see."

She unsnapped the briefcase which was stuffed with papers. I sat down on the vanity bench and leafed through the stack. "These are insurance policies," I said. "I think Melvin showed me all the ones he collected on."

"He never collected on these," Hannah said. "He would have though, if he'd had the chance."

I scanned the names listed on the forms. The names of the insured changed with each policy. I found Cassandra's name on one, also one on Laverne and Hannah. The list seemed to extend to everyone in the family.

It took a moment for me to comprehend what she wanted me to see. "He would have killed you all."

"Now, you can begin to understand," Hannah said. "When I found these, I confronted Cassandra with it. I told her Will was a murderer and that would kill us all. At first, she pretended not to hear me, but for once I forced her to listen, and then it got out of hand. Cassandra can be very dramatic."

"Is that so?"

"Once she gets going, there's no stopping her. She pitched a fit and screamed at me about how much Will had done for her, and for all of us. And it's true, he paid for a lot of the furniture in this house, and he helped with the bills sometimes. After my divorce, Laverne and I were really struggling..."

"You don't have anything to feel badly about," I said. "It can't be easy raising a child on your own."

"It really is," Hannah said. "Especially Laverne. She's so much like her father in that she can be... volatile."

"Volatility seems to run all through your family tree," I said.

"I took Will's help, but I never trusted him. Honestly, I tried to spend as little time with him as possible. You may have noticed how much I like to stay busy."

"So, your sister wasn't open to your accusations against her husband. She took his side over yours."

Hannah sighed. "Cassandra can't face the truth. Not while she's sober anyway. I probably shouldn't be telling you this, but I have to tell someone..." She paused as if trying to decide what to say next.

"You don't have to tell me anything you don't want to," I said.

She smiled then despite a tightly closed mouth, and I knew I must have said the right thing. "The same night I showed her the policies, Cassandra got very drunk. More than usual. She's always a little drunk. But that night she drank more than I've ever seen her drink before. She started talking, and she told me everything, all about her history with the Reverend. Some of it I knew, or at least, I'd heard stories, but she told me things I couldn't believe. It sounded like the plot of a movie. I thought she was making it up. Then, she got to the part about Lucy and the day she... you know..."

I nodded for her to keep talking. I was already regretting telling her that I would keep her secret. "What happened?" I asked. My heart was pounding.

Hannah covered her eyes with the back of her hand. When she moved it again, I could see water pooling in the corners of eyes. A quiver seized her bottom lip.

"What did she tell you?" I asked.

The Reverend
by Louella Harper

Chapter Twelve

Lucy stomped out of the kitchen and slammed the door behind her. She went into the living room, switched on the television set, and plopped down on the couch with her arms folded across her chest. The lamp was off and the shades were drawn; the only light was emitted from the television. Reflected images of a talking horse flickered across her scowling face. In the next room, she could still hear her mother and stepfather as they sat at the kitchen table talking in low voices.

"I know y'all are talking about me!" She stood up again and went to the television to turn up the volume.

In the next room, Cassandra and the Reverend turned toward the door, and the increasing sound of the television, then looked back at each other.

"It's time," the Reverend said.

"No. Not yet. I still need her."

Mr. Ed's theme song blared through the closed door.

"For what?" The Reverend sat with his back straight and his hands folded on the table in front of him. "She never helps you around the house anymore. She won't even clean her room."

Cassandra shut her eyes and shook her head. "No, Baby. There's got to be another way."

"Don't get emotional."

Cassandra stood up and paced the room. She opened a cabinet door and then closed it again. "I don't know."

"That girl is counting the days until she can leave you. She'll run away at the first chance."

"I was the same way."

"No," he said, giving her a wink. "You were a good girl."

"We both know better than that," she said, obviously pleased. "Remember that night at the Pines Motel?"

"Clarence thought he had us dead to rights."

"He did have us dead to rights. He broke down the door and found us naked under the sheets."

"He thought he was going to beat me down."

"I thought he was too," she said.

"He didn't count on the .22 I had stashed under the bed."

"I said to myself, 'Oh my Lord, the man I love has gone and shot my husband."

Baxter nodded his head approvingly. "I have to give him credit. He took it like a man. He kept his mouth shut and never pressed charges."

"Everyone believed I did it to stop him from beating on me." She sat back down in her chair and leaned forward so her chin was close to resting on the table. "Please, Baby," she said. "Pick someone else."

He said nothing, just watched and waited.

"I know you're mad at her still, but you have to let that go."

"The girl poisoned me."

"It was a prank. It gave you a little upset stomach, that's all. You were over it the next day."

"Next time it might be something stronger than laxatives."

"She learned her lesson."

"No," he said, the muscles tightening in his cheeks. "I doubt she ever will learn anything. I don't think she's capable."

"She did a stupid thing. Children do stupid things all the time. We all did stupid things when we were young."

"That's true," he said, giving her a sly look. "She is young."

Cassandra raised an eyebrow. "What do you mean by that?"

"Nothing," said the Reverend. "Just that she's a pretty young girl, about to be a beautiful young woman. Maybe, you're right. Maybe it would be better to keep her around for a while."

It was Cassandra's turn to look at him and say nothing.

Lucy was still watching television when the kitchen door pushed open, and her mother and stepfather entered the room.

"Come on, girl. Let's go," the man said.

Lucy turned around to face them but remained in her seat. "Go where?"

"To your cousins' house," her mother said. "We're just going for a visit, Baby. That's all."

"We just came from there," Lucy said. Both her mother and stepfather were standing behind the couch, Cassandra stood to Lucy's right. The Reverend was behind her to the left, where she couldn't see him.

"I know, baby," her mother said, "but we forgot something." She spoke in the high-pitched register she only used when she was lying about something.

"What did we forget?" Lucy asked. "And why are you talking like that?"

"Enough questions," the stepfather said. "Move your ass."

Lucy glanced back at him with an expression that mixed disgust and confusion.

"Over here, baby," her mother said. "Don't look at him. Look at me."

As she turned back toward her mother, the man's arm went around her neck. The tendons and ropy muscles tightened, and Lucy felt herself being pulled back against the back of the couch. Unable to turn her head due to the closing vice of her stepfather's meaty shoulder and forearm, her eyes bulged with terror.

"It's okay, baby." Her mother said. "You just need to relax and let it happen."

Lucy's feet shot up, knocking the underside of the wooden coffee table, sending women's magazines sliding onto the floor and overturning a candy dish.

"Now look what you did," the mother said. She flitted around the couch and pulled the table out of reach of her daughter's thrashing legs while continuing to utter soothing sounds as she picked up pieces of individually wrapped butterscotch candy. "It'll be alright Baby. Mama's here. It'll all be over soon."

From the Journal of Louella Harper

"I'm sorry to burden you with this," Hannah said when she had finished her story. Tears streamed down her cheeks. "I didn't know who else to tell."

"The police come to mind."

"No," she said. "I can't. She's my sister."

"She's a murderer."

"That was Will. Cassandra never would have been involved at all if it wasn't for him. She doesn't have it in her to be a part of something like that."

"She did have it in her. That girl was like her own daughter, but instead of treating her with love and kindness, she helped to end her life."

"You don't know what it's like to have a target painted on your back," Hannah said. "I do, and so does every other member of this family. She may not admit it, but even Cassandra knows it. That man would have killed us all so that he could collect all that insurance money. We were lambs waiting to be slaughtered. We had no idea when the axe would fall, but we had no doubt it would land on our necks eventually. Everybody knew it. Nobody did anything to stop it."

"The prevailing wisdom is that Lucy was the last straw. Her death was ruled a homicide. They had witnesses who would testify."

"They had witnesses after Taylor died too," Hannah said, "only they wouldn't testify. They weren't going to testify this time either. No one was ever going to testify. Will would have made sure of that. Everyone thought Calpurnia was crazy or foolish for marrying him, but that marriage bought her an extra year of life."

"She would have sent him to prison if she hadn't perjured herself," I said.

"He would never have let her take the stand if he wasn't sure what she was going to say. He would have killed her. I honestly believe he would have killed every one of us if Lester hadn't stopped him. He never cared about other people the way he cared about himself. He used people to advance his own interests. He'd probe a person for weak points he could exploit, and then he'd use them up and throw them away like trash. The devil is real, Ms. Harper. I knew him as well as anybody. He was coming for me, and Laverne, and I know as sure as I know anything that he would have come for Cassandra too."

Outside the door, a woman shrieked. I thought it might be Laverne, but Hannah knew immediately who it was making the awful sound. She opened the door to reveal Cassandra leaning against the wall. Mascara streaked down her face.

"You told her," she cried. "You went and told everything to the one thing you were never supposed to tell. She'll put everything in her book and then everyone will know."

"I can assure you the idea of writing this book becomes less appealing every day," I said, hoping to lighten the mood. "I curse the day I came to this town."

"What would you have me do, Cassandra?" Hannah asked. "Kill Louella Harper?"

Cassandra appeared to consider the suggestion.

"No, Cassandra," Hannah said. "Just stop."

"If you're entertaining the idea of murdering me, I would urge you to reconsider. I have informed several of my representatives of my itinerary for the day, and a professional reporter just dropped me off at your doorstep. It won't take Sherlock Holmes to solve the mystery."

"No one said anything about killing anyone," Hannah said. "Please. Let's all calm down."

"This woman is a murderer," I said.

Cassandra covered her eyes with her hands. "I didn't kill Lucy," she said. Her back slid down the wall into a pool of crossed legs. "I saved her. I'm the one who has to stay here and suffer."

"I bet all you ever do is suffer," I said. "And make the people around you suffer. I think you and Will Baxter were made for each other."

Hannah was crying. Cassandra just shook her head. Defeated, she said in a cold, scratchy voice, "You don't understand."

"I can't listen to any more of this," I said. I walked out, and no one tried to stop me. I went straight outside, and thank God Jim was out there parked at the curb. He must have known from my expression that something had happened.

"What's wrong?" he asked.

"Take me home," I said.

I had no idea what I was going to do next. I'd heard more than I ever expected, maybe more than I ever wanted to know, but the information was useless to me. I couldn't take it to the police. It was all just hearsay. I couldn't use it in my book without further corroboration. The only purpose of the knowledge I had accumulated was to torture me for the rest of my life.

Three days later, two middle-aged women sat on the wooden deck attached to the second story of Maris Harper Carlton's house overlooking Lake Robert. A double scotch and water rested on the table near my hand. Maris sipped from a tall glass of sweet tea.

"I don't know if I can do it anymore."

"I don't see why not," Maris said.

"I never asked for any of this. How did delivering justice become my responsibility?" I lifted my glass to my lips and let the scotch run down my throat.

"There's a cardinal," Maris said, pointing to a little red bird perched in one of the trees at the edge of the yard.

"I wish I'd never come down here."

"You've put all this time and energy into the thing, you might as well finish."

"How?" I asked.

"Maybe you're too close to the material," Maris said. "Do you see the blue jay?"

"I'd like nothing more than to get away from this material. I wanted to find the truth, and now I don't know what to make of it."

"You'll understand in time."

I swirled the ice in my tumbler. "I'm not sure I want to understand. I need another drink."

"Pace yourself, Louella. It's not even four o'clock."

"I'm a grown woman, Maris. I'll have a drink if I want one."

"Well, I expect you feel you are under some pressure."

"I am under pressure." I drained the last bit of scotch-flavored water. "You don't know what it's like to be in my position."

"Oh, pooh."

"Pooh yourself."

"You have everything and yet you still feel sorry for yourself. You don't even have to work if you don't want to. Do you know how many people would trade places with you in about ten seconds if they could?"

"Well, I might trade with them too."

"You'd be a fool," she said.

"Oh, you don't know what you're talking about."

"You're the smartest person I know, Louella. The person whose shadow I've been living in for most of my adult life."

"So that's what this is about? Jealousy?"

"Who wouldn't be jealous of you? You won the sweepstakes of life, and you don't even have the good sense to recognize or enjoy it."

I sighed. "It's not just the book, Maris. Lydia moved out."

She raised an eyebrow. "Did she?"

"She told me over the phone last night. She wouldn't admit it, but I think she's been seeing someone. I think she planned this whole thing, pushed me to come up here and write this awful book just to get me out of the house."

"I see."

"Do you?"

"I am your sister. If you want to talk to me about something, you can talk to me."

"I'd rather have a drink instead."

"You can do that too. I hope you don't but I'm here for you either way."

I heard what she said, and I appreciated the sentiment, but I was already headed for the liquor cabinet.

I spent the next few days puttering around my motel room, feeling sorry for myself, but not yet ready to abandon my efforts. There was still a strand of story I needed to follow.

Then, one morning found me on the edge of the bed with my body hunched into the light of the bedside lamp. My finger circled the face of the telephone until it found the zero. I spun the dial and waited until I heard the voice of the operator. "I'd like to place a person-to-person call, please." Less than a minute later, Lydia's voice came through the line.

"Hello," I said, my voice shaking. "How are you?"

"I'm fine." Her voice sounded cold, distant.

"This isn't turning out the way I thought it would," I said. I twisted the telephone cord around my wrist.

"Nothing ever does."

"I'm sorry to bother you. I shouldn't reach out. I just needed to connect with someone."

"We'll always be connected," Lydia said. "Our time together was very special to me."

"It was to me too." I wiped my eyes with some tissue, tried to add some steel to my voice. "This afternoon it's taking me to meet a convicted murderer."

"You're going to a prison?" Lydia asked.

"No. A funeral home."

"Is Jim going with you?"

"He has to work."

"What about Melvin?"

"It's just going to be little old me. Why," I ask. "Are you worried about me?"

"No," Lydia said. "I'm worried about him."

*   *   *

My tennis shoes sank into the thick, powder-blue carpet of the funeral parlor. A large bald man sat in silence on a stool behind the reception counter.

"Good morning," I said.

The man greeted me with a blank stare.

"I have an appointment to meet with the funeral director, Mr. Smith."

When the man stood up, it was like a mountain rising from the earth. I could feel the ground tremble. He led me down a darkened hallway to a conference area, where I was deposited into one of the oak chairs situated around a conference table. The floor was covered in the same blue carpet as the lobby. The walls were bare—not so much as painting of the savior. An elbow-shaped bar stood waist high in the corner. I soon discovered that it was fully stocked with liquor.

"Can I pour you a drink?"

As I whipped around toward the door, my hand flew up to my heart.

"Did I startle you?" He stood smiling at me from the other side of the table. He was six feet tall and appeared to be in his late forties or early fifties, with patches of gray coming through the bristles of his hair. His pockmarked face was clean shaven. He dressed in a rumpled black suit and a facade of sincerity.

"Mr. Smith?"

Ernie Smith came around the table holding out his hand. "And you must be Ms. Harper. It's nice of you to visit."

"I suppose it's nice to be wanted," I said, taking his hand.

"Did you want that drink?"

"It's much too early for me," I say. "Ask me again in five minutes."

He laughed. "We'll talk instead." He took a seat at the head of the table and motioned for me to take the seat beside him. "What can I do for you?"

"Well," I began as I open the satchel on my lap and removed a yellow legal pad. "I'm in town researching a book about a man you may know." I place the pad and a pencil on the table.

"I know why you're here, Ms. Harper, and I'd love to help you."

"You would?"

"Yes, of course," Ernie said. "I knew the Reverend as well as anyone could have known him. In fact, due to the nature of my business, I know just about everyone in town. I'm kind of a lightning rod for the community."

"Is that how you would describe yourself?"

"Ask anyone in town," Ernie says. "I'll introduce you to the Reverend's wife Cassandra. That's his third wife. I knew his other wives too—I buried them—and I know the rest of the family. Now, these are people who might not want to talk to outsiders, but they may open up if you give them an incentive."

"Will they?"

"Oh, yes. And I would be happy to facilitate such meetings with all of them for you."

"Would you?"

I picked up my pencil and began tapping the pad with the eraser. "How is it that you have so much control that you can... facilitate all these meetings?"

"As I explained, my business allows me to meet a diverse group of individuals, and, well, the Reverend's... activities... all seemed to require my services."

I stared at him for several seconds after he completed his sentence. "What would you say is your business philosophy, Mr. Smith?"

"Business philosophy? The only philosophy in business is make money."

"And in addition to your business philosophy, are you also in possession of a moral philosophy?"

"I go to church, if that's what you're asking. I love church so much I had a sanctuary built around my show room. What the hell does that got to do with anything?"

I did my best to ignore the menace in his voice. "Excuse my idle curiosity, Mr. Smith. I always ponder such questions when I encounter individuals in business. I like to know if they put their own selfish interests above the interests of other people."

"That's everybody. That's just life."

"No, it's a choice, Mr. Smith. It's a choice we make every day of our lives. We can make it better for people, or we can make it worse. Which will you do today?"

"It depends."

"It shouldn't. It shouldn't depend on how much money you will make or on what makes you look better, or more frightening, in the eyes of other people. Contrary to popular opinion, you are allowed to bring morality into your business. In fact, it's long-term survival depends on it."

"Why should I care about anybody else but me?"

"Because you need other people, Mr. Smith, "as much as you need the air you breathe and the water that you drink."

Ernie was silent for a moment. When he spoke, his voice quiet and laced with malice. "Thank you for your advice."

I spent much of the afternoon sitting on a cold bench along the hedge-rowed periphery of the town square. I huddled in my camel hair coat while the wind flapped the pages of the yellow legal pad resting in my lap and upon which I jotted down thoughts about the tragedy I was writing.

I often came to this place in the afternoons, after a morning of writing. With its close proximity to the courthouse, the public library, and the City Cafe—where I sometimes went for coffee—the square was the perfect place to sit and consider my options.

Unfortunately, a gray October sky loomed above me. A cold wind blew in from the northeast, causing me to turn my back to shield my flapping pages. I was writing down a thought about structure—specifically that I had none. No structure. No hero. No theme to pull me through other than a simple warning against the type of greed and narcissism that will march the entire human race to its annihilation if no one does anything to stop them.

Just as I was coming to this conclusion, I realized it wasn't just a hedge row standing behind me, and I almost leapt out of my skin. I jerked my head and body around and hid behind my legal pad.

It was a black man. Judging by the gray flecks in his goatee, he looked to be in his early-to-mid forties. His hair was short but impeccably combed in the afro style. He wore impenetrable black sunglasses despite the clouds, a navy-blue turtle neck sweater, and brown corduroy pants, along with a pair of tan moccasins.

"Don't be afraid, Miss Harper," he said.

"I can't think of anything more frightening than a strange man telling me not to be afraid," I said.

"My name is Kevin."

"I don't know you, Kevin. I'm busy, and I'd prefer not to be accosted, so if you don't mind skipping the pleasantries, I would prefer if you could go ahead and state your business. What is it that you want from me exactly?"

Kevin's face was calm and impassive. "I want to help you," he said.

"I can assure you I don't need any help," I said.

"I can help you with your story," he said. "I can tell you things no one else knows about, things everyone else would be too afraid to say."

Unconsciously, I drew my purse into my lap.

"I promise I won't hurt you," Kevin said, "though I work for a man who would."

"Mr. Smith, I presume."

Kevin looked down the street. I turned and followed his gaze toward a man pushing a large broom down the sidewalk by the pharmacy.

"It's just a street sweeper."

"We can't talk here. I'll come to your hotel tomorrow."

"I don't recall inviting you." I said, but he was already walking away. "Where are you going?"

"You'll want to hear what I have to say." He quickly strolled down a path in the opposite direction of the sweeper.

It annoyed me that I had not been given a time frame of when I might expect a visit from this person, and I had doubts about his ability to provide useful information, but a little voice in the back of my head told me that this one might be telling the truth. For one thing, he hadn't asked for any money.

It was getting late now. The pages of my legal pad were getting harder to control. The chances of me getting any more worked done approached nil, so I stowed my notebook in my purse and began the walk back to my car.

The man with the broom was gone, but I noticed a fair amount of litter. It occurred to me that I had never seen a street sweeper in town before despite frequent visits to the pharmacy and adjacent establishments, but what did that prove? Just because I didn't notice someone doesn't mean he wasn't there.

When I got home, my first thought—and my second and third as well—was to call Lydia. I remembered her voice the last time I called, how remote she sounded—more distant than the miles between us—and I knew by her tone that she was simply humoring me until I hung up the phone, and she could move on with her new life without me.

There was no one else I wanted to tell. Not even Maris. At that moment, I felt completely alone in the world. Tomorrow, a felon would be coming to visit me, and no one in the world knew about it. If things did not go well, and I went missing or dead, the crime would likely go unsolved. I decided to chance fate and face the man alone.

Kevin arrived at my door at 10 am precisely, wearing a suede jacket, a white button-down shirt, brown corduroy pants. He took off his fedora and bowed.

"Good morning, Mr..."

"Summers," he said. "Call me Kevin."

"Alright, Kevin." I extended my hand and he entered my room. He stood between the bed and the television looking anxious and awkward as he shifted his weight from one leg to another.

"Have a seat," I said while gesturing to the end of the bed. I turned the desk chair around and sat facing him. "I want to get a few things straight. I am writer. Anything you say will need to be corroborated with some form of evidence or it will not see print. If you want to tell me your story, I'll listen, but I am here to serve the truth even if it opposes your personal interests."

Kevin looked at me and nodded his head.

"Furthermore, I have no intention of paying you. If you have facts to share, you will share them freely. I am offering you nothing in return. If this arrangement is unacceptable to you, there's the door."

Kevin smiled then, and it seemed that some of his nervousness had drained out of his face. "That's fine," he said.

"Very well," I said, "Now, what do you want from me? What do you hope to get out of this?"

Kevin reached into his jacket pocket and removed a package of cigarettes. He tapped it against his hand so that one slid out, but rather than lighting it, he held it in front of him and turned it between his fingers.

"I have done things in my life that I regret," he said while staring at the cigarette. "Thing I can't undo." He spun the cylinder between his fingers. "But I feel like I need to do something, and I won't be able to do anything if I can't admit what I did."

"It sounds like you want to make a confession," I said. "Perhaps you should go to the police."

"I expect I will," Kevin said, "but not before I talk to you."

He proceeded to describe an unfortunate life filled with various misdeeds. He also detailed Ernie Smith's organization—if you can call it that—and his role within it. Mostly, he confirmed what I already suspected—that Ernie Smith was nothing more than an unscrupulous businessman, who knew how to seize a good opportunity, as well as an evil one.

While telling his story, Kevin made frequent trips to the window. He peeled back the curtain and stared for long intervals into the woods behind the motel. He mentioned several times that Ernie or one of his confederates might be watching.

"I feel sorry for anyone stuck staring at this building," I joked. "I hope whoever it is brought something to read."

"Ernie's not the type of person to take lightly," he said. "And he views you as a threat. If he finds out I'm here, you could be in real danger."

"And what about you?" I asked.

He lit his cigarette and said nothing.

Throughout the rest of the week, Kevin came by each day and spent several hours filling in gaps in my knowledge about the story I was trying to tell. During the time we were together he became more relaxed and made fewer trips to the window.

We soon settled into a comfortable routine. He came by most mornings, always parking his car somewhere far down the road, and then walking through the woods on some ancient Indian trail until he emerged a few feet from my door. We would then spend the several hours together, drinking coffee or tea, eating sandwiches and crackers, and sharing anecdotes about life in East Central Alabama.

He also told me in the most casual of terms about committing some of the most horrific crimes imaginable. He told me what he did to the Reverend Baxter's brother in exchange for a share of the proceeds.

"We got him drunk," he said. "We just kept giving him more and more. J. knew what we were doing, and he just accepted it. He didn't fight at all. I think he just wanted it over with."

"How is that you were able to do it to him? What did you have to tell yourself to make it okay?"

"I'm not sure," Kevin said. "I guess I didn't see him as a person at the time. He was just a bum. He had no money. No job. He was worthless, except for the money we could get from the insurance company."

He stubbed out his cigarette and continued to speak. "I've thought about him more than anyone else I've hurt through the years. J Christopher had some problems, but he was a good person. He cared about people. He didn't have much but he would help anyone. Over time, I came to realize he was much more valuable than a stack of little green pieces of paper. A guy like me or Ernie could stack up a million dollars on the table, and we still wouldn't be worth what J Christopher was worth alive. There ain't no hope for folks like us."

"What about Taylor Bennet?" I asked.

"I didn't know him that well," he said. "He was younger than me."

"Did you kill him?"

"The Reverend did that one himself," he said. "The same as he done his wives. We only helped with his brother."

"What was Ernie's relationship with the Reverend?" I asked. "Were they old friends? Army buddies."

Kevin shrugged. "Neither is the type to make friends."

Kevin was a man haunted by past deeds and the extreme folly of his youth, but he was ready to face responsibility. He fully expected to spend the rest of his life in jail. I think that was the whole purpose of coming to me. He wanted to confess his crimes to someone who would report the good things he did at the end and not just the terrible things he did at the beginning.

As strange as it is to say, I started to look forward to his visits. It was nice having someone to talk to who wanted nothing more than to tell me the truth. It was the perfect antidote to the shallowness of the cocktail parties I was still attending with some frequency. Perhaps he even assuaged some of the loneliness and feelings of abandonment caused by Lydia's departure from my life.

Kevin seemed to need me as much as I needed him, and in only a few short weeks I felt as if a dark cloud was lifting, and my days seemed brighter and full of purpose.

Then one morning in early November, the time for his expected arrival came and went. By 10:30, I was already on my second cup of coffee and I dug into the bagels.

I worked on the manuscript until one o'clock, when I had another bagel to go with a third cup of coffee. I wrote until four thirty or so, when I began to feel anxious. I usually take a walk in the morning and again before supper, but I had skipped both to wait for Kevin. There was also still the matter of the chili supper I had been invited to that evening. I had to get ready. Though it pained my pride, I took out my address book and found Kevin's number. I made the call and heard the phone ring five, six, seven times before it abruptly stopped.

"Hello. Kevin is that you? Is there anyone on the line?"

There was no response. It wasn't clear anyone was actually there or if I had been disconnected. I waited for a dial tone that never came. Eventually I hung up.

An hour later, I was dressed in my evening wear and putting in my earrings when I heard three sharp raps on my back door.

"What happened to you today?" I said as I pulled the door open, then recoiled at the sight of Ernie Smith.

He seized the advantage, stepping into the room and closing the door behind him. A smile expanded across is face as he came toward me. I backed into the television, rattling the rabbit-ears antenna and then continued around them. My screaming voice was lost somewhere in the pit of my stomach.

"What's wrong, Miss Harper? Were you expecting someone else?" He wore black workpants and a black long-sleeved pull-over shirt. His eyes made an inventory of the room.

"Where's Kevin?" I asked, though I already knew the answer. My initial shock was wearing off, replaced by a jumble of terror, grief, and desperation. I backed into the desk chair and then guided myself around it.

"He couldn't make it," he said, smiling, "so I came instead."

"What did you do to him?" I left the chair as an obstacle between us and continued backwards. He was between me and the only exit. There was a small window in the bathroom, but I doubted if I could even get through it.

"Me?" Ernie said in an expression of mock innocence. "Nothing." He started towards me.

"No, it wasn't you." I said. "You paid someone else to do it." My only chance was to lock myself in the bathroom, climb onto the counter, and scream out the window for help before he broke the door down and killed me.

"I'm here now," Ernie said. He grabbed the chair and flung it against the wall.

"Please," I said. "I don't want you here. Go away." The bed was against the wall. I thought about going behind it, but then I would be trapped against the wall.

"It's too late for that." His movement was slow but relentless. "You couldn't leave well enough alone. You brought this on yourself."

"You're right," I said. An involuntary tremor quickly spread all over my body. It was all I could do to hold my voice steady. "I never should have inserted myself into this story. Let me leave right now, and I'll go back to New York. You'll never see me again." The tears came now. I had already run out of places to go. I was backed against the counter in the open vanity area outside of the bathroom. I wondered if he could see his reflection in the mirror as he stalked toward me: a tiger approaching a lamb.

"It's too late for that," he said in the very same instant I realized I had lost my chance to bolt into the bathroom.

In the next moment, he had my wrist twisted behind my back, and I was pressed against the mirror. I couldn't look him in the eye, so instead I looked over his right shoulder and exposed the left side of my neck. It was a pose of complete submission, but somehow, I kept talking.

"Let me make you a deal.," I said. "I have money. I'll give you a large sum of money if you let me live."

A knife pressed against my throat. I couldn't see it, but I could tell it was long and sharp from the way it bit into my skin. I was suddenly keenly aware of its proximity to my jugular vein. The next wrong word would be my last.

In the room behind him, I homed in on my typewriter and a stack of manuscript pages and carbon copies rising from the desk.

"They already know about you," I said.

"Who knows about me?" His hot breath pressed into my ear.

"My agent and publisher in New York. The last thing I sent them were a chapter in which I described meeting you and told how hostile you were. They already know about your previous murder conviction. They know about Kevin. If anything happens to me, they'll come straight for you."

"Bullshit." The knife bit in my neck and I could feel a warm stream break through the slice in my skin.

I talked quickly to cover up my pain and fear. "Every week I make carbon copies and send the originals to New York. I sent the latest batch off today. See for yourself. The carbons are right there on my desk." With a shaking finger I pointed at the stack of carbons beside my typewriter.

Ernie considered my words for a moment and then released my arm and stalked across the room toward the desk. He picked up the top sheet from a stack of carbons and began scanning the words on the page. He found a page with my previous day's work.

Now was my opportunity to run into the bathroom and lock the door. I tried to calculate all the different possibilities, but it seemed most likely that he it would confirm his decision to kill me. He would kick down the door and slit my throat in the bathtub.

"You put my name in here," he said as he scanned through one of the carbons. "This is from the other day."

"I put everything in there," I said. "It's a true story. If I disappear, the investigation will lead straight to you."

He grabbed a fist full of carbons and shook them in the air a me. "Who all did you send this to?"

"To my agent and my publisher in New York. They run every word by their team of lawyers."

Ernie hesitated. "How do I know you won't send those lawyers after me if I let you live? When you publish that book, they'll come after me sure enough."

"I won't publish. I don't need the money, or the fame, or the headaches. And I don't want to stay in this town another second. There's nothing I would like more than to fade into obscurity."

Ernie shook his head. "I don't believe you. You're just saying that to make me leave. Once I'm gone, you'll send for the police."

"I won't. I promise. I won't as long as you do something for me."

"What's that?"

"Stop hurting people. Leave your neighbors alone. Recognize the fact that they have as much right to exist as you do. You do that for me, and I promise never to expose the truth about what you did here. Just... stop."

"Why should I believe you?"

"Because I believe in second chances. And I believe in forgiveness. I believe that even the worst among us can do better and should be given the opportunity to try."

"Oh, you're ready to forgive me, is that right? Even after what I did to your boyfriend?"

I grimaced at the thought of Kevin buried in a shallow grave somewhere or sunk down in the middle of Lake Robert. "You and Kevin have done horrible things in your life. Kevin wanted to make up for that, but he never got the chance. You still could. Once you realize what Kevin finally realized—that he had wasted his life—you might decide to change. When it comes down to it, all you have in this world is your influence. What effect will you have on other people. Now, I don't have the authority to offer absolution for your crimes, but I can offer you this deal. You try and change. You try and become a better person. You follow the path of the man you killed and robbed of his chance at absolution. You make his sacrifice mean something, and I won't call for anyone to hunt you down. I know all this must sound counterintuitive to a man like you,

Mr. Smith, but a man must possess the capacity to change if he expects to survive."

Ernie hesitated for a long moment, flexing the muscles in his jaw. The pupils of his yellowing eyes were affixed to mine, and I knew that my own survival depended on the landing of his mental tumblers. When the last one clicked into place, his facial muscles relaxed. He reached into his jacket pocket and removed the stub of a cigar. He stuck it in his mouth and, without saying anything, turned and walked out the door.

As the door slammed shut behind him, I became aware of my rapidly thumping heartbeat. I ran to the door and set the chain, and then I fell onto the floor and all the fear poured out of me in a great sob. I lay in the foyer for I don't know how long, shaking and gasping for breath. After a while, I recovered somewhat. Remembering the carbons, I walked over to the desk. My hands shook as I attempted to replace the copies on the stack of originals I hadn't yet bothered to send to my agent.

Chrissy

My brain was throbbing. All the squishy gray matter inside my skull squeezed together until I thought it was going to squirt out of my ear and go skidding across the floor. I could see my cranium exploding into a million tiny fragments that would rain down on Melissa Taggert like a bloody hail storm. The thought brought a smile to my face.

Melissa was just standing there—between me and the file cabinet—her arms crossed, a cellphone clipped in one hand, and a hateful expression clipped to her face. "You little thief," she said. "I knew you were up to something."

"Oh, this headache."

"That's your body's way of telling you you're a terrible person."

"You're a terrible person," I said. My head hurt too much to try and elaborate.

"You don't even feel any remorse about it do you? Maybe you're incapable of feeling remorse."

"About what? I borrowed a manuscript without permission. I'll pay the library fine."

"Oh, no. You won't get off that easy." She lifted her cell phone and began scrolling through her contacts. "Do you know how much a manuscript by Louella Harper is worth? You just committed grand larceny."

"I put it back!" My hands pressed against my ears as I tried to hold my head together. If I let go, it would explode for sure.

Would that be so bad, though? I just wanted the pain to stop. I just wanted it to all be over.

"I found the letter, you know? The one you sent Louella?"

Damn that letter!

"I think we may be able to find a whole string of charges to level at you."

"I didn't do anything. I did my job. The only thing I'm guilty of is borrowing a manuscript without permission, but then I put it back! If you want to fire me for that, go ahead. But I don't think I committed a crime. No one even missed it."

The one thing I had going for me was she had yet to make the call. I could still get out of this one if I could just get my headache to go away, so I could *fucking think.*

"You aren't the only one to try this crap, you know? People are always poking around trying to find her unpublished manuscripts. No one has ever been dumb enough to steal one before."

"I get it. I did something stupid."

"I knew you were up to something. You think I don't know what you were up to? You think I don't know you made copies? I bet you figured to sell a million pirated copies over the internet before anyone caught on to what happened, and by then you'd be off in Paris or wherever. I think I'll go ahead and call the police now."

I tried to speak as clearly and as softly as I could. "I wasn't trying to make any money. I just wanted to know what happened." Subconsciously, though, I must have wanted to get caught. Why else would I have mentioned to Louella where I was from?

Melissa put the phone to her ear. "You're lucky I caught you. You probably won't get more than six months in jail. If you were caught trying to sell this, you could have gotten ten years."

"Six months in jail for borrowing a book?"

Melissa ignored me.

"Hello Nurse K," she began. "This is Melissa Taggert. It seem that once again you have sent a thief to come work for us...

Yes... Uh huh... A manuscript... No, I'll be calling them as soon as I get off the phone with you..."

The whole time she was talking to Miss Cotton, she stared at me as if she really enjoyed the pained expression on my face. The pain made my head feel heavy. I felt like it was weighing me down so much my feet were sinking into the floor.

"Go ahead and make yourself comfortable," Melissa said after she'd ended the call. "Pretty soon this will all be over, and you'll never have to look at my pretty face again."

"Can I at least say goodbye to Louella?" I asked in a squeaking voice.

"No, you may not say goodbye to Louella," she said in a mocking tone. "If you think I'm letting you anywhere near her again, you're crazy."

Crazy. There was that word again. Through the pain and haze of my thoughts, I caught an image of Lester Woods, smoking gun in his hand, standing over the Reverend's corpse. "You are done having power over me." That was the gist of what he'd said.

Melissa was looking down at her phone again. This time she was dialing the police. I glanced over at Louella's Olivetti typewriter. I imagined the coolness of the metal against my skin. It was such an exquisite object. I drifted toward it. I don't even know if my feet moved or if I just floated across the room.

I looked down at the keyboard as if I could use it to write my destiny. My fingers drifted across the ivory keys where Louella's fingers sometimes still danced in the frenzy of creation. My hands flattened against the sides of the machine. My fingers bumped across the cold grooves and contours as I lowered my face into the keys, letting the cold metal caress my cheek. It felt so solid—this thing—and so comforting. My hands slid under the base and I felt the jutting metal bite into the joints between my fingers as I lifted the Olivetti from the table. It was heavy, but not as heavy as I had anticipated.

"What do you think you're doing?"

I could barely hear her at this point. I no longer felt capable of speech. I kept walking.

"You're insane," she said, as if this was the first time she fully grasped the seriousness of the situation. I sensed a change in the power dynamic. I detected hesitation, confusion, and then fear. She looked down at the phone to finish dialing. Her finger seemed to shake above the screen as if it couldn't find the number she needed to press. In her eyes, I saw the light of recognition. Her finger found the number just as the typewriter came down upon her head.

She never saw it coming. I heard a sickening thud and watched her fall to the floor. The typewriter slipped out of my hand and careened off of her and went tumbling onto the carpet.

I didn't stay to see what happened to her. Whether she was dead or alive, I had no idea, but my headache was gone.

Later, I would be told that I went to the bathroom. They found my hairbrush sitting on the side of the sink. I guess I freshened up and made myself a little more presentable before leaving. I don't remember that. I don't remember splashing my face with cold water and then patting it dry with one of the expensive hand towels investigators found crumpled on the bathroom floor. I don't know if I looked at myself in the mirror or if I avoided the sight of my own reflection.

I do remember walking outside, being amazed at the blueness of the sky and the sunlight reflected off of all those luxury cars. I remember walking up to the black Mercedes and watching as the passenger side window disappeared into the doorframe. Louella turned her confused expression from me to the door of her apartment and back again. "Where's Melissa? What's taking so long?"

I walked around the front of the car and climbed into the driver's seat. "She's on the telephone. She said something came up and that I should take you to lunch." I don't know how the lie tumbled out of my mouth so easily. The words were just there.

"Melissa said she would be right back. That was ten minutes ago."

Ten minutes? It felt like a year.

"She said it was nothing to worry you about but that it might take a while, and that I should take you to lunch."

"That's not like her," Louella said. She grasped the door handle.

"You can go ask her if you want," I said. "I'll keep the car running." She took a moment to process this idea, and I filled the silence with whatever words happened to stream out of my mouth. "It sounded like regular business call to me. You know, lawyer-type stuff."

She hesitated a moment longer before her hand moved from the door handle to the automatic window button. The glass raised to the top of the doorframe. I put the car in reverse and soon we lurched out of the parking lot.

As we approached the main gate, I saw Dorothy walking down the steps of Building One. I rolled down the window and waved, laughing at her gawking expression.

Look at me. I'm driving Louella Harper.

I'd never driven a Mercedes before. I'd never driven a car with leather seats. It was nice. Every time we came to a stop, I found myself fiddling with the knobs and buttons on the dashboard or under the seat.

"What does this do?" I asked.

"Chrissy! Would you please keep your eyes on the road?"

"Whatever you say, Boss," I said. I was in a silly mood for some reason. I felt like a humongous weight had been lifted off of me. "Where are we going?"

"We were going to have lunch at The Arrowhead. Melissa said she had to check on something first."

"The Arrowhead, huh? What do they serve? Indian food?" I laughed so hard at my racially insensitive joke, my sides started hurting. "I'll like my curry heavy on the chutney."

"Chrissy, are you okay?"

"I feel great," I said, "but I am hungry. I skipped breakfast."

"Maybe your blood sugar is low."

It was nice how Louella worried about me. It was like she was embracing our time together. We were finally becoming friends, just like I knew we would. "I wanted to tell you how nice it's been working for you these last few months, Louella. You really are a good person."

She smiled. "Well, it hasn't been completely terrible having you around. You've been a big help to me."

We rode along in silence that was only broken when Louella needed to give me directions or bark out the occasional criticism of my driving. "Slow down. You'll miss the turn," and so forth. I didn't care. I was going to lunch at a fancy restaurant with Louella Harper.

When we arrived at the restaurant, we were greeted by the owner, and old man who looked like he'd come straight from a fishing boat. He wore a tan vest and white bucket hat dangling fishing hooks. "Louella," he said, giving her a hug and a kiss on the cheek. "Where's that lawyer of yours?"

"That's what I'd like to know," Louella said. "I brought along my assistant instead." Her hand flapped over her shoulder to indicate my presence behind her. "Milton, this is Chrissy."

"How do you do, young lady," Milton said as shook my hand.

"Charmed, I'm sure." I was still beaming from being recognized as her assistant.

"Chrissy's from Atlanta," Louella said.

"Well, I won't hold that against her, not as long as you both brought your appetite." He led us away from the other guests to a table situated by a wall of windows partly obscured by potted plants hanging from the ceiling. On the other side of the aisle were a few empty tables beside a long wall decorated with old maps and Native American artifacts.

"Mmm," I said. "It smells wonderful in here. Seafood?"

The Arrowhead, I would soon learn, specialized in lake trout and fried catfish, neither of which are favorites of mine. Louella ordered a grilled chicken salad. I ordered a porterhouse steak cooked medium rare with a loaded baked potato. I told the waiter he could keep his salad.

An elderly couple came up and talked to Louella after we ordered. I paid them little attention and they ignored me completely. It was a little annoying having them try and steal away my time with Louella, but I tried not to let it bother me. This was, after all, a dream come true. A server brought us a plate of cornbread for the table, and the couple politely excused themselves.

"So," I asked when we were alone again and waiting for our lunch to arrive. "What are you writing these days."

"Nothing to speak of," Louella admitted, "sometimes I put my thoughts on paper to try and get them organized, but nothing of interest to the public."

"You might be surprised," I said, tearing apart one of the muffins. "You know, I'm a closeted writer myself."

"Are you?"

"Yeah, I'm working on something right now."

"Do tell."

"It's a book. Not a novel. A true story. Just the facts, you know? It's about a girl who was led by God into the life of a famous writer. The two are connected because of a story that took place in the girl's hometown. So, the girl gets a job working for the author, and she finds the manuscript, and she reads it, and she loves it so much, but she understands why the author had to put it in a drawer for all those years. She understands that choices had to be made, but she also knows that somewhere inside her she holds the missing piece, the thing that would make the story worth putting out into the world. I only came because I have something to offer in return."

"That's where you're wrong," Louella said. She balled up her napkin and placed it in the center of her salad, which she had hardly touched. "I'm ready to go home now."

What followed was the longest silence I have ever had to endure. She knew. It was obvious. I had to acknowledge it.

"I'm sorry I took this job under false pretenses, Louella, but it was the only way I could get close enough to meet you."

"Maybe you weren't supposed to meet me."

"Oh, but I was. I've never known anything as strongly as I knew I was supposed to meet you, Louella Harper."

"You need to see a doctor," she said.

"No, Louella. It's not like that. You don't understand. I'm not crazy." My eyes filled with tears.

"Please be careful." We were passing through the gates of Lakeview Estates.

"This isn't going how I wanted it to go." I was bawling now. Streams of mascara ran down my face. I wheeled the Mercedes into the parking space directly in front of her door. I couldn't look at her any more. I just stared down at the gearshift thingy. She handed me a tissue and then craned her neck toward her apartment.

"Is my front door open?"

I dabbed the tissue against the area around my eyes as I peered at the door. Had I left it open? "It could be a burglar," I said. "Maybe we should call the police."

Louella just looked at me. She seemed to be studying my face, trying to determine whether or not I was making a joke. She had yet to come to a decision when police lights flashed behind us, illuminating everything in silent, blinking blue light.

Police officers surrounded the car. They opened the passenger door and whisked Louella away. I watched her go, still trying to make sense of what was happening, when my door flew open and I was ripped out of my seat and thrown down against the concrete.

From the Writing Desk of Louella Harper
2011

"How in the world did that girl end up working for you, Louella?"

That's the question I hear most often.

"What was wrong with her?" comes in a close second.

"Funny you should ask," I respond invariably. "My personal attorney set her mind to answering those very questions, plus a few more."

Melissa was released from the hospital the same day she was attacked. Thank God there was no skull fracture, or brain hemorrhage, or Lord knows what else could have happened had that typewriter struck her with a touch more force. As it happened, she received a gash from crown to temple, a purple grapefruit on her cheekbone, and an eye "swole shut", as my grandmother used to say.

After less than two days of recuperation, Melissa summoned me to her office. Her head was still bandaged, and she spoke out of one side of her mouth due to the swelling. "I'm going to learn everything there is to know about that psychotic b---h," (You can fill in the blanks yourself), and then I'm going to own her."

"Melissa, you've just suffered perhaps the most traumatic event of your lifetime. Maybe this isn't the time to make decisions."

She swiveled her chair from side to side. "She attacked me, Louella. Look at me. Look at my face. I'm not supposed to respond to this?"

"It's best not to commit a sin just because you see someone else doing it. Clinging to hate is the same as worshipping the devil."

"Damn it, Louella. That isn't fair."

"You're getting so worked up, you're liable to pop your stitches. You need to take some time; that's all I'm saying. Put vengeance to the side for now."

"I've taken all the time I need," she said. "Honestly, Louella, I don't believe what I'm hearing. She could have killed me."

"I know. Believe me, I am sorry. It is only through monumental effort that I am able to offer that girl forgiveness."

"You aren't the one who should be giving it."

"I may be the only one she'll take it from."

"I don't believe what I'm hearing."

"I am sorry, Melissa. I feel responsible. If it wasn't for me, that girl never would have come here. I drew her to me like a gnat to a bug zapper."

Melissa plopped down into my mother's antique rocking chair. "Maybe it was your sexual magnetism."

"Don't try to joke your way out of this conversation, young lady. You tried to protect me. You were acting on my behalf when you were attacked. Where was I? Sitting idle. Going out to lunch with the perpetrator while you lay bleeding on the carpet."

"You were kidnapped. You just didn't know it."

I don't believe I was ever in danger, but I had to consider Melissa's feelings. I told her I was sorry, and if she wanted to hire a private investigator to follow the girl around, she could send the bills to me.

"Absolutely not. I'm paying for this myself, Louella Harper. I'm only keeping you in the loop as a courtesy. I'm calling Brub."

"What's Brub?"

"Brub is my guy." She winked at me with her un-swollen eye. "I've got a guy."

"And his name is Brub apparently."

Not only did Melissa call Brub, she also called a friend of hers who served on the board of directors of the company that owns Lake View Estates and the other assisted living facility that employed our little friend with the ironic name, Christian Hope. She left him a message.

He eventually confirmed that Chrissy's references had been called and that they had checked out. No one at her work ever suspected anything was wrong with her.

"How did she pass her background check?"

"She passed," he told her. "No hospitalizations. No criminal history."

Melissa's man, Brub, spoke with friends and family members who confirmed that Chrissy was eccentric, and that in the past she had acted obsessively towards people and objects. She was prone to manic episodes and had gotten into some unspecified trouble in her youth.

At work, however, the girl was a consummate professional. She never gave anyone a peak at the secret world inside her head. She showed up to work every day and treated her coworkers with friendliness and respect. She was neither the best worker, nor the worst. She was just another cog in the wheel of the health care industry.

Outside of that structured environment, however, the truth began to reveal itself. Police searched her basement apartment and found copies of one of my manuscripts and sections of my personal diary hidden behind a tile in the drop ceiling. She was planning to write something and then somehow connect it to my work—some kind of stitched-together experimental nonsense with about as much resemblance to my previously published work as it does to Mary Shelley's *Frankenstein*.

"How could she publish my work?" I posed the question to Melissa. "No publisher would go near it."

"It's a new era in publishing," Melissa said. "These days, he can publish it herself online."

"We'd sue."

"What would she care? She doesn't have any money. She'd get the attention though, which is probably all she really wanted in the first place."

"It's all so bizarre."

She just got carried away—that was essentially the argument her lawyer made in court, after the judge determined she was fit to stand trial. She'd never been arrested before, never even been accused of a crime. Her illness just got the better of her.

Not so, said the prosecutor, who also happened to be a close friend to Melissa and myself. The police had a signed confession which showed knew exactly what she was doing.

Statement Selected from the Signed Confession of Chris Hope

From working at Lake View, I knew that some of the nurse's aides had keys to the residences in which they worked. I knew Summer worked for Louella and that she was kind of a ditz who would leave her keys lying around. One day, I saw them on a table in the breakroom, and I picked them up and slipped them into my pocket. When I took my lunch break, I went to a locksmith and had a copy of Louella's door key made. Afterwards, I put the keys on the floor beside Summer's locker. She assumed she had dropped them.

I only used the key once, about a week after I took it. I offered to cover the overnight shift one night when no one else was available. The residents slept most of the night, and I had a lot of down time to read or whatever. About three o'clock in the morning I went over to Louella's apartment and slipped the key into the lock. I knew the residences were monitored by cameras, but I also knew when the security guy that watched the camera took his break. I wasn't even really nervous about breaking in. I knew how the apartments were set up—the master bedroom was all the way on the other side of the building—and I knew from my research that Louella was slightly deaf; she would have taken out her hearing aids to sleep.

Louella's office was the first room I came to. I didn't have a flashlight or anything. I just flipped on the light switch. When I saw the typewriter, I knew I was in the right place.

There was a diamond brooch sitting beside it, and I picked it up and put it in my pocket. Then, I went through the file cabinets until I found where her writing was stored. I saw that it was all sorted by years and that the year would include whatever stories or novels she had been working on at the time. I took a couple of short stories written in the 1990s to read later. I would have gone on looking for The Reverend, but I heard a sound at the other end of the apartment.

Louella was moving around in her bedroom. She'd either heard me making noise, or else she had just gotten up to go to the bathroom; I wasn't sure. I wasn't afraid she would catch me either, but I also wasn't trying to get caught. I figured I could always come back after I was moved to the nightshift fulltime.

But then, a week or so later, Louella finally noticed her brooch was missing, and I happened to be on shift when she falsely accused Summer. In that moment, I felt like it had all been preordained. My getting that job seemed to confirm something I'd somehow known all along—Louella and I were meant to be together.

End of Statement.

It made my blood shiver to read those words. The idea that a stranger could come to believe that she knew me so intimately based on simple happenstance defied comprehension. The fact is, Chrissy Hope barged into my life uninvited. She stalked me, lied to me, broke into my apartment, inserted herself into the sanctuary of my home, stole my property, brought chaos to my household, and almost murdered a dear friend of mine.

Melissa Taggert, if you ever find yourself reading these words, I hope you know how much I need you, how much value you bring to my life. Honestly, I don't know how I could have made it as long as I have without you. You are the living embodiment of all the virtues I look for in a person, and I am proud to call you my friend.

I completely agreed with you when you went down her list of criminal code violations and then asked, "Shouldn't this person face consequences for her actions?"

"Yes," I said. "She certainly should."

She did face consequences. She was sentenced to seven years in prison for assault with a deadly typewriter. (The official charges differed in language but not in meaning.)

"She probably won't serve more than three or four," Melissa responded gloomily the day the sentence was handed down. "They should have given her the death penalty."

Melissa had a right to be angry, but I refused to harbor such bitterness. For every heinous act the girl committed, something always came along threatening to make me feel sorry for her. For instance, that boyfriend of hers—James—he wasn't real. She just made him up. Apparently, she did most of her writing during her manic phases.

"He's just another one of her lies," Melissa said.

Phone records showed the only calls made to or from her cell phone belonged to her mother, who also signed the lease on her apartment in Atlanta. None of the neighbors Brub interviewed recalled ever seeing any visitors to her apartment.

Melissa thought maybe James was an ex-boyfriend, so she called her mother to find out. The poor thing just kept apologizing.

"I'm so sorry my daughter did this to you. It's not like her. She's never done anything like this before. She's never been violent."

That wasn't what Melissa wanted to hear right then, so she brushed the message aside. "I'm trying to get in touch with a friend of your daughter's. I'm hoping you can help me out. His name is James."

"James?" she said. "The only James I know is a stuffed animal. It's her teddy bear."

"Do you believe that s---?" Melissa asked me when she got off the phone.

I told her I didn't know what to believe.

As for the girl's prison sentence, I had an entirely different reaction than Melissa. The notion that the girl needed help more than she needed a prison sentence toppled onto me like a falling building.

"I don't believe she is mentally ill." Melissa said. "She planned this whole thing and executed it to the last detail. She didn't care who she hurt and showed no interest in differentiating between right and wrong. She deserves to be punished."

"I suppose she's the justice system's problem now," I said, but I was already feeling guilty and wondering if there was anything else I could do for the poor girl.

"You don't owe that girl anything, not even a second thought," my friend Franklin told me one evening over a game of Bridge. Franklin is a professor over at Auburn.

"You were violated," his wife, Evelyn, added. "You probably have PTSD."

"You may be right. That's certainly true of Melissa, but I see myself as having a choice about how I respond. It's a choice between hate and love, between vengeance and forgiveness."

"She's not your responsibility," Franklin said.

"That's true. She is responsible for her own actions, but I'm responsible for mine."

It was with no small amount of effort and favors called in that I managed to get the girl reevaluated and transferred to the psychiatric hospital in Tuscaloosa after less than a year in prison.

"As your lawyer, I'm telling you this is a bad idea," Melissa warned me just before my phone call with the governor. "Let's say you get her hospitalized. You get her meds straight. She loves you for it. What's to stop her from coming back?"

"I've thought about that, and I have an idea for how to deal with the problem."

"I'm beginning to think you are as crazy as she is."

After Chrissy was transferred to the River Road facility up in Tuscaloosa, I paid her a single visit as a courtesy. Melissa insisted on driving me to the small collection of brick buildings that served as a campus. She parked behind the building known as Somerville, where they housed the most violent offenders. I left Melissa smoking a cigarette in the parking lot and went inside. I just needed answers to a few simple questions.

The facility seemed well secured. I was patted down and searched by security guards who had to buzz me into each inner layer of the mazelike facility. The most dangerous prisoners were spaced throughout a cluster of hives at the center of the maze, but I never made it that deep into the inner sanctum. Instead I was ushered into a waiting area with seating along the walls and a wall-mounted television tuned to a 1970s-era sitcom.

I found Chrissy curled up in one of the seats angled away from the television. She wore pink pajamas decorated with ice cream cones and a pair of white converse all-stars. He hair was pulled back in a ponytail. Her knees were drawn up to her chest and she was reading a well-worn copy of my book.

When she looked up and noticed me standing there, her face transformed into something resembling joy. "Louella, you came to see me."

I was taken aback by this response. It was a deliberate decision on my part that she not be informed of my visit ahead of time. I wanted to see how she would react. I expected shame. I expected tears.

"Look," she said. "I'm reading your book."

"I see." It was not a fact I found comforting.

An orderly brought a folding chair and set it up facing her.

"I won't be staying long," I said. "I just came to ask a few questions. I wanted to find out why you did what you did."

The girl looked surprised. "I was just doing what you were doing—uncovering a mystery. I followed your lead."

"I never stole anything. I never hurt anyone."

She smiled. "Of course not, Louella. You only did what you had to do. And I did what I had to do."

"You didn't have to do anything."

She looked down at the pages of my book. She was only a few chapters from the end. "I had to find out the truth."

"What truth did you find? All I see are lies."

"No, there is truth in the story," she said. "Lots of it."

"But when it's all mixed together," I said. "It all turns to lies."

"But if we put our truths together, maybe we can come up with something better than what's happened in the past, something better than what's happening now even. Unless of course..." She looked down at her book. "... I'm just another person you don't care about."

That one got me like a knitting needle through the aorta.

It reminded me of a conversation I'd once had at a family get-together. My niece, Madeline, asked me why I always got so upset when people talked about me and wrote about me. "Isn't that every writer's dream: to write a book so good everyone talks about it and about them?"

"No," I said. "A book is not an invitation for people to come interfere with the author's life. We don't forfeit our rights—including our right to privacy—just because someone felt a connection to something we wrote."

"You're a public figure, though. The rules change when you put yourself into the public eye."

"If I'd known such rules existed, I never would have written that damned book."

"Really?" she asked. "I always heard you were so driven to write. I heard it was all you ever wanted to do."

"That was a long time ago," I said.

Madeline is a sweet girl, but she was poking at an open wound. Here was Chrissy doing the same thing.

For a long time, I made it a policy to cut people out of my life for the sin of talking about me in the press. I have always treated such an action as a betrayal, necessitating swift and brutal punishment: complete loss of access to my life.

At the same time, I considered myself a Christian. My intention has always been to try and reconcile my behavior with the principles governing my faith: peace, love, forgiveness, and helping the less fortunate.

However, I have sometimes struggled to live by those principles. Sitting in a visiting area of a psychiatric hospital, I found myself once again questioning my obligation to the person who inserted herself into my life and attacked my friend. Why did I feel responsible for her?

Once upon a time, I wrote a story that, through a combination of hard work and blind luck, became immensely popular all over the world. I was blessed that my words had a positive effect on so many people. Wasn't that enough? Must I also try and save all the people I come in contact with in my daily life? Is it my job to reach out to all the people making the world worse through hate, anger, selfishness, and narcissism, and try to point them in the right direction? It seems like such a simple thing to understand: you can either make things better for everyone or you can make things worse.

Years after my first improbable success, I went to Jackson City, Alabama and I had to ask myself whether writing that book would make things better for everyone involved, or would it make things worse.

It's always easiest to make things worse. All you have to do is criticize and belittle, hunt for insecurities in a person and then draw attention to them. Focus on the flaws of others with the tenacity of a schoolyard bully.

I have now lived for 87 years and from what I can tell there are only two directions you can go in this world: toward the better or toward the worse. Stupid is going toward the worse and pretending it's better. Stupid is a choice, or, perhaps, a series of choices people make every day in every country and culture. Stupid is the act of gratifying our most immediate and prurient interests while sacrificing whatever principles we pretend to hold dear. It's putting ourselves over the people and plants and animals we need to sustain life on this planet. Stupid is maintaining loyalty to those who would follow the path of darkness because it makes us feel better about our own bad choices.

Well, I feel no regrets about not publishing *The Reverend*. I based that decision entirely upon my own guiding principles and a unitarian ethic. I simply asked which would be better? To publish the book or not to publish the book? You know the choice I made.

The Reverend was a book without heroes, only people struggling to get ahead, and not caring how they did it. I can tell you now the same thing I said at various times to Ernie Smith, Cassandra, and even Melvin Little: you can't outrun God's judgement. The truth will come to light and your name will be attached to the sins you committed. You might outrun the consequences during your lifetime, but the truth always comes in time.

Last year, I had Melissa's man Brub track down Ernie and Cassandra to find out what happened to them. Cassandra seems to have mellowed some in her advanced years. She married for a third time and lived the rest of her life in deserved obscurity. She spent the rest of her life trying to forget her past, although I don't know how well she succeeded.

From what we can tell, Ernie Smith honored our detente, though he had help from the police and the reporters, who kept a close watch on him, which caused much of his business to dry up. A new funeral home competing for Ernie's market put the proverbial nail in the coffin of the Temple of the Smith. By adding the novel service of not murdering its clientele, the new business quickly cornered the market, while Ernie was left on the verge of bankruptcy. (His ambulance service had gone out of business years before.) He was only saved from complete financial ruin by a fire that incinerated his building. It turned out the *Temple of the Smith* was heavily insured. Ernie took the money he made from the settlement and retired. He lived out the remainder of his life as quietly as a church mouse.

As I sat in the waiting room of a psychiatric ward, looking at a woman who left her senses to follow her misguided adoration for me, I thought about how I could make the situation better for everyone. "I do care about you," I told her. "That's why I'm giving you that old manuscript."

She looked up again from her book with a perplexed look on her face.

"I'm not using those old words, so you might as well have them. I'm transferring the rights over to you."

Her expression changed from bewilderment to amazement.

"But I'm only offering you this gift under certain conditions. If you intend to publish my words, they will require proper editing. I insist on final say about how they are to be presented to the public. You're also going to have to work to bring your own writing up to my standards."

She was sitting up in her chair now, leaning toward me. "Of course, I'll do whatever you say."

"You won't see a dime from the venture. Any money generated by the book will be divided in half. Half will go toward private psychiatric treatment you are to receive once you get released from this place. The other half will be donated to a local charity benefitting the people of Jackson City and the surrounding area. If you cease to participate in your treatment, the money earmarked for that purpose will go instead to pay for a private investigator who shall ensure that you are not a threat to society. Do you accept these conditions?"

"Yes," she said with complete focus and seriousness. "But why? Why are you doing this?"

"I don't know exactly," I said. "When I went to Jackson City all those years ago, I hoped to come away with a good story, but I couldn't find any good in it. I never found my hero. Maybe you can succeed where I failed."

"I can find the hero in the story," Chrissy said. "I've already found her."

Some people will say this decision of mine is out of character for me. That's fine. I've never saddled myself with other people's expectations, and I don't intend to start now. People will always believe or disbelieve according to their own inclinations.

"Before you get too excited," I told Chrissy, "you should know there is one other condition."

She raised her eyebrows in anticipation.

"This book is not to be published during my lifetime."

All the joy drained out of her face.

"Did you think I would be so willing to sacrifice my personal privacy? If so, you don't know Louella Harper."

I'm afraid it's true. If you find yourself reading these words, it means I have shed my mortal coil. Regardless of what happens with any book published by Christian Alexis Hope—and any publicity she manages to generate—you can rest assured that it will have no effect upon me whatsoever. Consider me at peace.

I don't suppose I owe anyone else any more explanations for my actions at this point. I expect to live out the rest of my life in relative comfort, surrounded by dear friends and family members, and in possession of an iron-clad restraining order preventing Chris Hope from coming within a thousand feet of me.

Chrissy
2019

Louella pulled a prank on me by dying. She gave me permission to use her material. She did so verbally and in writing. "You can have those old words of mine. You need them more than I do." That's what she told me that day at Somerville. I could publish my words, my thoughts, my experiences alongside hers. We were going to write a book together. We did write a book together.

But no one will ever know.

The lawyer tells me I have to change the names. I can't even use the real name of my hometown. I have to pretend I'm from some other place that doesn't exist but is eerily similar to my hometown. And even though I got permission directly from Louella, I can't even call her by her real name either because her own lawyer will sue me for doing the one thing I had planned to do all along.

The truth is, her name wasn't Louella Harper. It was something else. I can't say what it was because I'll get sued. Let's just say that it belonged to one of the most famous writers who ever lived and leave it at that.

It really pisses me off though. Louella never said I had to change any names. She said I could have her manuscript. Period. I could publish the book after she passed away. Period. (RIP.)

It all comes down to her lawyer. (Melissa Taggert was not her real name either.) She never wanted me to succeed. She wanted me to spend the rest of my life behind bars all because I hit her with a typewriter. Ever since that day, she's been manipulating behind the scenes, doing everything in her power to make my life miserable.

I can't prove anything. I don't have any evidence. I never saw her, or Louella, at any of my hearings. Neither the lawyers nor the judge mentioned either one of them. I asked my court-appointed attorney why it was no one mentioned them. He said, "Don't worry about it. I'm going to take care of you."

He took care of me alright.

Everyone kept referring to Victim 1 and Victim 2, and I figured out through context which one was Louella, and which was Melissa. I tried to tell my lawyer Louella wasn't really a victim. She went along with me willingly. She was never in danger. I would never do anything to hurt Louella Harper. Never in a million years.

It wasn't until after sentencing that I realized what had happened. When the judge banged that gavel and sentenced me to seven years in prison, I wanted to scream out, "For what? I only did what I was supposed to do." I followed the path that was laid out for me by the universe.

Six months after my sentence was handed down, I was sitting on my prison bed, planning how I would exact my revenge on Melissa Taggert. A guard came up to my cell.

"Pack your shit, Hope. You're going to the loony bin."

"What are you talking about, Shorty?" He hated it when I called him Shorty.

"You heard me. You're being transferred."

I'd already known about the transfer. The day before I made a bet with him that I'd be out of prison within a week.

"You lose the bet, Dip Stick. You owe me fifty bucks."

"I'll mail you a check," he said, but he never did. The last I heard from him, he was muttering something about liberal judges.

Little did he know, I was benefitting from old-fashioned, good-old-boy justice. You know how it goes. Some rich kid gets arrested for driving under the influence of alcohol, fleeing the scene of an accident, or assault. Calls are made. Favors are exchanged. Pretty soon the kid is back on the street with a freshly expunged record. Well, Louella Harper was the rich daddy who got me transferred from prison to a temporary stay at a luxury psychiatric facility.

Louella looked out for me. She cared about me. She wanted me to succeed, to move forward and become a better person.

You have no idea how many people are out there actively trying to make other people fail. Backstabbing, name-calling, always pointing out the shortcomings of others, I saw it all the time in prison.

Louella Harper wasn't like that. She wasn't the type of person to turn her back on anyone. I'm alive because of her. She saved me. Then, she made my biggest wish come true.

Louella Harper and I wrote a book together. Her part may have been written forty years ago, but she proved to be a supportive editor as I worked like hell to finish my part of the story. How many times did I send her drafts, only to have them returned to my mailbox filled with corrections and notes scribbled in the margins in red ink? There was always a yellow Post-It note with a message scrawled in her chicken-scratch handwriting.

"Keep at it."- LH

You can't imagine how much that meant to me.

It's just sad that people won't get to know the truth, and even if they figure it out, they probably won't believe it. Oh, they'd probably believe me if the story ended a different way—with me still in prison and her murdered and robbed of her manuscript. I bet readers would have no trouble swallowing such a sordid ending, since it's the kind of story that pops up every few minutes in a smartphone's newsfeed. Of course, you would have heard about the murder of the most famous author in the world—it would have dominated an entire news cycle.

BLOOD CRIES

    I feel sorry for people who act out aggressively against each other. I really do. I only did it myself that one time, and I'll probably pay for the mistake until my dying day. I think a lot of these "lone wolf" acts of violence could be avoided if we all did a better job listening to people's cries for help. I bet most violent offenders never had a Louella Harper in their life to reach out to them with compassion and forgiveness. Chances are, the people they do have in their lives don't know what to do with them, so they throw up their hands and hope it will get better on its own.

    It never will.

    We can't just turn our backs on each other. We have to reach out to each other. We have to form connections. We have to try and make things better not just for ourselves, but for everyone. We have to try and save one another, just like Louella Harper saved me.

###

CHRIS HOPE

Thank you for reading *Blood Cries*. If you enjoyed your experience, please consider leaving a short review wherever you buy books.

Discover more titles by the author

By Chris Hope

Blood Cries

By Christamar Varicella

The Reverend

Two Weird (stories)

There Are Sneetches in my Breeches (and Other Parodies)

Acknowledgements

I would like to thank the following people without whom this book would not have been possible: Harper Lee, Tom Radney, Robert Burns, E Paul Jones, Al Benn, Jim Earnhardt, Lois Brasfield, Judy Willis, Joy Lynn Brasfield, Brian Bice, Judy Willis, Joel Martin, Alexander City's Feast of Sharing, Keelia Brasfield, Pa Bice, M.S. Brasfield III, Baron Brasfield, and Greg Akers.

In writing this fictional story, I depended on the following factual resources: *To Kill a Preacher* by E Paul Jones; the author's interview with Tom Radney; *Reporter: Covering Civil Rights and Wrongs in Dixie* by Alvin Benn; *The Devil and Harper Lee* by Mark Seal, *Furious Hours* by Casey Cep; "With a Saw and a Truck: Alabama Pulpwood Producers" by John C. Bliss and Warren Flick; Author's interview with Alvin Benn and Jim Earnhardt; *Mockingbird: A Portrait of Harper Lee* by Charles Shields; the trial transcript of the State of Alabama vs. Robert Burns; transcript of the Independent Life and Accident Insurance Company, a corporation v. Willie J. Maxwell; extensiv reporting by Al Benn, Jim Earnhardt, Lou Elliott, Phillip Rawls, Phyllis Wesley, David Granger, Ray Jenkins, Casey Cep, and Jim Stewart.

BLOOD CRIES

Made in the USA
Columbia, SC
25 June 2019